substitute

isobel rey

sourcebooks
casablanca

Published by Sourcebooks Casablanca, an imprint of Sourcebooks, Inc., in
conjunction with Xcite Books Ltd.
P.O. Box 4410, Naperville, Illinois 60567-4410
(630) 961-3900
Fax: (630) 961-2168
www.sourcebooks.com

Originally published in 2013 in the United Kingdom by Xcite Books Ltd.

Library of Congress Cataloging-in-Publication data is on file with the publisher.

Printed and bound in the United States of America.
VP 10 9 8 7 6 5 4 3 2 1

Prologue

FINDING YOURSELF IN THE en suite bathroom that adjoins the company boardroom may not be all that unusual. Finding yourself hiding in there while two people are about to fuck on the boardroom table—well, that definitely doesn't happen every day. Certainly not to Alexia.

She eased herself as far back into the bathroom as she could, hoping to stay hidden. How the hell did she get here? Two days into a new job and she was hiding in a bathroom? She had run away from her old life, a life that had cornered and trapped her. And yet here she was, cornered again, praying hard she wouldn't be discovered, and holding her breath. But then, it felt as if she had spent years holding her breath…

One month earlier

She didn't look back at the house, not until she'd gone through the gates that led out on to the street. She pulled her car into the road to drive away, desperate to slam her foot to the floor and get as far away as possible, as fast as possible. But she found herself pulling the car over to the side of the road and taking a last look back at the front door.

It was an impressive house, large and double-fronted, surrounded by trees, with a pretty cherry tree swaying in the front garden, soft pink and fluttering, so inviting. She remembered the first time she'd seen it, at the end of a whirlwind first date. She had trotted behind Carter as he strode up the drive and the taxi that had delivered them retreated into the night. He'd proudly opened the door to his mansion for his new girlfriend.

She shivered. How could she have been so stupid? It was obvious throughout that first evening that he was controlling. He had ordered the wine without asking her what she liked. He'd insisted on a certain table without checking if she was happy. She'd missed her train home and he insisted she stay at his house. He'd made it a *fait accompli* before she'd had time to object. Then he'd insisted she share his bed when she asked for the spare room. It was their first date, and Alexia wasn't the type to jump into bed so soon. But he made it impossible to say no. He managed to make her sound petulant and unreasonable for daring to object.

She had moved in with him two weeks later, just as a temporary measure. Her flatmate had sold the apartment she'd been living in since leaving college. Alexia was now homeless and jobless.

"Of course you should come here," Carter had said as he'd brushed her objections aside. He was tall, powerfully built, with a strong voice and a stronger grip. He was a human bulldozer, physically and emotionally.

She wasn't sure quite when he had gained control over her; it seemed to happen slowly, incrementally, like water dripping on a stone. He played on her lack of experience with men, and bit by bit she became passive, complying. She dared to argue, but less and less, as it always ended with him shouting her down until she acquiesced.

She was in his house, and he made sure she felt beholden to him. By day, he was mercurial; one minute charming and loving, the next petulant, controlling, bullying, and difficult. By night, he was worse. That first evening she should have known. The sex had been demanding and hurried. She hadn't enjoyed it, but then she thought, I've had a few drinks and so has he; it'll get better, he'll get softer. But it didn't get better, and he didn't soften.

He didn't believe in making love. He would grab her hair to make her look at him as he pounded her, his jaw tight and his eyes hard and staring. Or force her facedown as he took her from behind without ever testing whether she was ready. He liked her before she got too wet. He told her it felt better, but deep down she knew it was because it gave him a sense of control.

He owned her and didn't care what she did or didn't want. She had sex like an automaton. She'd never really enjoyed sex that much before Carter. No one had ever lit a fire inside her, making it easier for her to avoid it or blank out each encounter. He wasn't often demanding of her, and she suspected he got his bedroom kicks elsewhere. Instead of feeling betrayed, she was relieved he would leave her alone.

Alexia sat in the car, the engine still running. She took a last, long look at that huge oak door, the one she'd run out of so many times. With nowhere else to go she had always gone back, hearing it shut behind her. The noise of the slamming door reminded her each time of her failure. Not this time. This was the last time.

Carter had gone to some business meeting, leaving her alone in the house. The overwhelming feeling of incarceration had suffocated her, tightening around her stomach, her ribs. She'd paced through the house, tearing at her own clothes. This feeling had been getting tighter and tighter around her until she could barely breathe. He had screamed at her again that morning, another of his flashes of temper that erupted from nowhere over nothing at all. This one had been a bad one. He'd left her shaking on the bathroom floor.

As she paced the hallway she cried out like a wounded animal. She had to go, she had to get out, but where? Anywhere was better than this. She was leaving. Now.

Alexia ran upstairs and started throwing all her things in bags, stuffing them blindly. She ran out of the house, filling the back of her small car. When she was done she turned around and ran to the door. Her keys were inside the house; if she pulled the door now, she couldn't get back in. She froze, contemplating what closing the door would mean. She could feel her heart pounding against her ribs; her breathing was ragged. Then, with one big heave, she pulled the door. The final slam. She had heard it shut so many times, but this time the sound echoed like someone had struck a giant bell. She fled backward to her car and leaped in, thrusting the keys into the ignition and speeding out of the drive, gravel flying out from under the wheels. But then she stopped the car on the far side of the road. She was across the street, looking back.

"This is the last time I look at this house. This is the last time, the last time." Saying it out loud made it more real. She was the mistress of her destiny, not him.

She slammed the car into first gear and roared away down the street.

Chapter 1

RUNNING INTO ROMY HAD been unexpected. The kookiest girl in school, Alexia always knew she'd end up doing something crazy or glamorous. It turned out to be both. Gone was the pink hair, punky jewelry, and drop-dead attitude; here was her old friend smartly dressed, working as a personal assistant at a sports agency. Not just any agency, but the hottest one in London. Fallon Sports Agency had the biggest and sexiest client list. A-listers of track and field, soccer players, and tennis stars were represented by Nathan Fallon and his team of agents. Romy had landed on her feet all right, in her brand-new red-soled Louboutins. What happened to the Doc Martens? Alexia thought. If the old Romy could see the new one, she'd laugh herself hoarse.

Over a coffee and then too many glasses of wine, Alexia had poured out all her troubles to the new-look Romy. It was a night that was to change her life forever. Romy's flatmate and former work colleague had just upped and left for Australia, leaving an empty room at the flat, and an empty chair in the office at Fallon's. In less than a week, Alexia had moved in and started work as a temp at the agency. She had found a friend's sofa after her flit from Carter's house, but she couldn't stay there much longer. So this was perfect, and it came with the prospect of a lasting job.

"If I make a good impression maybe they'll keep me," she told Romy.

"Yeah, just one thing though, Alex; they're quite a fast lot. You know, work hard, play hard. And you're—well—not really used to that, are you?"

Romy was concerned her shy, beautiful blond friend would be eaten alive at the agency. Alexia was petite and unassuming, completely unaware of her attractiveness. She had a cool air about her that made men think she wasn't interested. But she was just a little shy and very naïve.

"Seriously, Alex, it's great I've got you a job, but it's not an ordinary office!"

But Alexia was determined. "Oh, don't worry, Romy, what's the worst that can happen?"

That was a week ago. Now, as she pressed herself against the tiles in the tiny bathroom off the boardroom, Alexia remembered the conversation all too clearly.

She pushed herself further into the darkness in the cramped room as she tried to stay hidden from the couple who very definitely thought they were alone.

She'd crept upstairs at the company offices to use the boardroom en suite as the downstairs bathroom was full of people intent on snorting cocaine. It was a party after the first press event for a huge new client. Romy was right. She had told her they worked hard and played hard, but Alexia really hadn't been prepared for this.

Alexia peered out through the crack between the door and the frame. She'd seen the couple before, the two people who were now in the boardroom; she'd seen them in the office, but had never met either of them.

Phillipa Greenwood was walking backward toward the board table. She was the commercial director, a very confident and attractive fortysomething bottle blond with a taste for tight silk blouses, fuck-me heels, and younger men. In her hand was a tie, still attached to the young man she was pulling into the room with her. Tony was the kind of man every girl noticed. In his midtwenties, he was a young would-be agent, with rock-hard abs and tousled dirty blond hair. Alexia watched his face. She didn't recognize the expression in it. He was young, but he looked very calm and in control, despite the fact that he was being led like a dog on a leash.

Phillipa tugged Tony's tie and pulled him to her. He was only a few inches taller than her as she stood in her towering heels. He eyed her coolly.

"Ever fucked a cougar, Tony?"

He lifted one eyebrow and a small, crooked smile curled his lip. His fingers found their way to her breasts, hitched up by a very tight Wonderbra. She always wore her blouses with one button straining to stay shut, so every man she dealt with would be distracted enough to give her what she wanted. And she always got what she wanted. Tony was going to be no exception.

He walked forward purposefully but slowly, forcing Phillipa to move backward. They were face to face, chest to chest, groin to groin, stepping slowly across the room. It was like watching a tango, a very slow, deliberate, sexy tango.

As Phillipa's backside hit the edge of the board table they stopped. They stood staring at each other for a moment, as if each was waiting for the other to make the first move. The air was heavy with electricity and Alexia was terrified they would hear her breathing.

Then suddenly Tony jammed Phillipa against the table. Alexia felt a jolt in her groin. She clutched her hand to her stomach. The couple's faces were centimeters apart, like two fighters eyeing each other in the ring before a fight. They didn't kiss but their mouths hovered close together, breathing each other in, daring each other not to kiss.

Alexia's heart hammered in her chest; she was terrified she'd be discovered. But then, they were in a far more compromising situation than her. Perhaps she wasn't scared, perhaps she was something else. Excited?

She realized she was squirming slightly, watching as Tony ran his hands down Phillipa's arched body. She felt a tugging lurch in her panties as he reached down and grabbed the bottom of Phillipa's pencil skirt, hiking it up so the pink flesh above her stocking tops was exposed.

Alexia bit her lip to stifle a moan. She noticed his hands: long, elegant fingers, with silver Celtic rings usually worn by long-haired surfers rather than corporate types.

"Well, well, it seems like young Tony is more of a tiger than I thought," Phillipa teased, twisting her exposed hips against his groin.

But Tony was still dancing, and he was going to make sure she knew he was still leading. He lifted Phillipa up and sat her on the edge of the table. Alexia felt a squirt of dampness hit her panties. She had to force herself to stop squirming. They'd hear her!

But Phillipa wasn't about to relinquish control. She grabbed Tony's belt, and pulled it hard to let the little metal pin unhook itself. The leather strap started to slide through the buckle, as if she was slowly unbridling a horse. He put his hands on her knees and held her there for a moment, looking into her eyes, eyeing her like a fighter again. His strong fingers curled around her knees, locking her to the table. The air between them was heavy with desire and power play. They stayed there, breathing hard, looking into each other's eyes. No words. No fucking. Just watching… Waiting.

Alexia wanted to moan again; she'd entirely forgotten her fear of discovery. All she could think about was how she didn't want them to stop.

Slowly, achingly slowly, Tony inched Phillipa's knees further apart, never taking his eyes off hers, daring her to stop him. Holding his gaze, Phillipa reached out for his fly and slowly unzipped him, rolling his trousers over his hips. It wasn't easy, his bulging erection made it difficult, but she was clearly practiced.

Alexia could see his cock, so hard and stiff it looked almost painful. As he breathed heavily it bobbed slightly, moving gently up and down as he breathed in and out. The small muscles in his flank and buttocks were taut and twitching. He reminded Alexia of a racehorse, standing straining in the stalls, waiting for the race to begin, waiting for the chance to explode forward.

Phillipa curled her long, scarlet-tipped fingers around his cock, wrapping her hand around it one finger at a time. She was looking deep into his eyes, looking for the smallest sign that he was losing his grip on his self-control. This was a battle, to see who would yield to their passion first. Tony stayed impassive. As Phillipa worked her, fingers around his length, their eyes stayed locked together.

Alexia realized her own hand had crept to her crotch. She was holding herself in her palm and pressing down. The tension between the couple was almost unbearable for her to watch. The tension of the last months seemed to have been building in her, and now, it seemed it would be contained no longer. The tension had a will of its own and it wanted attention, it wanted passion, it wanted…

Without warning, Tony let go of Phillipa's knees and grabbed her ass, a strong hand covering each butt cheek as he yanked her toward him. She slid the few inches across the desk toward him in an instant; her pussy, covered only by a thin sliver of damp, blood-red satin, slammed against his naked, hot erection.

Alexia's gasp was masked by Phillipa's own. She wanted to feel him, the way Phillipa was. She rubbed the hard heel of her hand against her clit. She was not in control. And neither was Phillipa.

Victory was Tony's; she'd lost control first. It might only have been a small gasp and a widening of the eyes, but he knew it and he felt her increasing wetness as her pussy pressed up against the underside of his cock.

She needed to get her composure back.

"Well, this is a party, I hope you brought a party hat," Phillipa purred.

He looked at her intently.

"Oh well, a good girl guide is always prepared." She reached into one of the cups of her overflowing bra and pulled out a purple foil packet.

She slowly and very deliberately put the corner of the packet between her beautiful, straight white teeth and started to slowly tear it open, millimeter by millimeter, watching the anticipation on Tony's face.

The foil opened achingly slowly, and Alexia found she had to move her hand inside her panties to feel skin on skin, and stifle the ache. She was soaking. Her middle finger slid through her wetness to find what she was looking for. As she rubbed the engorged nub, her knees started to weaken with the delicious feeling.

The foil was off and Phillipa was expertly covering Tony's erection with the condom. Alexia marveled that anyone could do that so quickly. But she didn't have time to dwell on Phillipa's hidden talents as Tony grabbed his partner's hands and pinned them to the table.

His cock was aimed at Phillipa's pussy, like a missile. It looked even bigger in the condom, like the rubber was straining against his size.

There was a moment, a hiatus when nothing happened. The two stared at each other again. Who was going to start?

Alexia was rubbing now, desperate to feed the starving need in her groin. She could hear her own wetness as her fingers moved and curled around her pussy. But she was past caring if anyone heard her. She leaned against the wall with her other hand, steadying herself as she rocked. There was music floating up from downstairs; she could only hear the beat, and it chimed with her heartbeat and the throb inside her.

"Come on, come on, please," she silently urged Tony. She needed him to start; she needed to watch the last, explosive movements of this dance, so she could find her own release.

Tony pushed Phillipa down and aimed his cock right at the crack of her pussy. With one hand he tugged her panties to one side and exposed the yawning, raw wetness that waited to accept him. Then he expertly maneuvered himself to thrust into her. He waited, teasing the tip of his cock against her. Phillipa panted. He plunged. Phillipa and Alexia both gasped at once. Alexia was pressing her clit so hard now, desperate to feel what Phillipa was feeling. Phillipa's legs hung open, dangling from the edge of the table as Tony pumped into her. He was really driving; Alexia could see his cock, glistening and hard, as he pulled back and plunged again, over and over.

Alexia watched as every muscle on his flanks and his hard ass compressed and relaxed with each thrust, all working together like a piston engine. Compressing then relaxing, compressing then relaxing, thrusting over and over, he rammed into her as he gripped her hips to keep her on the edge... On the edge of the table and on the edge of coming.

At the end of each thrust he pressed against her clit, in up to the hilt. But each time Phillipa's moans sounded as if she was close to coming, he would lean his body back away from her, leaving that quivering nub of flesh exposed and needy. She clawed at him to make him come closer and press against her. But then he would stop. He would stand there motionless, his long, muscular legs taut with the tension of staying still as he watched her exquisite agony. She was desperate, desperate for him to keep thrusting, to keep hammering her clit into submission and explosion. But he was in control and he would decide when she came.

Each time he stopped, Alexia thought her heart would leap into her mouth as she had to stop too. She was so wet, her entire hand was smeared with her own juices; she was wetter than she had ever been in her life, and she could hear her juices squelching as she rubbed.

Then Tony would start again, slamming into Phillipa. She'd given up her fight for supremacy and was now arching back, getting the ride of her life. Tony's cock must have been hitting all the right spots as her lower legs were hanging limply like a rag doll over the table, and she moaned with every burning thrust of Tony's hips. Harder and harder, until she threw her head back.

As Phillipa came, Alexia pressed and rubbed herself with furious pressure, desperate, desperate to come and end this excruciating torture. Tony kept thrusting, his eyes now fixed on Phillipa but glazed and unseeing as he climbed and climbed to finally hit the target.

Alexia leaned on the wall with her elbow, stuffing her fist in her mouth to disguise her stifled moan as she came with him. She came so hard she thought her legs would buckle. A sudden warmth she'd not felt before rushed from her groin to her stomach and down her legs to her toes. This was not an orgasm like she had ever known before. She had very little experience of sex; one pale and earnest college boyfriend, and then Carter.

She breathed heavily and watched the couple on the table. Phillipa was lying back, her eyes closed, her mouth open, her lungs clutching for air. Tony stood over her, his cock still deep inside her, as if he was leaning against her and into her, to steady his legs.

Alexia straightened up and slowly pulled her hand from her panties. She realized it was soaking wet, and looked around desperately for something to wipe her juices away. There was a towel on a rail. Silently, she wiped her hand and tried to smooth down her clothing.

When she looked through the crack in the door again, Tony was zipping himself up, and Phillipa was trying to compose herself. The sassy, in-control woman Alexia had seen in the office was gone. She saw Phillipa flushed and breathing hard. She did up her clothing and smoothed her hair. Slowly the calm and powerful professional returned, on the outside at least. But there was no mistaking that she looked like she'd been fucked, hard.

She put a hand on Tony's chest as he buttoned his shirt.

"Give it a few minutes before you leave," she told him, back in control.

"Sure thing… boss!" Tony smiled sarcastically.

Phillipa made for the door. The red soles of her killer Louboutins showed a very small unsteadiness in her walk. She opened the door and the music from downstairs flooded the room. She paused, then went out, closing the door behind her.

Alexia was leaning against the wall, still slightly out of breath. The throb that had spread through her limbs and her stomach was subsiding now, and she was left with the warm afterglow of pleasure lying languidly in her veins. I'll wait here a couple of minutes until Tony leaves too, she thought. She closed her eyes, waiting for her breathing to return to normal. The room was quiet again, save for the dull thud of the bass line.

"What the hell…?"

Alexia's eyes burst open to see Tony standing in the small bathroom, staring at her with disbelief.

"Were you watching us?" Tony demanded.

"What! No… No… I… I mean…"

"You *were* watching us… Get a kick out of it?"

Alexia stammered, "You don't understand. I was already in here, and when you came in… I…" Her voice trailed away.

Tony studied her for a moment. Those same wicked eyes that had fixed Phillipa now rested on her. He might have only been around twenty-five, but Alexia could see why it had been such a battle for the strong and controlling Phillipa. He was no boy; he knew he was attractive, with his dirty blond, surfy hair and fit body. He loved himself and he loved to see himself reflected in the eyes of others.

"Maybe you'd like a turn? Give me a couple of minutes to get my breath back!"

"No!" cried Alexia. "No!"

She caught a panicky note in her voice. He regarded her coolly for a moment.

"You're the Ice Queen, aren't you?"

"The what…?" Alexia was confused now.

"That's what they call you, the boys downstairs. Cool as anything, with that 'look but don't touch' thing going on."

Alexia was dumbstruck.

"Hey, that doesn't matter, ice can—melt." He said the last word as if the breath of his voice alone could accomplish the task.

"Alexia isn't it?" His full lips formed her name as if he were sucking her in as he said it.

She flushed, unsure what to say or do. Then Tony stood straighter and finished buttoning his shirt.

"Don't worry, little ice maiden, plenty of time for that. Though spring is coming. Thawing season might be just around the corner."

He laughed to himself and disappeared from view. Her stomach lurched with relief and embarrassment. It seemed unreal, but it was real all right. She'd just watched two people fuck and now one of them had caught her. She moved to look out into the boardroom to make sure he was leaving, but as Tony got to the door it flew open, and in strode a tall, dark-haired man in a perfect dark suit, carrying a briefcase. He stopped and eyed Tony, then his eyes flashed to Alexia. She felt her stomach somersault so heavily she thought she'd fall backward.

The smell of sex hung unmistakably in the air, and Alexia's flushed appearance made it all too obvious that some serious fucking had just taken place in the room.

"Finished?" said the man coolly.

His voice was hard and commanding, without a hint of sarcasm. He was clearly Tony's superior, in every way. Tony half raised his hands in a "you got me" gesture and walked out, leaving Alexia standing in the doorway of the bathroom.

The man eyed her coolly. She didn't know who he was but she wouldn't forget him in a hurry. He was very tall, at least six-foot-three, with broad, strong shoulders. His hair was very dark brown, almost black, and well cut, but strands escaped and hung down over his dark blue eyes. He had an aquiline nose, slightly French-looking, which gave him a haughty appearance.

"Don't let me keep you!" he said with mock civility. He strode over to a desk and put down the briefcase. Alexia couldn't help noticing that his legs were long and athletic. He looked tired, as if it had been a very long day and he was eager for it to end.

"I… It's not what you think—" she stammered.

He raised an eyebrow in a gesture of tired indifference.

"As long as people do their jobs in my company, then I will put up with a certain amount of excess, but don't insult my intelligence, young lady…" He almost spat out the last word.

His company? Oh my God, thought Alexia, this is Nathan Fallon, the Fallon Sports Agency, my boss!

She had never met him; she'd been at the company only two days and he had been away on business.

"Please go and find your boyfriend, and do whatever it is you do somewhere else. I have work to finish." He walked back toward the door and opened it. The music flooded the room again. Shame and mortification flushed through Alexia's face.

"But—" she protested.

"Look, it's been a long day, I've had a long flight. Now kindly go and find yourself—" He looked at the table where the fucking had just finished. "Find yourself a more comfortable bed."

He walked behind her and ushered her out before she could protest any further. She could smell his aftershave, soft and warm; it filled her nostrils and its heady effect seemed to find its way into her panties. But she didn't have time to ponder on it for long, as she found herself propelled into the hallway by a strong hand and the boardroom door shut firmly behind her. She could hardly breathe.

Alexia was dumbstruck. It was like a bad dream. She gasped suddenly and clutched her forehead. She ran down the corridor, straight into the main office where the party was still in full swing.

Romy was sitting on some guy's lap, and he was clearly intent on getting the kind of action Tony had got. "Hey where you going?" she slurred, a little drunk.

"Home!"

Alexia grabbed her coat and handbag and ran the gauntlet of the partying staff to get to the door. As the cold night air hit her chest, she sucked in a lungful of it. A taxi was drawing past the office; its yellow roof light blinked invitingly, signaling her salvation. She waved him down frantically and fell into the backseat.

"Good night?" said the taxi driver, regarding her in his rear view mirror.

"Oh God!" she whimpered. "How the hell am I going to get out of this one?"

"Don't worry, love, it can't be that bad. Whatcha do? Kiss the boss over the photocopier?"

Alexia's mind was swirling. "No... I... Look, I'm sorry, I just need to get home."

She gave him the address and he obliged, moving the cab away from the curb and away from the scene of her shame. Alexia looked out at the office and saw the boardroom light still on. Nathan Fallon was standing in the window. Was he looking at her? His lone figure in the window grew smaller as the cab drove away; he turned away from the window and was gone, just as the cab turned the corner. Her misery was complete.

Chapter 2

ALEXIA WOKE UP SLOWLY. She was exhausted; the last few months with Carter had really worn her down. After her sudden flight from captivity, and being catapulted into a new job, her nerves were in shreds. She rubbed her eyes and peered groggily at the sweet little room that had become her new home. She hadn't had time to make it her own yet, but it felt good to have a bedroom door that was hers and hers alone. No man could enter unless invited.

She sighed heavily and stretched her long legs to the cool patch of the bed. Why did that feel so good in the morning? Cool cotton sheets slipped against her freshly waxed legs. The waxing was Romy's idea.

"You have to up the grooming if you're going to work here, sweetie!" Romy had laughed as she dragged Alexia into the salon.

She'd drawn the line at a Brazilian wax, though; that was a step too far. She settled on a neat triangle. That was as radical as she wanted to get.

She moved her hand down to her pussy and felt the triangle of hair and bare upper thighs. She was still foggy, not fully awake. But as her hand slid over the curls, a jolt of memory snapped her into full wakefulness.

"Oh God!" she cried out loud. So loudly she heard Romy's voice through the door.

"Hey, I thought you came home alone, girl!"

Romy came into the room carrying two huge, steaming mugs

of coffee. Alexia felt her face flush violently with the embarrassment of remembrance and she flung the sheet over her face as if it
would cover her shame. She needed to hide from last night, from the
memory of Tony's invitation and—worse, much worse—of Nathan
Fallon's disgust and disappointment. He was her boss and their first
meeting had been a car crash. She was on three months' probation at
the firm, and now she would never get the job.

She groaned under the sheet. Romy pulled it roughly away from
Alexia's face.

"What the hell's the matter with you? Here, I made you coffee.
I don't know about you, but my head's banging!"

She proffered the steaming cup of salvation. Alexia sat up slowly
and took the offering; she sipped. The scalding hot liquid seemed to
be a reproach for her behavior and her shame. She bit her lip.

"Hey, the coffee's not that bad! It's the expensive stuff from the
deli, thought we could do with a treat. Celebrate your new job!"

"Oh God, Romy!"

"What did you do last night? I saw Tony looking at you when
you ran out."

Alexia groaned with shame.

"Oh my God, did you fuck him?" demanded Romy.

Alexia was horrified. "What? No!"

Romy raised her eyebrows.

"No, I didn't!"

"Mmm, thought not, you're not the office fucking type. Mind
you, you might feel better if you had shagged him. Might loosen you
up a bit. Get Carter out of your head. Out of your snatch, certainly!"

"Romy!"

"Well, if you had a bit more—you know, experience—you
might not let bastards like Carter get their claws into you. I think
you should give Tony a ride. I certainly wouldn't mind, I bet he's a
bloody good shag."

Alexia nearly spat out her coffee and started coughing violently.

"Oh, come on, sweetie, I know you're a good girl and all that, but you must admit he looks like he's got a cock that could keep you happy for hours!"

Romy giggled at the thought of Tony and his tool.

"Well he has, actually," said Alexia, who'd finished her mini coughing fit.

"Eh? I thought you didn't…?"

"I didn't! But I saw who did!"

Romy was understandably confused.

"What happened last night? Because you ran out like your ass was on fire. And not in a good way!"

Alexia took a deep breath and put her head in her free hand, trying to smooth away the memory by rubbing her temple. She took a long glug of her cooling coffee to steady herself.

"Alexia?"

"Okay, okay… Look, I just needed a pee. I went in the bathroom and it was full of people snorting coke so I went to look for another toilet. There's one off the boardroom."

She stopped, flushing again at the memory of the previous night.

"Well…?"

"I was in there, and I couldn't find the light, so I was just feeling the wall, looking for it, when two people came into the boardroom. They didn't know I was in there, in the bathroom. I couldn't just burst out."

"Why not?"

"Well, it was Tony and that Phillipa woman and they'd come in…"

"To fuck! Oh my God, this is too good. So what happened, what did you do?"

"What could I do? I just had to hide."

"Did you see them—you know—do it?"

Alexia took a long, slow slurp.

"Oh my God, Alex, you did! Oh, details, details. Come on…"

"Well they just—you know—got on with it."

"Phillipa! She's a right bitch; she's like a praying mantis. Did she rip his head off and eat it afterward? Bloody hell, Tony's brave!"

"Oh no, he won that bout!"

Romy looked at Alexia, her eyes wide.

"Seriously, it was like watching a couple of tigers or something, you know, big cats… Circling each other, like they were trying to decide who was hunting and who was…"

"Getting eaten?" Romy smirked at the double meaning.

The two girls slurped their coffee, both imagining the scene.

"God, that sounds hot!" said Romy.

"Yeah," Alexia said quietly to herself, remembering.

"Hey, you were turned on!"

"No, I bloody wasn't. I was trapped. It was awful!"

Romy remained unconvinced. "Well, when you ran out of there last night it looked like *you* were the one who'd been royally fucked."

Alexia flushed violently.

"Come on, Alex, what's wrong with that? It's just like watching porn, only live. Did you see it all?"

Alexia nodded as she drank her coffee.

"Is he good?"

"He left Phillipa looking like she'd been filleted."

Romy screamed with laughter. Alexia relented and had to join in; it was funny, after all. The two girls rocked with laughter on Alexia's double bed.

"Well, it's about time someone brought that cow down to size," said Romy. "What did he do to her?"

"Well, it wasn't so much what as how. He was making her virtually beg for it. And the way he was…"

Alexia faltered.

"Way he was what?" demanded Romy.

"Well, hammering into her... Literally."

Romy bit her lip. "Is he big?" she asked.

Alexia nodded "Yeah, he is... And rock hard. It was like a nightstick!"

The two girls dissolved into laughter again.

"So, what were you so torn up about when you left?" asked Romy.

Alexia stopped suddenly. The laughter abandoned her as she remembered the finale to the little pornographic operetta she'd witnessed. She groaned.

"Phillipa left, then Tony found me!"

"Oh my fucking God!" Romy's mouth fell open.

"And he... Well, he said..."

"What? He said what?"

"He offered to..."

Romy's eyes rolled with realization. "Oh yes! Go for it. Every girl in the office wants to fuck him. He's been with us for six months and he doesn't seem to have done anyone yet, except Phillipa, obviously. He must be more into fucking management. Although I hear he's fucked quite a few clients. If Nathan knew he'd be out on his ear."

"He told me everyone calls me the Ice Queen or Ice Maiden or something."

Romy's enthusiasm evaporated. She looked uncomfortable.

"Romy? Oh my God... Is it true? They call me that?"

Romy sighed. "Well, you have this untouchable look, sort of virginal. And you don't give off vibes that you might be up for it, which is unusual."

Alexia suddenly looked like a child and Romy felt huge guilt. She wanted to protect her friend; her doll-like beauty always made her look so vulnerable, and never more so than now.

"Don't take any notice," said Romy. "The girls are just jealous 'cause you're gorgeous, and the boys just all want to get there first. You take your time." She blew out her cheeks. "Although Tony… I wouldn't mind tripping him up and making sure I'm underneath him when he lands!"

"Romy!"

"Look, he's gorgeous. And it wouldn't be serious… You should think about taking him up on the offer. You need to get over Carter. I'm just talking about a damned good fuck, not an affair. You need it."

Alexia couldn't deny that. Watching Tony last night, she realized that she needed it, and badly.

"That's not all that happened," she said quietly.

"There's more? Bloody hell."

"Well, after Phillipa left and Tony found me, and I told him to get lost… After that, he started to leave, but… Oh God!"

Alexia collapsed on the bed and closed her eyes.

"Oh God… What?"

Alexia just lay there shaking her head, her hands covering her face.

"What? What?" Romy was desperate.

Alexia sat bolt upright. "Nathan Fallon walked in."

"Oh, buggering hell!" Romy looked startled for a moment, then started to laugh with the craziness of it.

Alexia was beside herself. "He took one look at me and knew that Tony had been…"

"He thought Tony had fucked *you*!"

Alexia was miserable again. She buried her face in her hands. Romy gave a low whistle.

"Wow! The white whale thinks you shagged Tony."

"The white what?"

"The white whale," repeated Romy. "It's what we call him. The big one no one can catch. No one knows why, but he doesn't fuck around—well, not so that anyone knows if he does. And it's not because no one's tried. God, I'd give anything for a night with him, he's fucking gorgeous. I've been his PA for a year now and he's never flirted with me once. He's just a good boss... Damn him! He built that company from nothing, he knows everyone, goes to all the best parties; he's the catch of the century. I saw him in tennis shorts once..." Romy closed her eyes in remembrance. "*Tight* tennis shorts. Oh God, is he ever a mouthful. Not sure I could cope... I'd love to try though." She giggled.

"You should have seen the way he looked at me, Romy. Like I was a cheap little tart!"

"Oh, I'm sure he didn't... It was a party, and he knows how people behave in this industry. Just 'cause he doesn't join in doesn't mean he doesn't know about it."

"No, I know he thinks that... It was the way he..." Her voice trailed away.

Romy pushed a blond lock away from Alexia's pale face. There was a tear running down her pink cheek.

"Oh, sweetie, don't. So he thinks you fucked Tony, so what?"

"Because it's a temp job and I need to keep it. If he thinks badly of me then he might not give me the job permanently."

"Listen, as long as you do your job okay, you'll be kept on. It's only temporary while they try you out, so stop worrying..."

"But then..." Alexia bit her lip.

"Then what? What?"

"Nothing. I just... I don't know." Alexia looked desolate again. "I don't want him thinking that about me."

"Why? Want a shot at the white whale yourself?" Romy cocked an eyebrow.

"Well, that could never happen *now*, could it?" Alexia realized what she'd said and tried to backtrack. "I mean, could never *have* happened..."

"Hmm," said Romy knowingly. "Be careful who you have a

crush on. Tony you could fuck and throw back into the pond, but Nathan Fallon—he's not catch and release. And you don't need your heart broken again."

The two girls fell silent. Then Romy jumped up.

"Mind you, if you just want to get back on the bike Richard is going to be here in a minute."

"Who?"

"He's an old mate. He needs somewhere to crash for a bit so I told him he could have the sofa. He's American, very pretty, complete tart but great fun. He could pump your tires up! Come on, get up, he'll be here soon and you look like a fright. I'll run you a bath."

She flounced out of the room, singing to herself. For a moment Alexia could see the old Romy, punky and proud. You can change on the outside, she thought, but not on the inside, not really. The thought made her sad. She knew she needed to change, to reinvent herself the way Romy had done. She couldn't bear to think that the office staff thought she was frigid. But maybe she was. Her sexual encounters with her college boyfriend had been uninspiring. She'd slept with him because that's what you did. And Carter? That was horrible; she didn't want to think about him or his bedroom.

But then last night had proved to her that the aching in her loins was as strong as any woman's, stronger perhaps because she had been so starved of satisfaction.

Alexia heard Romy turn the tap in the bathroom and heard the water running into the bath. She swung her legs over the bed and looked at the floor. There was her laptop. She thought for a moment, then reached down to pick it up. She turned it on and found herself slowly typing a name into Google. She was jittery and her fingers were jumpy. She seemed to have trouble typing straight. N-A-T-G—no wait, that's an H-A-N…

She tapped out the twelve letters that made up the name but her finger hovered over the search button. Why was she nervous? She made the final tap and half a dozen pictures of the gorgeous Nathan Fallon jumped off the page. Her stomach flipped, a jolt of electricity running down the invisible line from stomach to pussy.

There he was: Nathan Fallon at Wimbledon; Nathan Fallon with Premier League soccer managers; Nathan Fallon with his arm around that gorgeous women's Olympic sprinting champion; Nathan Fallon alone, in black tie, smoldering into the camera. Looking into those eyes, the same eyes that had looked down at her in the boardroom, the surge to her pussy was undeniable.

He was like a panther, with his black hair, black suit, and searing blue eyes. He was handsome, but not in the conventional sense; his face had a smoldering intelligence. He was in his late thirties and very self-assured. Nathan Fallon, star sports agent. His image stared out at her from the screen. He's my boss, she thought. The boss who thinks I'm a tart.

She threw herself back on the bed. Images of Nathan swam before her eyes and her face burned again. She hadn't done anything wrong and here she was feeling like it was she who'd behaved appallingly, when her only real crime was being in the wrong place at the wrong time. How could this have happened to her?

She lay on the bed, prostrate with searing shame and horror. She could hear the water tumbling into the bath as if it were far away in the distance. She closed her eyes and listened; the sound of the liquid was soothing, warm, and inviting, just waiting for her to step into it and wash away her shame.

She realized her hand was on her chest. She felt a deep urge to rub her nipple. Slowly, almost guiltily, she moved her hand and ran her fingers gently over it. She felt a tiny spark of electricity. She did it again; the same spark. She pressed a little firmer and curled her toes at the soft and lilting pleasure. She pulled down the strap of her nightie and exposed the nipple.

It was pink and hard now, proud and begging. She held it

between the tips of her thumb and forefinger and increased the pressure into a slow pinch. The pressure revealed that straight line connection between her nipple and her pussy. She pinched it again and the tug got stronger. She pushed her other hand under the covers and ran her middle finger down into her now damp curls until she found the nub. It was already engorged.

She began to rub gently. She could hear the water fill the bath as her own wetness began to increase. She rubbed the flat of her middle finger up and down as her other hand pinched and tweaked her erect nipple. She dug her heels into the bed. Romy was just the other side of the open door; she could hear her humming in the kitchen. She had to stay quiet.

She rubbed harder, pressing the length of her finger against her clit, trying to imagine it was a cock. But whose cock? She had started thinking about Nathan, but realized that Tony's face kept swimming into view.

Nathan's face, then Tony's face. Nathan, then Tony… Nathan's face, then Tony's face… Nathan's face, then Tony… Tony's face… Tony's cock…

She stopped abruptly and gasped. What was going on? She didn't like Tony; he was arrogant and cocky. Cocky! Literally. But Romy was right: he would be a hell of a ride. Nathan, well, he was altogether different. Thinking about him felt dangerous; he *was* dangerous. Too dangerous for her? He wasn't a man to be played with, not that she knew how to play with men. Romy was right again. She needed to learn. Maybe Tony was the man to practice on, even if it was just in a fantasy?

She started rubbing again, this time harder, picking up speed. She arched her back as Tony's blue eyes heaved into her imagination. She could hear his voice. "Ice can—melt…"

She groaned and thrust a finger into her soaking pussy, but it was a poor substitute for Tony's cock. But she rubbed and rubbed and bucked underneath her own hand until she came. It was a short and almost perfunctory orgasm, but she needed it so badly after the tension of last night. The orgasm she'd given herself in that bathroom was intense, but nothing close to what she needed.

She lay still, breathing hard. The sound of the bathwater, which had seemed so far away a moment ago, now reentered her consciousness.

She got to her feet and looked at the laptop, still brazenly flaunting pictures of Nathan. She slammed the lid shut and walked into the living room.

"Hey there!" said a scruffy young guy.

"What?" she gasped.

"Hey, sorry. Didn't mean to startle ya!"

She heard a southern American drawl and looked at the disheveled guy, wearing torn jeans and an old T-shirt. He might have needed a tidy up, but there was no denying he was sexy. His hair was collar-length and a little greasy, and he was unshaven, which gave him a lived-in look.

"I'm Richard… Sorry, I thought Romy told you I was coming."

Alexia composed herself. "Yes, she did. Sorry, I was—er…"

"Yeah, I'm sorry I've disturbed you two…"

Alexia thought that he was referring to her and Romy when he said "two." But she realized Romy was in the kitchen and Richard was nodding toward the bedroom.

"Two? No, there's no one else in there, just me… I just got up."

"Got up?" he said. "I thought maybe you'd just got off!"

Alexia flushed.

"Don't worry," he said, lowering his voice. "A little morning self-love is a great thing. Keeps you healthy."

Alexia was still stumbling for a reply when Romy walked in.

"Hey, you've met! Richard, this is Alexia. Alexia, this is Richard."

Richard took Alexia's hand and kissed it theatrically. He stopped for a moment, holding her hand and breathing in. A tiny half sniff.

Alexia realized it must still smell of her come. She yanked it away as her face reddened.

"I'm making breakfast," said Romy and went back into the kitchen.

Richard's eyes twinkled at Alexia. "Maybe I could help you out one morning." He cocked an eyebrow and sauntered into the kitchen.

Alexia stood in the living room, her head swirling.

"Alexia, get in the bath before it runs over!" shouted Romy.

"Oh my God, the bath!"

Alexia dashed into the bathroom and shut off the taps. She locked the door, then wiped the mirror with a towel and took a look at her reflection. She looked like a wood nymph, all wide-eyed and innocent. But her little hand job had left her flushed and wanton-looking.

She stepped away from the mirror and took off her nightie. She looked down at the little triangle of hair over her pussy. Blond curls still glistened. Her lips were pink and swollen. She got into the bath, lowering her body into the water to wash away the evidence of her morning's pleasure. The warm water lapped her lips and soothed her after her frantic rubbing. She closed her eyes and sighed heavily.

Romy was cooking bacon, and the smell of it was wafting into the bathroom. Richard was helping himself to coffee and sat on the windowsill in the tiny kitchen.

"She's nice."

"Hey, she's had a rough time, so watch it," warned Romy.

"Okay, okay, just sayin'…"

"Yeah, and you were just thinkin'…" She copied his American drawl and curtailed verbs.

"Actually, she looks real sweet."

"She is, and she's been with a complete bastard. Took a huge amount of guts to leave him."

"How do you guys know each other? She's not like your usual friends."

"I know. School together—hadn't seen for years, then ran into her. She was always a quiet one. But she's nice, you know. And I wanted to help. She needs…"

Richard's eyes glinted.

"Hey!" Romy slapped his arm.

"Am I wrong?" asked Richard teasingly.

"No. No, you're not." Romy sighed. "I think she'll come out of her shell once she's settled down at work."

"You got her a job too?"

"Er, yeah. But…"

"She no good at it?"

"No she'll be great… But you know what it's like at my office. It's a bit on the wild side for her."

"Well, then she'll definitely come out of her shell." Richard smirked.

"Yeah, I just hope she enjoys it, I don't want to see her hurt again. She needs to get back in the saddle but not with another asshole."

"*I'm* not an asshole!"

Romy threw a tea towel at him.

"Hey, watch it, sister!"

Richard folded the towel up neatly and put it on the countertop.

"Look, I won't touch her if she doesn't want me to, and if she does, I'll be real gentle, in every sense… okay?"

Romy shook her head. "Well, she is a grown woman, and a gentle jiggle with you might do her good. Better than Tony—or Nathan."

"Who's Tony…? Nathan? How many guys does this chick have lined up?"

"You've seen her. They're queuing around the block. She just doesn't know it."

"That's kinda what's sweet about her."

Romy sighed. "Yes, yes, it is… But you can't stay sweet forever."

"And ain't that the truth!" Richard laughed. Then he smacked Romy's ass and sauntered back into the living room. He walked past the bathroom door. He stopped and contemplated Alexia's body in the bathwater and felt himself harden slightly. He blew out a long breath and moved on into the living room.

―⁓―

In the bathroom, Alexia was lying back, still staring at the door. She'd heard every word from the kitchen.

She looked down at her newly manicured muff. It *was* time to change, she knew that. It was time to claim her place in the world as a woman; not a good little girl, but a fully rounded, sexual woman.

"You can't stay sweet forever." She repeated Romy's words to herself—and she knew it was true.

Chapter 3

ALEXIA SPENT THE WEEKEND in a daze. She tried to busy herself making her bedroom look more like her own room, buying cushions and baubles and new curtains. Her credit card was complaining, but she needed to nest and feel secure.

When she'd finished, her room looked like a French boudoir in beautiful blues and greens, with jewel-colored cushions on her bed and gorgeous drapes framing the floor-length window.

"Wow," said Romy. "Who's the lucky guy who's going to get seduced in here?"

Alexia felt good about her new little haven. It was the first time since she'd left college that she truly had a space of her own. It was tiny, but it was hers, and that was all she needed.

Richard and Romy spent most of Saturday and Sunday out and about, leaving Alexia to her own devices. They'd invited her along, but she wanted some alone time.

She couldn't get Friday night out of her head. The sight of Tony's buttocks kept intruding on her thoughts; the way the muscles in his perfect, tight ass twitched and flexed as he pumped Phillipa over and over. She didn't want to think about it, but the images just invaded her mind. Whatever she did to distract herself just reminded her of that night...

She was washing dishes, and the slurping water made her think of the wet, slapping sound of Tony's cock in Phillipa's cunt. She leaned over the table to pick up her handbag and saw Phillipa's arching back

and begging eyes, urging Tony to pump faster and harder. She went
to the kitchen door and saw Nathan stride through it, saw his eyes,
and how he looked at her. Nathan.

She still couldn't fathom the expression on his face when he'd
found her. He'd looked at her with what? Hostility? Disappointment?
She couldn't pin it down, but the image kept looming into view,
nagging at her, reproaching her. But she hadn't done anything
wrong, so why did she feel so wretched?

"Get a grip!" she barked out loud to herself.

There was only one way to tackle this; she'd have to get out.
She put on her running shoes, shorts, and a T-shirt and grabbed her
keys and iPod as she headed for the door. I'll have to run it out, she
thought, and headed for the street.

Running always cleared her head. But this time she needed to
clear more than her head; she needed to get rid of the nagging ache
in her groin. She headed for the park near the flat where runners
pounded the paths every day. She hit the circuit and found her stride.

She wasn't very tall, but her legs were long for her body and she
had an even, rhythmic stride. She was engrossed in her music and
her own footfall. She found the steady motion to the heartbeat of
the music, and it calmed her mind. Thud, thud, thud on the asphalt.
She wanted to feel free and calm, but the strong, insistent beat of
the music and rhythmic pounding of her feet on the floor made the
pounding in her pussy even stronger.

It started to rain softly, but she didn't care; the water felt good
on her skin, cooling and healing. She ran for almost an hour and
then, exhausted, she made her way back to the flat.

It was Sunday evening and the sun was hanging low in the sky,
one of those lazy London days where the city seems to take its rest
from the hectic bustle of the week.

She padded softly up the stairs to the flat and let herself in. She
caught sight of herself in the mirror; blond tendrils had escaped from

her ponytail and were hanging around her face. Her hair was damp, but she was glowing, and the wet hair made her look even sexier. Her blue eyes were clear, betraying no sign of the heaviness she felt.

She went into her newly decorated bedroom. The room needed air; she walked over to the long window and opened it. The glass was draped with soft white voile that shifted lazily in the breeze from the open pane, diffusing the light in the room.

"Beautiful," said a soft voice behind her.

Alexia wheeled around, startled. Richard was leaning against the doorway, arms folded, assessing her.

"You have a great eye," said Richard. "This is quite a little love nest!"

"It's just a few bits and pieces to make it, you know, cozy," protested Alexia.

"Cozy. Ah, that's one word for it. Sumptuous. That's a good word. Inviting, there's another, but not quite right." He thought for a moment. "Enveloping… Oh yeah, that's it. This room could *envelop* you."

His mouth caressed the word as his eyes roamed over her. Bedroom eyes, she thought, quite literally. She felt a lurching in the pit of her stomach, and lower down, which surprised her. He was attractive, soft, and as laid-back as his southern drawl. Alexia suddenly felt very naked in her flimsy running gear.

He had been leaning against the door; now he stood up suddenly and turned to go into the living room. Alexia felt a surge of regret and relief that he had removed that knowing gaze from her.

"Romy's gone out with some guy she met. Glass of wine? Looks like you could use one."

"I—er—need a shower," Alexia stammered.

"Sure thing. I'll have a glass waiting for you when you come out. I've made some pasta too; you'll need it after all that exercise."

Richard retreated to the kitchen and Alexia breathed out. He was very attractive, and the way he'd looked at her made her unsure whether the dampness in her shorts was all because of rain and sweat.

She jumped into the shower and stood under the spray, letting the warm water wash off the perspiration. As she soaped her body, she kept thinking that Richard was just the other side of the door. Was it time to throw away the little sweet girl? Or was it too soon? She couldn't just jump on him, could she? Or could she? Her soapy fingers were circling her stomach. And then they started to circle lower, and lower, almost involuntarily. The suds caressed the curls and her middle finger slid slowly and seductively down…

Don't be silly, she told herself. Just get dressed, have some pasta and a glass of wine, and get to bed; you have work tomorrow. Work! Oh yes, there'd be the office tomorrow and work—and Nathan. Her knees felt weak at the thought of having to face him again. She'd spent barely thirty seconds in his presence, but the very thought of him made her head swim.

She came out of the bathroom to find Richard holding two large glasses of red wine. She was wearing a towel that barely skimmed her backside.

"After you…" He stood to one side to let her pass.

She didn't want him walking behind her, she knew he'd be looking at her too-short towel, but she had no choice. She dived toward the bedroom, her towel riding up at the back, exposing the very barest hint of the curve at the top of her thighs. She felt Richard's eyes burning into her. She knew he was watching. She shut the bedroom door behind her and stood against it, breathing hard, clutching her towel. The silence was broken from the other room.

"Food's on the table," shouted Richard through the door.

Alexia pulled on her soft, velvety pajama bottoms and a T-shirt and reemerged into the living room.

"I preferred the last two outfits," said Richard with a little tone of reproach. "Nice T-shirt, though."

Too late Alexia realized that she'd pulled on a pale pink top that showed only too clearly that her nipples were standing to attention.

"I'm really tired, Richard. This is really sweet of you, but I think I'll just have a little pasta and go to bed. I've got a big day at work tomorrow and I—"

She didn't get to finish her sentence as Richard strode over to her and grabbed her, pulling her into his arms. It happened so suddenly she had no time to protest. His face was inches from hers; she could smell his masculinity and the warm red wine on his breath.

"I have never met a woman who needed this more than you do right now." His voice was low and warm.

His mouth was on hers. She felt her legs buckle with the sudden rush of pleasure that flooded through her. He was only kissing her, but her belly and her pussy felt as if a sudden rush of water had coursed through them on its way somewhere more urgent. As his kiss deepened, she felt the surge build.

She wasn't sure why, but she found herself kissing him back, her mouth hungry for his. She felt the need to breathe him in as he kissed her. Her need was sudden and raw, and he felt it.

He pushed her backward to the wall and their mouths parted. She looked into his lazy brown eyes. They stood motionless for a moment, breathing, watching. He didn't take his eyes from hers as she felt his hand find its way into her pajama bottoms. She gasped. His aim was spectacular. With one smooth, silent move, his hand had buried itself in her curls. She wanted to protest, but his mouth was on hers again. His lips were warm and insistent as he kissed gently but deeply, so she felt as if she might only be able to breathe while he was kissing her.

His fingers circled in the soft, downy hair on either side of her sex, but avoided the middle, the place that ached to be probed. His fingers circled round and round, never parting her lips. It was torture. She was breathing hard as his mouth had been on hers without release. She wanted him to touch her, really touch her. Then, without warning, he pressed down and found her clit. A desperate moan escaped from her mouth into his.

There was no hiding from him. She was wet, really, really wet. He had found her out. She did need this, she needed it very badly. He worked her nub with firm, even strokes which matched the rhythm of his moving mouth. Stroke, stroke, stroke… With each one she felt the wetness increase and her need get stronger. She parted her legs slightly and he gave a little laugh. But the laugh broke the moment and suddenly she could see Nathan's face in front of her. She opened her eyes and saw Richard's cloudy gaze looking into hers.

She pushed hard against him. She felt his hand yank out of her pajama bottoms and away from her pussy.

"No," she stammered. "I can't!"

He put both hands up.

"Okay, okay."

He looked at her and saw the confusion in her eyes. He lowered his hands and his voice and spoke very gently.

"I'm sorry, really, but you looked like you needed…"

"I can't… I'm sorry, I—I just can't. Not right now." Alexia felt exposed, scared, turned on, and oh so needy. But she couldn't, she just couldn't.

"Hey… I'm real sorry." Richard moved to put his arms around her, but she squirmed away. "Listen, Alexia, I'm sorry, I overstepped. I'm used to girls who are a little different from you. I know you've had a bad time, Romy told me, so I'm sorry… Really."

He looked genuinely pained. His soft American drawl made him sound sweet and vulnerable. Alexia breathed out. She felt suddenly foolish and petulant.

"No, it's okay. You weren't wrong, I do need…" She looked down. "I need to get my bearings."

She looked at him and gave a weak smile.

"Hey, kiddo, I hear ya. Look, just think of me as a friend who's here to make you feel better, *whichever* way that is… okay?"

"Okay," she said softly.

They stood in silence. Then Richard moved to the table, and she could see the straining bulge in his trousers. The material was stretched tight across his groin. He was being gracious and seemed very in control for a man who was clearly so turned on. Why couldn't she have that same level of control?

"Well, the food's still hot, you need to eat, and I promise, no more moves. Just food, wine, and some friendly conversation."

"Thanks, but I'm not really hungry. I'm going to go to bed."

"Okay," Richard said, looking slightly crestfallen. "Am I forgiven?"

Alexia sighed and smiled at him. "Yes, yes, you are."

He was very attractive. Alexia knew she wanted him and she must have been giving off some pretty strong signals. She didn't blame him; he was being very sweet. She turned to go into the bedroom and stopped. She looked back at him.

"When I'm ready, then maybe."

Alexia smiled at him and he dropped his head and looked back up at her through thick lashes.

"I'll be here," he said.

Alexia went into the bedroom and closed the door. She turned off the light and climbed into her big bed and pulled the covers up tight. She suddenly felt howlingly lonely. The ache she felt was raw, like an ancient need nagging inside her. But she was too tired and worn to give it what it wanted. She closed her eyes.

When the hideous screech of her alarm clock burst into her consciousness Alexia felt as if she had only just fallen asleep. It was 7:00 a.m.

It had been a torrid night, with Nathan's and Tony's faces swimming in and out of her consciousness again, now joined by Richard's face.

She crawled out of bed and went about getting ready for work. Washed, dressed, and with makeup more carefully applied than usual, she could hardly remember the journey to the office. She'd been alone, mercifully. Romy had gone in early to finish a pressing contract.

Alexia sat at her desk in the open-plan office and tried her best to look composed. She felt as if everyone in the company knew something about her; perhaps they'd heard about Tony. But as she studied the faces she realized she was probably just being paranoid.

The morning went past in a blur of typing. It was boring work and she found it hard to concentrate. But the monotony wasn't to last long. Tony appeared from nowhere and sauntered past her desk like a cat who's just managed to steal the last bowl of cream in the fridge.

"Good morning," he said. He was almost licking his lips.

She felt her stomach lurch; well, not just her stomach. She was feeling it much lower down.

She glanced up at his retreating figure. He stopped to talk to one of the junior staff, standing with his back to Alexia. His trousers couldn't hide the muscularity of his ass and legs. As he shifted his weight from one leg to the other, the fabric molded around the cheeks of his bottom and Alexia felt a squirt in her panties.

"Hey." Romy appeared from nowhere and sat on the end of Alexia's desk. Alexia flushed. Romy leaned forward conspiratorially and whispered, "Well you have seen his butt before, only last time it was naked."

"Be quiet!" Alexia hissed.

"Don't worry, no one will hear. Oh my God, you've gone bright red! Come on." She grabbed Alexia's arm and her handbag. "It's time for lunch, let's go to Joe's."

Joe's was a little Italian café close to the office. Alexia was whisked along at a cracking pace by Romy and found herself propelled into the corner of the snug little eatery, almost breathless.

"Right!" said Romy, rolling up her sleeves. "Time for some lessons in office hotties."

"Romy, please…!" Alexia's eyes darted around the room; she was terrified they'd be overheard.

"I'm not listening. Right, then… Tony is gorgeous, we know this, and there are quite a few shaggable guys in there. I should know, I've had two of them. But most of them are fussy beggars because they get loads of women around them at press events. That shouldn't worry you as they *all* want to get in *your* panties!"

"What? Don't be silly! They're not interested in me. They're really cool toward me. They don't like me."

"Exactly!"

"What?"

"You're the untouchable one, but they all want you. It's easy to check them out. When they're being cold, just see what's going on in their pants. And when they think you aren't looking, just look back quickly as you walk away and you'll catch them ogling. You have to pay more attention to the signals."

"That's ridiculous!"

"I know what I'm talking about. I can see I am going to have to be your new governess and give you a thorough education in men. And as for Tony—he's gagging for you!" Romy took an enormous bite of the sandwich that had just arrived. Mayonnaise squirted out onto her lip as if to emphasize the point.

Alexia flushed again and felt wetness in her panties. She wanted to squirm. That ache seemed to have been there since last week, since last Friday night at the party—all weekend, in fact.

But Romy hadn't finished. "And then there's *la balena bianca*!"

"The what?"

Romy's family was Italian, and she usually broke into her mother tongue when she was being particularly naughty or needed a damned good swear.

"The white whale, of course. Mister—drumroll, please—Naaaathan Fallon."

"Oh, stop it!" said Alexia, nibbling halfheartedly at her own sandwich.

"Look, I'm his PA," said Romy. "And he asked about you this morning."

Alexia nearly choked on her bread. Romy knew she'd dropped a bombshell and was playing innocently with the spoon in her coffee, stirring in a slow, suggestive circle, the tiniest trace of a smile dancing on her red-painted lips.

"What do you mean he asked about me?" Alexia was panicked.

"He just asked who the new girl was." Romy feigned an innocent air. "He doesn't normally ask when we get someone junior in; he's too busy to care about staff who come and go. You obviously made quite an impression."

"Oh God, that's what I was afraid of!"

Alexia felt miserable again. She kept seeing his face glowering at her. The face that looked out at her from her laptop screen—dark, unforgiving.

"Hey, don't panic," said Romy. "He didn't look cross, just…"

She didn't finish her sentence but sat thinking about it for a moment, keeping Alexia waiting, playing to see if she'd reveal an interest in him.

"What? What? He looked what?" pleaded Alexia.

"Hmm, and you're not interested in him?" Romy smiled knowingly.

Alexia flushed.

Romy was pleased with herself. "He looked *intrigued*." She let the word hang in the air for a moment, floating like a parcel full of possibilities and secrets. "Yes, I'd say intrigued. It was like he couldn't quite figure out what to make of you."

Alexia sat staring. Romy went back to drinking her coffee. She'd dropped the stone into the pond and now she was watching the ripples.

But Alexia was sticking to her story. "I'm worried about my job."

"Hmm!" Romy was theatrically unconvinced.

"I am!" Alexia insisted.

"Don't worry, you'll keep your job."

Alexia looked relieved. Romy arched an eyebrow.

"And you can stop all that whale nonsense, he's my boss and that's it." Alexia pursed her lips.

"Who happens to be the *one* guy in the office—no, in this whole business—every single woman wants to fuck!"

"Well, he won't be fucking me!" said Alexia, a little too loudly, she realized, when several male customers turned to look at her.

"Oh God, this just keeps getting worse." She sank down into her chair, trying to make herself as small as possible.

"Okay. Well, time for your first lesson in learning about men— properly. Back to the office, and this time you are going to pay close attention to whoever is paying close attention to you."

They went back to the office in silence. Romy was almost skipping along; Alexia just wanted to go back to bed and pull the covers over her head.

They walked through the double glass doors that greeted any visitors to the agency, past the manicured and identically clad receptionists. As they walked down the corridor to the main office, Nathan emerged from the boardroom. Alexia's stomach gave such a lurch she felt it was almost audible.

"Nathan," said Romy with theatrical breeziness. "I don't think you've met Alexia… She's new."

Nathan regarded Alexia. His cool glance made her legs feel unsteady. He was probably the most magnetic man she'd ever met. Now that she had more time to study him she realized what a presence he had. And there was that aftershave again, subtle but oh so sexy. The smell of it sent her right back to Friday night, standing in the boardroom. He looked at her. She felt a clutching feeling in her cunt. It was almost unbearable.

"Alexia." His professional veneer was perfect as he repeated her name. He put out his hand.

He's going to pretend we haven't met, thought Alexia. She wasn't sure if she was relieved or just very confused. She put out her hand and he grasped it. The warmth and strength of his fingers sent a warm rush up her arm.

"Hello," she said shakily.

He obviously hadn't told Romy *how* he'd seen her in the office, just that he'd seen her. But Alexia knew that Romy knew, and this pantomime was excruciating.

Romy was still playing hostess. "Alexia is also my flatmate."

"Indeed," said Nathan, releasing Alexia's hand. She was relieved to be free of his grasp, but slightly bereft also. The energy from the touch of his skin was shocking to her.

"Well, we're not quite one big happy family here, but we're pretty close…" As he said the last word, he looked directly at her. He certainly hadn't forgotten Friday's encounter in the boardroom.

She smiled weakly, wanting the ground to swallow her whole, right then and there.

"Welcome to the company, Alexia." As he repeated her name he inclined his head slightly. It was a small gesture but it induced a huge tug in her loins. Then, suddenly, he was striding away; elegant, tall, confident. Down the corridor, sweeping out through the double doors like a gunslinger from a saloon, and gone.

Alexia let out a pent-up breath, the exhalation one of relief and mortification, mixed equally.

"Well," said Romy breezily. "That wasn't so bad, was it?"

"I need to sit down." Alexia hurried off to the main office.

"Hey, don't forget I gave you homework. Observation class!" Romy called after her, laughing as she sauntered away to Nathan's office.

Back at her desk, Alexia couldn't collect her thoughts. "Welcome to the company," he'd said. "We're pretty close!"

Oh God, she thought, he really thinks I'm a tart. And that thought hurt, really hurt. But why? She hardly knew him. Yes she was attracted to him, but then Tony and Richard were both attractive. What was different about Nathan? But he was different. Very different.

She was in a daze, staring at her computer, unseeing. Her head was swimming, her lips felt numb, as if all the blood had drained from her head. She took a deep breath and looked up to orientate herself. But as she did she saw two of the jocks who worked at the company looking at her. They both looked away hurriedly. Alexia blinked. These guys were very good looking; she'd seen the girls flirting with them, trying to catch their attention. Alexia pretended to look back at her screen but she sneaked a look at one of the guys and, sure enough, she saw a small bulge in his pants. She suppressed a small giggle. Did I do that? she thought. Was Romy right?

She felt a sudden jolt of power. It was a strange feeling, and one she wasn't used to, especially after so long with Carter. She wanted to know more. Slowly, she got up and walked to the water cooler. She bent over to fetch a cup, but the cup store was empty as she knew it would be; she had seen it from her desk. She had her back to the boys and realized they would have a good view of her behind in her tight pencil skirt. She stood up very suddenly and whirled around.

"Anyone know where the cups are kept?" she asked.

One of the guys nearly fell off his chair. They had clearly been transfixed by her rear end. Neither spoke.

"Oh, don't worry," she said. "I think they're in the supply closet."

She smiled and walked away, suppressing a giggle of disbelief at her boldness and the reaction of the guys.

She left the office and felt a jolt of pleasure as the door closed behind her, taking her out of sight. She knew their eyes had been on her departing figure. She was wearing borrowed heels from Romy. They were far too high for her, but she'd wanted to look her best today. She'd been a little unsteady on them all day, but now she stalked down the corridor with absolute steadiness. She felt taller and it wasn't just because of the four-inch stilettos she was balancing on.

The supply closet was tucked away at the back of the building, far away from any office space or people. She found the light switch and went in. There was a large table being stored in the room that made it hard to get at the supplies. She leaned over it to reach the cups. She couldn't quite reach and had to strain forward.

"Can I help?"

She whirled around to see Tony. He'd come in silently and was closing the door behind him.

Alexia couldn't form a word.

"I just thought I should say hello properly as we haven't really been introduced—formally, that is. Tony Schaeffer, at your service." He extended a hand.

She looked at it but didn't move. He didn't seem to be as wolflike as he had on Friday night. His smile was warm and seemed genuine. She put out her hand and he took it. It was softer than Nathan's grip, but his skin was warm and it felt good. He didn't let go.

"You're still holding my hand," said Alexia, her eyes never leaving his. He was very pretty; not handsome but pretty. His boyish face was framed by blond curls. He looked like a slightly fallen angel.

"I know," he said quietly. "I'd rather not let go."

He held on to her hand with his right and, with his left hand, he traced up her extended arm until they were standing too close and his fingers rested by her armpit, grazing the side of her breast.

She gasped, but didn't move; she couldn't. There was nowhere to go in this tiny space. But then, she didn't want to move. Her breast was aching with the brushed touch and it wanted more.

"I'm sorry you saw me with Phillipa on Friday. I'm not always so rough. She likes it like that. You, on the other hand—" He thought for a moment. "I think you deserve to be treated more *gently*, don't you, Alexia?"

He knew her name. He was speaking softly as if trying to calm a skittish horse. She felt that now-familiar spurt of wetness between her legs. His hand slid gently under her right breast and cupped the weight of it. His eyes never left hers; big, blue pools she could dive into. His face was angelic but, now she studied him, his mouth seemed quite cruel; his lips had a curl to them that wasn't quite in keeping with the rest of his face.

He inched toward her. As he closed the distance between them, he bent his head and brushed his lips against the side of her mouth— not a kiss, but almost. She couldn't breathe.

"Very gently," he repeated.

He was right up against her now. She could feel his hardness, and she knew what was straining beneath the cloth of his trousers; she'd seen it on Friday. The hand she'd extended to shake his had found itself resting against his chest and he put his hands on the sides of her rib cage. He would be able to feel her breathing hard.

The wetness in her panties was getting warmer and her pussy was aching so much she felt as if her juices would stain her skirt. She wanted to press her pussy against his cock. She could picture it, just as she had seen it days before: rock hard, circumcised, the helmet marble smooth.

But he pulled back and looked at her. She couldn't read the look in his eyes. Without taking his gaze away from hers he put his hands to work undoing the buttons of her blouse. The fabric was tight around her breasts, which seemed to have swollen, straining the buttons.

He expertly undid the fastenings, traveling down from her collar bone to her waist. Then, with one sudden tug, he lifted the sides of her blouse clear of her skirt, leaving her lacy white bra exposed. The shock of it made her gasp, but she didn't move; she was transfixed. His gaze traveled down from her eyes.

"Oh, beautiful," he breathed. "Really magnificent!"

Her chest was heaving as he studied her breasts. The shock of his gaze on her exposed chest terrified and excited her. Carefully, with strong fingers, he teased down the fabric of her bra and lifted each straining breast so it was free of its cup. It made her tits stand even higher and prouder as they rested on top. Her nipples were engorged and pointing straight at him; dark pink, quivering, desperate to be touched. But he wasn't going to give her what she wanted. He traced his fingers around the orbs of her breasts, leaving the nipples orphaned and unloved, aching for attention.

"I knew you'd have gorgeous breasts. You look like a girl with really, really beautiful tits. Good enough to eat."

He bent his head, his tongue escaping his mouth to touch her left nipple almost imperceptibly. It was barely a touch, but it sent a shock wave right through Alexia. She had never felt this kind of electricity in her life. Was it Tony? Or was it the fact that they could be discovered at any moment? She didn't know why; all she knew was that she didn't want him to stop.

He took her nipple in his mouth and ran his tongue over it. She moaned and he smiled on hearing her reaction. With his free hand he reached for her other nipple and gave it a gentle tug. Alexia thought she would come then and there. Could that be possible? Just from having him play with her breasts? But the pressure was mounting and she wanted release; oh, how she wanted it.

Suddenly Tony stood up. "Damn, we can't!" he said.

"What?" The word almost exploded from her mouth. She felt as if a blast of cold air had suddenly enveloped her.

Tony's blue eyes were slightly cloudy. She felt his hardness pressing against her and knew he wanted her. What was he playing at?

"God, this is crazy, but Nathan needs me in the office. I only came in to get some blank contract copies. He'll be wondering where the hell I am."

Nathan? Her head swam. Alexia suddenly felt very naked and very exposed. She pulled her blouse over her exposed breasts.

"Oh God, that's a shame!" said Tony, and buried his head once more in her cleavage.

She almost fell back over the table. He picked up his head again.

"We have to do this—we absolutely *have* to—" He gave a low growl. "But not now."

Alexia was embarrassed and furious. Her emotions were flying around faster than her hormones.

"No, we don't!" she spat.

"Hey, come on. It's just bad timing. We have to…"

"No, we don't." She was emphatic. She frantically did up the buttons of her blouse, her breasts tucked safely back into the embrace of her bra. She was pushing her blouse back into her skirt and trying to compose herself.

"You want to, you know you do. What's wrong with that?" Tony protested.

"Look, you caught me. I was… I wasn't thinking."

"Well, that's your problem. Too much thinking. You just have to feel it—and, gorgeous girl, you are definitely feeling it…"

He reached to put his hand on her hip but she twisted away.

"No, Tony, stick to Phillipa. She's obviously happy with a knee-trembler in the office, but not me, okay?"

She pushed past him and dashed out into the long corridor; she wanted to get away as quickly as possible. What the hell was going on in her life? She seemed to be spending all of it running away.

As she reached the end of the corridor, she went to grab the door handle but stumbled on her heels as the door was flung open toward her. She suddenly found herself crashing into someone, then strong arms grabbed her shoulders and stopped her falling over. For a split second, she wondered what had happened. And then she smelt it, that soft, sexy aftershave. She looked up and realized that the person who was holding her up, holding her at arm's length, was Nathan.

They stood staring at each other. She was startled; he looked puzzled. She wanted to fall, fall straight into his arms as they seemed the safest place to be at that point.

"Are you all right?" he asked, his voice as soft as the musk that invaded her nostrils and wrapped itself around her.

He was tall and lowered his head to look into her eyes. She knew she must look strange; slightly wild, upset, flushed. Their eyes locked. There was an expression on his face she couldn't read. Not like the last time, this one was... Was what? Concern?

She tried to speak, but couldn't find her voice; she felt as if her lips were trembling. He looked down at her. His eyes seemed cloudy, troubled. She thought she felt him pull her toward him, but it was a tiny movement, almost imperceptible. Was she dreaming it? He looked at her mouth, and his own opened slightly with the merest hint of an intake of breath. Was he going to speak, or was he...?

A noise behind her broke the moment. She saw Nathan lift his head to look past her. His face darkened and he let go of her, suddenly setting her back on her feet and withdrawing his hands. She turned and saw Tony coming out of the supply closet, adjusting his balls through his trousers. The only thing at the end of the corridor was that closet. It must have been obvious where she'd been.

She turned back to Nathan, who looked thunderous. But he kept his eyes fixed on Tony.

"When you're ready, Tony, we're waiting for you." He was too classy to be openly angry or sarcastic, but Alexia could feel his displeasure. She was so close to him, how could she not?

Then he was gone, through the door again without a backward glance.

Tony sauntered up behind her. "Well, now the boss definitely thinks we're doing it, we might as well make it official—when you're ready, beautiful!"

He ran a hand up the side of her hip, then disappeared through the door after Nathan.

She stood for a moment, alone in the corridor, struck dumb.

Then she heard herself spit out the words, "Bastard! You arrogant fucking bastard!"

Pent-up emotion exploded from her. Hot tears welled up behind her eyes and she felt her lungs heave. She was almost hiccupping, trying to catch her breath. She ran into the nearest bathroom, straight into a stall, and locked the door behind her. She stood breathing hard, leaning her head against the door, her hand still on the lock, as if just getting in and slamming the bolt shut was the most she could do before all her energy abandoned her.

She felt so confused, emotions whirling, writhing, competing for attention. Nathan, Nathan, Nathan, Nathan. She was banging her forehead against the door and saying his name out loud. When he'd held her shoulders, the way he'd looked at her, what was he thinking? She felt there was almost—almost—a "moment" between them? She didn't trust herself, she must have imagined it.

But then what did it matter now? He'd seen Tony. Then she knew exactly what he was thinking. He hadn't even looked back at her as he left, just put her firmly back on her feet and disappeared. The tears were running down her face now. She let them fall and just waited until they stopped. She stood with her eyes closed. An eternity seemed to pass. Just breathing in and out. She opened her eyes and remembered Tony's words about "making it official" now that their boss thought they were "doing it."

She hated him! But she couldn't deny she was so turned on by him. Her panties were still soaking. She pulled some toilet paper off the roll and pulled up her skirt to wipe herself lest she stain her clothes. As she pressed the tissue to herself she felt that deep need still there, lurking, reproaching her for thinking she could ignore it.

Her fingers seemed to move on their own, without her permission. She started to stroke her clit, like a robot. She had to get rid of this feeling as it raked at her. She pressed and stroked, the pleasure suffusing her core, but almost as if the pleasure was happening in a dream. She parted her legs, her calf muscles taut as she balanced on her heels and the tension filled her limbs.

She closed her eyes and this time it wasn't Tony's face that flooded her imagination but Nathan's. Nathan's soft gaze as he'd held her at the door. She stroked and stroked, remembering the smell of him, the heat of him. She let out a sharp, almost silent gasp at the thought of him. She clasped her free hand to her mouth; the room was empty but the tiny sound echoed around the tiled walls and came back to her ears as if the cry came from someone else. She stood breathing hard. Her palm was cupping her pussy, as if trying to comfort it, comfort herself. She needed comfort, but she also needed release, a release that seemed so far away.

Suddenly she heard women's voices, outside the door at first, and then inside as two secretaries came in, chattering. She tidied herself and smoothed down her clothes, wiping her juices off her hand. She flushed the toilet and came out to the washroom.

The girls were in the stalls, still chatting to each other. She saw herself in the mirror. Her eyes were moist, but she didn't look as if she'd been crying; she looked strangely calm, or was that empty? She washed her hands then smoothed down her hair.

She took a deep breath and pulled the door. As she went back through the corridor, she didn't see Nathan look up from the office and see her going past, ash blond, beautiful, troubled. He was troubled too.

She went into the open-plan office and sat in silence. She plowed through the rest of her work, trying to blot the afternoon from her mind. She was aware that she was getting glances from some of the men, but she didn't care.

At 5:30 she grabbed her coat and made for the door. She didn't wait for Romy; she just needed to get home, back to her bedroom, her haven, as far away from work as fast as possible, away from Tony—and from Nathan.

Once home, she ran into her bedroom and threw herself on the bed, burying her head in her beautiful blue-green cushions.

Chapter 4

ROMY CAME INTO THE apartment and padded into Alexia's bedroom. She found her friend facedown on the bed.

"Hey, what's happened?" she asked.

"I have to leave, I can't work there. I just can't…"

Alexia was crying softly, not wracking sobs, but little miserable moans that made her speech sound like a long one-note wail. She told Romy about her flight from the closet, and her gut-wrenching encounter with Nathan.

"Oh, sweetie!" said Romy.

She scooted up on the bed and sat with her arm around Alexia.

"Come on, it's not that bad."

"Bad? It's awful!" Alexia moaned.

"Nothing's happened really, it's just that—well—Tony's being a twat. And Nathan, well, he's…"

Romy took a deep breath and looked at Alexia's face and crumpled shoulders. She was dripping with misery. She gave her a squeeze.

"Look, Nathan is a really good guy. He's not all strutting and full of piss and wind like the others, and you know, once he gets to know you…"

"Well, that's never going to happen, is it? I'm just a temp, remember."

Romy thought for a moment. "Well, you never know. Perhaps we just have to make sure he does get to know you."

Alexia snorted. Romy eyed her for a moment as if calculating her next words carefully.

"We just have to make sure he gets to know you because, after all, a boss needs to know…" She stopped for moment and chewed over what she might say next. "Needs to know his employees, and he does like to do that. Really he does."

"I thought you said he never bothered with the junior staff?"

"Did I? Oh well, that was when you were worried he was going to sack you."

Alexia looked unconvinced. Romy was undeterred.

"Look, you want him to think well of you, so we'll make sure he does!"

"How? He thinks I'm Tony's office shag who does it on tables and in closets."

"Well, you nearly did do it in a closet!"

"Romy!"

Alexia shook off Romy's arm.

"If Tony hadn't stopped, would *you* have?" Romy arched a perfectly groomed eyebrow to emphasize her point.

Alexia sat, her mouth opening and shutting. No words came out, just confused noises. Romy was right: would she have stopped him? His face flashed into her thoughts. The feel of his hands on her breasts, his mouth…

She felt her nipples harden as she thought of what had happened. She crossed her arms in front of her, afraid Romy would see. But she couldn't deny the yen she felt in her pussy. The ache wasn't going away, and it was getting stronger all the time.

She breathed out heavily. Romy tilted her head to show her sympathy.

"Hey, come on, Alexia. It's okay. God, if I thought he wanted me, I'd jump on him before he'd had time to clear his throat to say 'fancy a fuck?'"

Alexia laughed weakly. Romy pressed on.

"Look, he is a terrible flirt and a tart, obviously, but it would help you get Carter out of your system. Or you could just laugh and flirt with him and concentrate on your job, and Nathan."

The mention of Nathan's name yanked at Alexia's loins even harder. Just the thought of his hands on her shoulders… But it was crazy. She didn't know anything about him; he thought she was a flighty office tart. Her stomach lurched at the memory of his disapproval. Why did he have this effect on her?

"And as I said," said Romy, watching her friend closely to judge her reactions, "we can work on him getting to know you. Anyone who has spent any time with you can tell you're…"

"Can tell I'm what?" asked Alexia. "An ice queen? Frigid?"

Romy sighed. "I was going to say more discerning than many."

"I thought you said I needed to learn more about men and get Carter out of my system?"

"Hey, there's nothing wrong with getting a good seeing-to when you need it, but first things first… You think Nathan's got a downer on you and we're going to make sure he doesn't."

"*We* are going to make sure?"

"Yes, we." Romy winked at her, then got up slowly. "Actually, I'm not feeling too hot this evening. Feeling a little achy and I've got a bit of a sore throat. I think I'll go and watch TV in bed and get an early night."

"Oh," said Alexia. "Do you need me to do anything?"

"No, no," said Romy breezily, "I'll see you in the morning. Night, night." She left the room, the grin on her painted lips barely suppressed.

Alexia got up and put on her nightie and a cuddly dressing gown and went into the kitchen. Richard was making pasta again. Is that all he cooks? she thought.

"Hey there, darlin'. I've made a huge panful, and Romy's not eating, so plenty for us. And there's some crisp Californian Sauvignon to wash it down. You look like you could do with a drink."

Alexia couldn't deny that, and smiled as she accepted a very large glass of wine.

She took a long sip of the chilled liquid, all grass and gooseberries. It cheered her.

"Now sometimes what a girl needs is a boy friend, and I stress that's *boy friend*, as in a friend who's a boy." Richard pointed at himself. "One with wide shoulders and two good ears."

He dished out the spaghetti and handed Alexia a fork and a plate.

"I need a spoon as well," she said.

"No, you don't. Romy taught me to cook pasta like her Neapolitan mamma and eat it Italian style. So into the living room and let's chow and pow-wow!"

He turned her around and scooted her into the living room. The feel of his hands on her back was comforting and sent a little charge through her midriff. He had a wicked smile but he was soft and gentle and there was a kindness to him. And suddenly she wanted that kindness very badly.

They sat on the floor listening to soft jazz. Alexia had never been a fan, but Richard was a Miles Davis fan, and somehow it seemed perfect for her mood.

Richard expertly twirled the pasta on the tines of his fork, then delivered the spaghetti into his open mouth. The last two centimeters of a strand lingered on the outside and he sucked it into his mouth, the tomato sauce coating his lip. Alexia watched his mouth. He saw her watching and licked it. She felt another jolt. She looked down and grabbed her drink, swallowing two huge gulps.

Richard laughed softly. "I cook it better than I eat it!"

She laughed.

"That's better," he said. "You look beautiful when you laugh."

Alexia felt his eyes on her, but they were kind as well as wanting.

"Bad day, huh?" he said.

"You could say that."

Richard looked inquiringly at her, his soft eyes languid under his lashes.

Alexia picked up her fork and started to twirl the spaghetti on it as Richard had done. She was used to using a fork and spoon, and she found it difficult.

"Just a couple of strands at a time on the edge of the plate," he said helpfully.

"Oh, okay." Alexia complied.

She moved two strands of spaghetti as instructed, and twirled slowly and carefully until it was neatly wrapped around the fork. She lifted it to her mouth, but as she tried to deposit it, one long strand escaped, forcing her to suck it up noisily, the sauce coating her chin. She giggled and dropped her fork to wipe it away.

"No, no, no… It may not be an Italian tradition, but I am going to make it mine." Richard leaned forward and ran his finger along her soft, white chin. He put the sauce-coated finger into his mouth and sucked it.

Alexia felt a rushing surge in her pussy. She looked at his hand and couldn't help remembering how his fingers had felt when he'd plunged them into her pajamas and caressed her intimately.

She grabbed her wine again and drained the glass.

"Hmm, really tough, I guess." Richard smiled and poured her another.

They were very large glasses, and in the space of fifteen minutes Alexia had drained the better part of a bottle while eating her pasta. The sauce was incredible. Deep, dark flavors of tomatoes and sunshine. Its slippery oiliness helped the pasta to glide over her tongue.

She twirled the strands and put them in her mouth. Each time she missed, Richard obligingly wiped the red, silky sauce from her mouth, the last time running his finger along her plump lower lip.

She wanted to suck his finger, to pull it into her mouth and run her tongue over it, licking all the sauce. But he removed it before she had a chance to embarrass herself.

He poured her another glass.

"What happened today?" he asked quietly.

Alexia was a little drunk. She was warm too. She shrugged off her dressing gown, revealing creamy bare shoulders covered by the dark blue straps of her knee-length satin nightie.

Richard sat very still, trying to keep his attention on her face.

Alexia was exhausted and in need of unburdening.

"Do you think I'm an ice queen?"

"A what? God, no!"

"The men in the office call me that, apparently. Maybe I am. You said the other night that I"—she faltered—"needed *it* more than anyone you know."

Alexia looked miserable. Richard wanted to pull her into his arms, but he sat looking at her.

"Yeah, you did, and I think you still do, but that doesn't make you icy, sweetheart. You're no ice maiden, you just need…"

"Need what? A good fuck?"

Alexia was slightly startled by her own frankness. But she felt as if she needed to be blunt and to let everything go.

Richard was silent. He reached over and smoothed a strand of her wavy, ash blond hair from her face. She looked up at him with her big blue eyes. She was very beautiful and she was wearing a look he hadn't seen before. She gazed levelly at him.

"Well, I nearly fucked someone in a closet today."

"Okay…" He nodded slowly, taking in her statement and trying to sound as if she'd just said something very ordinary like, "I bought a new dress today."

Alexia looked down, thinking. There was a long silence.

"The man I left, to come here—to come and live with Romy…

His name was Carter. He—he was a complete bastard. He was a bully. A selfish, nasty, horrible, bullying, bastard, selfish…" She was on a roll but she'd run out of words. "Cunt!"

The last word came out as an explosion, as if all the pain and stress of her time with Carter needed to be ejected in one go. Tears started to roll down her face but she wasn't going to stop.

"He got me when I was vulnerable and then he played on it. I'd only ever had sex with one other guy, in college, and he was—well…"

Richard tried to finish her sentence. "Crap in bed?"

She scrunched her eyes shut, trying to stop the tears.

Richard plowed on. "Came too fast? No foreplay?"

Alexia blurted, "Boring!"

Richard roared with laughter and Alexia found herself joining in.

"Man, that hurts!" said Richard. "I feel for the guy."

Alexia was giggling now.

"He was really bright and brainy and he was all about the books. And he was sweet, I really liked him, but sex was just so pointless! I couldn't understand why everyone else was raving about it. It was, well, just not…"

"Fun?" asked Richard.

"No, it was definitely not what you'd call fun."

"Then he definitely wasn't doin' it right." Richard laughed.

Alexia went quiet again. "No, no, he wasn't," she said after a long pause.

Richard got up and walked into the kitchen. As he stood, Alexia noticed a bulge in his trousers. She was drunk and feeling the lust that comes with intoxication. She was sure Richard knew how to "do it right"; the confidence in his fingers in her pussy had shown her that. She wanted that again, she wanted to feel that fire. She shifted on the floor; she could feel her pussy getting wet, and she didn't want leave a puddle on the rug.

Richard returned with another bottle and filled her glass and then his own. She took it gratefully and swigged down the thrilling, cold, gooseberry taste.

Richard waited for a moment before he spoke. "And then…?"

"I met Carter," Alexia said flatly.

"The cunt?"

She snorted to hear her words coming back to her. Had she really said that? "Yes," she said, blushing.

"Was he boring in bed too? I'm guessing not, but not in a good way."

"No, not in a good way."

Alexia went quiet and Richard waited. He could tell she needed to share, but he knew she shouldn't be rushed. She took another long swig of wine.

"He didn't like me too wet." She was being very bold this evening, the wine loosening her tongue as well as her inhibitions. She felt Richard's gaze on her.

"He didn't want me too wet, because he said it felt better if I wasn't."

"That's crap… God, half the fun is to feel a hot, *wet* pussy clamped around your cock."

Alexia felt another hot squirt of moisture at Richard's bluntness. God, then Carter would hate me now, she thought. She felt the wetness in her own pussy. She was absolutely soaking; she could feel it on the top of her thighs.

"That guy was just an asshole, honey. That was about control, not about sex."

Alexia looked at him. He smiled with closed lips and raised his eyebrows, nodding gently to assure her he was right.

"He only ever really liked it"—Alexia realized she was talking in intimate detail, but the wine had made her bold and she wanted to unburden herself—"liked it from behind. He was always trying to stick it in my"—she faltered—"and it hurt so I used to shout for him to stop. Then he'd ram into me, you know, normally, because he couldn't get what he wanted. He used to hold my head down. Sometimes I felt like I was suffocating, but I just wanted him to finish and get off."

"Oh, sweet girl, that ain't right. Hey, anal can be great, but only if you're with someone who wants you that way. No guy should ever force a girl. If she wants it, great; if she don't, move on, buddy, find another girl or another way to please the one you got!"

Alexia listened to his soft drawl. It was so seductive, those deep, southern vowels, like melted molasses.

"It's about pleasing a girl?"

"Hell, yeah!" Richard smiled. "A hundred percent."

She looked into his face and knew she wanted him now, really wanted him. He wasn't like Nathan, he wasn't powerfully masculine, but he was all man. The stubble on his chin looked as if it would be soft and caressing. She imagined it plunged deep into her pussy.

She tried not to look at Richard's stiffening cock, tried not to imagine what it looked like. Was it big? Would it be circumcised? Romy told her American men usually were. Did it have a marble-smooth helmet like Tony's?

Richard was definitely hard now; the zip of his jeans was straining to contain his erection. But he remained remarkably contained.

"You still ain't told me what happened today," he said.

"Oh." Alexia sighed, brought back to reality. "Today… Well. It kind of started the other day when I was at an office party. I'd only been there a couple of days, so I didn't really know anyone. I needed a pee and the only free bathroom was off the boardroom, which is part of the boss's office—there's an en suite. So I went in, but then these two people came into the boardroom and I had to hide. The guy's called Tony, he's a bit of a player, and the girls in the office are always flirting with him. Well, he and this woman, they…"

"I think I get the picture." He took a long, suggestive gulp of wine. Alexia watched as it moistened his lips. She knew Richard was imagining the boardroom and she was wishing she was in that fantasy with him, splayed on the table, waiting to be speared. She thought of Tony's cock, then tried to imagine Richard standing there, with trousers peeled down, his erection standing to attention ready for action. But she kept seeing Tony's face, Tony's cock as she tried to imagine Richard. Maybe it was because she knew what it looked like, and Richard's was still a dark secret hidden under the straining denim.

"So, I watched them," said Alexia, and let the words hang between them.

Richard was no longer so completely still. The image of Alexia watching a fucking couple from her secret hideaway was clearly cracking his composure. She could see him pulling his hips backward as if trying to ease the pressure on his manhood. It aroused her.

"He was pretty merciless, but it wasn't like Carter, it was… She wanted it that way."

Richard's breathing became slightly ragged.

"He kept making her wait; he was playing with her and it made me…"

Richard finished her sentence. "Made you want it too."

"Yes!" The word tumbled out of her in a half whisper. She realized she'd answered a little too quickly, too eagerly. She blushed again.

"Well, what's so bad about that? You're a healthy young woman, and watching people fuck should make you have that reaction."

Alexia looked down and took a deep breath, then another glug of wine.

"It wasn't that… It was when they'd finished. The woman, she left the room, but he came into the bathroom and caught me."

"Oh fuck!"

"Quite! He offered to do me the same service—and I panicked. But that's not the worst of it."

"Oh God." Richard snorted. "There's more?"

"As he was leaving, this man came in. He's the boss of the company, Nathan."

Richard nodded. Suddenly, all the names Romy had mentioned in connection with Alexia were making sense. Carter, Tony, Nathan. Quite a collection for a quiet little girl.

"He took one look at us and thought it was me Tony had been shagging!"

Richard nodded and let out a long, slow whistle. Then his eyebrows knitted and he looked quizzically at her.

"Um, where'd the closet come in?"

"What?" Alexia was confused, then remembered how she'd opened their conversation.

"Oh… Well, today, I had to get something from the supply closet. It's a huge closet and it's well away from the offices, and while I was in there…"

"Nathan came in?"

"What? No." Alexia felt a huge, curling rush in her pussy at the thought of Nathan in the closet with her. "No, it was Tony…" She stopped.

"I can see how this would be a little confusing," said Richard, trying to keep up. He took a huge glug of wine and shook his head, as if the act of shaking it would make all the pieces fall in the right place.

"We—he was… I…"

Richard stepped in to help. "Tony?"

Alexia pursed her lips and nodded.

"And you…"

She nodded again. Richard studied her for a moment.

"Yeah, but you didn't go all the way, did you? You didn't fuck." Richard smiled softly. "What happened next?"

"He stopped because he was on an errand for Nathan so he

just said he had to go but that we should do it another time. I was angry, upset, ashamed. It was horrible, I just shouted at him that I'd never…"

"Hey, it's okay. I bet you were pissed."

"I ran down the corridor and straight into Nathan and he—he caught me. I thought I was going to trip, I was wearing Romy's shoes and I…" Alexia was babbling now.

"Hey, slow down. It's okay."

"He was holding me to stop me from falling and I thought… He looked like he was going to—I don't know—something. But then Tony appeared and…"

"Oh jeez. He thought you'd fucked this guy Tony again, in the office!"

"Yes." Alexia looked completely crestfallen. Richard thought how adorable she was.

"Look, honey, everyone has these stories, not as funny as yours, some of them, but hey, I gotta few. When you're old and gray and lying on your deathbed surrounded by your grandkids, you'll be glad you have something to look back on and laugh at. It'll keep you warm when you're ninety, wrinkled, and dried up."

He tapped the end of her nose with his finger. She laughed softly.

"I hope you're right, because at the moment… Tony told me I'm known as the Ice Queen. I probably do look frigid to most people. Maybe I am."

"Oh, honey, you are *not* frigid." Richard moved over to her and put his arm around her, but didn't pull her in. "You just need a guy who's gonna guide you. Show you how it should be done. Let you flower in your own time."

He smoothed her hair again and desire flamed up inside her.

"I need…" Her voice trailed away.

"There's just one thing you need, honey."

Suddenly, she was off the floor. She wasn't quite sure how,

but Richard had managed to pick her up and he was now carrying her into her bedroom. He kicked the door shut behind them and laid her down on the bed. He was standing over her, his erection straining against his jeans. She looked at his face; his lips were parted. Alexia felt an overwhelming rush of need surge down through her cunt. It was throbbing now, the blood thundering like a jungle drum.

He got onto the bed, but he didn't lie on top of her, he lay beside her. Alexia was confused. She turned and tried to kiss him, but he stopped her.

"What you need is to come, to come slow and hard. But I am *not* going to fuck you. God knows I want to, but to quote the late, great James Stewart"—he broke into an impersonation of the actor— "'You're a little the worse for wear, and there are rules about that.'"

She blinked and looked at him closely. She wanted him; she had never wanted anything so badly.

"I am not going to take advantage of you, but I am going to give you what you need, baby."

He reached his arm around her and pulled her toward him. His mouth was on hers and his kiss was soft and sensual, not demanding, but oh so seductive. Her breasts were pressed against his chest and she wanted to be naked. She tried to pull her nightie up, but his hand stopped her. This was going to be slow and at his pace.

She could feel his hardness pressing against her pussy and she ached to feel it inside her, feel it driving its way into her over and over. She felt her hips undulate in an involuntary wave, trying to feel his erection more. His kiss deepened and his arms held her tight, crushed up against him.

Then, suddenly, he let go. "Oh no, sister. That way madness lies."

He turned her. With strong but gentle arms he turned her onto her side, facing away from him, and he curled in behind her, spooning her perfectly. His strong arms were around her from behind. She stopped still, breathing, waiting. Was he stopping? Please no, don't stop, she thought, please God no...

But he hadn't stopped; he was pausing to settle her. They were both lying on their left sides and, slowly, his right arm moved down over her thigh and eased up the shimmering blue satin of her nightie so that it floated around her waist. The exposure was thrilling and Alexia felt herself push her bottom back against his erection.

His fingers circled her thigh and her pussy as they had done the night he pushed her up against the wall. It was exquisite and painful. The thrill of him not touching her clit was heart-stopping. Round and round his fingers circled. His mouth was on the back of her neck now, on that sweet spot that buckles a girl's knees when a man knows how to find it. Just a kiss, a nibble, and Alexia moaned with pleasure.

"That's it, beautiful." Richard's voice was low and warm. "You just lie back into it and let go..."

His fingers moved slowly down the slit of her pussy and Alexia gasped.

"Oh, honey, you are wet, so wet—so..."

He waited to make sure she heard his words.

"So delicious." His stretched out the word as if tasting it, experiencing it.

Alexia rocked her hips against his hand, coating him in her slipperiness, reveling in her wetness for the first time. Carter had made her hate it. She heard the sounds it made as he worked her clit and stroked against her swollen, begging lips. No more Carter, no more painful screwing. She was wet, really wet, and it was glorious.

Moans escaped from her mouth with each stroke. The quivering nub of flesh he was pressing suffused her entire abdomen with pleasure.

Then she felt two hard fingers as they found their way deep into her. She gasped loudly, not caring who could hear. His fingers had slipped in easily, guided by the slick of her juices.

He pushed his knee between her legs and tilted his hips so that his knee was lifted, pulling her leg up and draping it back over his, opening her pussy to him completely.

Alexia was clutching at the pillow, holding bunches of cotton in her fists as she rode the pleasure of being completely open to his hand. She felt him curl his fingers in that "come hither" movement that found the sweet spot inside her pussy. She pushed her head back and her chest forward as she felt his teeth suck and bite on her shoulder. Her strap slipped down and she could feel his ragged breath, feel its warmth flowing down over her shoulder, down over her now exposed breast, the whisper of it dancing on her hard nipples.

And Richard just kept stroking, pulling his fingers out to stroke her clit, and then plunging them in again to find its hidden counterpart deep inside her.

Her leg was curled backward around his and she was clamping it tight as she felt the waves coursing through her cunt.

He stroked harder and harder, increasing his speed as he felt the contractions. And then she came. His palm cupped and held her mound as his fingers pressed inside her; she felt her inside clutch around his fingers as the contractions racked through her cunt. Her hips bucked in perfect timing.

Her head was pushed back against his and she gasped for air and rode the waves. She lost herself; one minute she was coming, the next she was floating. It was almost as if she had lost consciousness for a fleeting moment. She felt her breath return to normal and realized her eyes had been shut. She opened them and turned her head back toward Richard. She felt his mouth find hers and his lips held hers in a long, soft, motionless kiss, as if he was breathing life back into her. After what seemed like an eternity he pulled his head away.

"That's what you needed," he said softly. "Close your eyes again."

She looked at him.

"I said close your eyes."

Suddenly she felt an overwhelming tiredness sweep over her, mingling with the tingling afterglow that swirled in her veins. She obeyed like a child who has just been put to bed, and in a few short breaths she was asleep.

Richard waited until her breathing became steady, then gently removed his leg from between her thighs and slid off the bed. He pulled down the satin of her nightie and pulled the quilt up over her.

"Good night, my little ice queen," he said softly and padded out of the room, closing the door behind him. He walked to the bathroom and stood against the door. He tore open the buttons of his fly and grabbed his rock-hard cock. All the gentleness was gone from him now as he rubbed frantically, bracing himself against the wall. The slapping sound betrayed the speed and frenzy as he wanked hard. It took only moments before his come shot out in an arc into the bath. He breathed out hard and laughed to himself.

"It's a shame it's not gonna be me who gets to fuck you, Alexia," he said quietly. He knew that was for someone else. But she needed to know how to embrace her sexuality, and he could certainly help her out there.

Chapter 5

SHE HAD SLEPT MORE soundly than she could ever remember and it took what seemed like an eternity to reach full wakefulness. Slowly, she opened her eyes and blinked. Her body felt warm and relaxed and more at ease than it had for weeks. It was still dark outside and she rolled over to slip back into that delicious slumber. As she pulled the quilt up under her chin she caught sight of the illuminated display on her clock—7:45 a.m.

Oh fuck! She leaped out of bed. She hadn't set the alarm for 6:45 last night. Last night? The memory crashed in on her and she felt the room wobble for a moment. Richard. The orgasm. *The* orgasm! But it was 7:45; she would be late for work. No time to think. She dashed into the living room, then crashed into the kitchen. Romy should be up. Where was she?

"In here!" came a plaintive voice from Romy's room.

Alexia ran in to find Romy in bed, surrounded by crumpled tissues and the room heavy with the smell of eucalyptus.

"I told you I was feeling rough last night. Well, I've got a shitty cold, so I can't go in today."

"Oh!" said Alexia, moving toward her bed.

"No, stay away. You have to be well, because you've got to take over."

Alexia stopped in her tracks.

"Take over… Take over what?"

"The soccer press trip. I was supposed to go with Nathan to handle everything, so you have to go."

Alexia felt a clutching panic in her stomach.

"What? No, I can't. That's… No!"

"You have to."

Alexia was wide awake now.

"But I'm just a temp. What about all the other girls who could do it?"

"Look, it's done… You're going."

Romy gave a theatrical cough and splutter.

"What do you mean it's done?"

"I rang Nathan last night on his mobile and told him I was ill. I told him I'd brought the file home to work on it and the easiest thing was to bring you up to speed on it because you live here—and he said yes."

Alexia was dumbstruck. She slumped onto the end of the bed and put her face in her hands.

Romy watched Alexia from under her lashes. Time for the clincher…

"How do you think he'll take it now if I tell him you won't go?"

Alexia looked up suddenly, panic on her face.

"Exactly!" said Romy, triumphant.

"How could you do this to me?" wailed Alexia.

"Look, you want him to get to know you so he knows who you really are. Well, this is your chance!" Romy suddenly sounded remarkably less ill, she realized. She coughed again, for dramatic effect.

"But I can't. You haven't briefed me," said Alexia, clutching for excuses.

"He's not in till lunchtime so we have plenty of time. There's a file on the table over there. Go and make yourself some tea, get dressed, read the file, and then I'll fill in any blanks."

"Romy…"

But Romy wasn't listening. "Look, I feel like shit, I need rest for a bit. Please, *cara mia*, just get the file!"

Breaking into her mother's soft Italian made her sound pleading and vulnerable. Romy squashed down into the bed and put a hankie to her nose. She blew it noisily, then pulled the quilt up and closed her eyes.

Alexia realized there was no use fighting; it was done, as Romy said.

It was done.

Alexia walked to the dressing table and picked up the file. She moved miserably into the kitchen and clicked on the kettle. Two days with Nathan, in a hotel. She opened the file and saw the travel arrangements. He was driving and she was traveling with him. Two hours in a car with him before getting to the hotel. Two hours alone with Nathan!

Her stomach lurched with dread, but her pussy had a different reaction. As Nathan's image flashed into her head she felt that now familiar surge in her loins.

"Get a grip, girl!" she said out loud.

The kettle clicked. She grabbed a cup and the tea caddy and made a very strong cup for herself.

She went to the kitchen table and started to read the file. It was a press event involving three Premier League soccer players. Alexia knew nothing about soccer, but she knew how big these players were. She knew they were always in the gossip columns with their million-pound lifestyles and taste for wild parties.

Fallon's agency had organized for these star players to be the faces of an incredibly stylish brand of aftershave, and the press conference was in a country house hotel outside London, in keeping with the styling of the TV commercials they had shot. The team from Fallon's had to stay the night before to make sure everything was set for the press conference and that the players would actually be there on time.

Nathan would be there himself, as this was a huge account,

and stars want their babysitter to be the boss and not an underling. Nathan's PA would be there to ensure everything ran smoothly and to support Nathan.

Nathan's PA? That was her now. She closed her eyes and imagined him striding into the room of photographers and journalists, commanding and in control. She felt a squirt down below. She was still wet from last night. She must get in the shower.

"Morning, beautiful... Sleep well?" Richard appeared, tousled and still half asleep.

Alexia, flushed with embarrassment, tried to stammer a reply.

"Hey, last night was great. And you, my sweet girl, look really blooming this morning. And I don't think it's that coffee."

He leaned over and kissed her forehead. Alexia was confused for a moment. It was such a fatherly gesture, after the passion of last night. What was this relationship she now had with Richard? Were they lovers? They hadn't had sex but it was pretty intimate.

Richard poured himself his own cup of coffee. "I have to get to a job interview. Just a local bar, but it'll keep me outta trouble. Aren't you late for work?"

Alexia was still confused by the normality of the conversation.

"Um, no. I'm going in later today..."

"Cool," replied Richard breezily. "Okay, I better get my duds on and get down there. See ya later, beautiful."

He smiled a huge American smile and winked. Then he disappeared into the bathroom.

Alexia sat stock still, trying to take in this latest encounter with their temporary flatmate. Romy appeared, wrapped in a dressing gown and clutching a tissue.

"Well, it's all in there, nothing to it. Just common sense, really. I'll be on the end of my mobile if you're not sure about anything."

Alexia looked unconvinced.

"Look, there's no way I'd convince Nathan to let you do it if I thought you'd screw it up, or it's my neck on the line too. So, you know, have a little faith."

Alexia smiled weakly. Screwing up was the least of her worries. She realized how crazy that was. A new job, a new chance, and all she was worried about was...

She stood up sharply and took a deep breath.

"I'll be fine. Like you say, it's common sense. There isn't a problem. There isn't!"

It was clear she was trying to convince herself more than Romy, but her friend pretended to buy into the performance.

"Absolutely. Right, I'm going back to bed. Call me later?"

"Okay," said Alexia, but as soon as Romy was out of the room she felt her knees weaken.

She spent the morning studying the file, familiarizing herself with the details and the people, and then dressed for work. She chose her clothes carefully. Pale blue blouse and a smart black pencil skirt with good heels. Not too much jewelry, and she put her ash blond waves into a neat, low bun. Every inch the executive PA, she hoped. She studied herself in the mirror. Who was this girl? She didn't recognize the cool professional who returned her gaze.

She grabbed the file, put it into her bag, and set off for the office. The journey was tiresome as usual, but she was in no hurry to walk through those doors, to walk into Nathan's office...

The bus lurched to a stop and jolted Alexia out of her daydream. She jumped off and walked the last five minutes to the polished glass doors of the Fallon Sports Agency. She crossed the street and was just mounting the pavement when a strong grip encircled her right arm and she was whirled around to face Carter. A very angry Carter.

Alexia gasped.

"Not expecting to see me?" he snarled. "It's taken me a while to track you down, but you don't think I'd let you just disappear, do you?"

His mouth had a cruel downturn, as ever, and his dark brown eyes were hard and beady, betraying his dark nature.

His grip was tightening and she struggled to free herself. He grabbed her with his other hand. He was really hurting her, and the look on his face was more aggressive than she had ever seen. She couldn't speak; she was breathing hard and trying to make sense of this. How did he find her? Why was he trying to drag her back? He shook her hard and almost knocked the wind out of her.

"No, Carter, please—just let me go!"

"What the hell do you think you're playing at? You can't just bugger off like that and think it's okay. You're *my* girlfriend and you're coming home with me!"

"The hell she is!"

Suddenly, there was the sound of a hard thump and an "ugh" from Carter, who released her arms as he crumpled to the ground.

Alexia looked up to see Nathan, his nostrils flaring, though otherwise in complete control. He'd floored Carter with one sharp jab to his kidneys, leaving him gasping for breath.

"I don't know who you are, but that's the last time you touch Alexia," Nathan commanded.

Alexia couldn't speak, couldn't think. "The last time you touch Alexia," he'd said. Hearing him say her name seemed unreal. He turned and fixed his eyes on her. She looked up at him, completely unable to respond.

"Come on, let's get you inside," he said.

Carter moaned and swore on the ground.

"Stay down, or I'll put you down, again," said Nathan. He was not a man to argue with.

Nathan put his arm gently around her shoulder, not rushing her, but guiding her toward the door. He cast a swift backward glance at Carter to make sure he wasn't getting up off the pavement, then walked Alexia in through reception. The two girls on the desk were openmouthed, but he silenced any thought they might have of questioning him with a curt shake of his head. The girls shut their mouths and stood back. Does everyone do his bidding? thought Alexia.

He took her into his office and offered her a stiff drink. She shook her head.

"I'm guessing an ex-boyfriend?" asked Nathan.

Alexia nodded dumbly. She tried to speak, but her voice was nowhere to be found. She was in shock. Nathan looked at her and saw that her eyes were glistening with unshed tears.

In one swift move she was in his arms, and he was holding her, really holding her. The subtle smell of his aftershave filled her nostrils and she melted into his embrace. His body was hard and strong and she spread her hands on his chest as she rested her head against him.

"It's okay, he's not going to hurt you. He can't get to you now." Nathan's voice was soft and gentle. She had not imagined it could sound so soft; she had only heard the commanding boss, never the soothing one.

He cupped the back of her head with his strong hand, and she felt him rest his cheek against her head. His other arm was wrapped around her, holding her close.

She stood there as he rocked her ever so slightly, almost imperceptibly in his arms. It was so comforting and felt so right. Her tears had stopped. He drew back slightly to look into her face.

His black hair was disheveled. Strands normally perfectly in place had escaped and were hanging over his forehead. His eyes were heavy with—what? Concern? Alexia couldn't read him. She just looked up at him, her face inches from his. She felt his strong fingers move from her head and run down her cheek. Her knees buckled and that wetness filled her again.

She felt her own fingers on his chest and had to stop herself from curling them into the fabric of his crisp white cotton shirt. She realized the tips of her fingers had crept underneath the lapels of his dark suit, dislodging the shoulders slightly. She felt her breathing become heavier, and she felt his chest. Was he breathing harder too?

She stared at him, slowly realizing that his mouth was inching toward hers. His lips were smooth and firm. They were slightly parted as he moved toward her. He stopped. The lurch of disappointment almost tipped her into grabbing him and begging him to kiss her. He must have read her thoughts as, suddenly, his mouth was on hers.

She was completely enveloped in his arms and his kiss was overwhelming. The need inside her roared into life. This was like no other kiss she'd had. Tony and Richard had made her needy but this—this was completely different. Nathan was no callow boy, he was all man.

Pressed against him, she could feel his hardness. His cock nudged against her stomach. Damn him for being so tall; she wanted to feel it against her own loins, to feel its hardness against her pussy. He was so hard and the length of him seemed to go on forever, up her stomach. She could feel it pulsing against her soft belly. She wanted to climb up, up his tall, hard frame, to open her legs around him and slide down onto him. She wanted to feel him inside her. She realized how Phillipa must have felt that Friday night in the boardroom, without a thought of her surroundings. Only feeling, no thinking; her need, her deep, aching need.

She felt herself almost lifting off into his arms, into him. His mouth was searching hers, his lips hard and needy. His tongue traced hers and she felt as if he wanted to devour her.

She heard a low moan escape his lips as he pulled away from her to look at her face. She couldn't read the expression. She'd expected lust, but there was something else.

In the distance she could hear voices, like a gentle babbling from a faraway radio. Suddenly his eyes grew clear and hard and he stiffened, his arms going rigid. He stood like an animal that has scented a predator, frozen, listening for its approach. The voices grew louder. One of them she knew. Tony's. Coming down the corridor!

Nathan's blue eyes darkened. Without warning, he set her back on her feet and strode away from her to his desk. She almost collapsed, her knees still weak from the surging in her body. The sudden absence of him felt like a rush of cold water through her loins, quashing the fire that he'd set roaring.

She whirled around to look at him; he was smoothing his hair down and picking up a file on the desk. There was a loud knock on the door behind her. Without waiting for an answer, Tony strode in.

"Hey, boss…"

Tony faltered when he saw her, his playful eyes suddenly puzzled. He locked eyes with Alexia and she felt a lurch in her stomach.

She couldn't help herself; she turned to look at Nathan, to see his reaction. His eyes were hard and his jaw tight as he regarded the two of them standing close together.

He strode over to Tony. "This is the file you need. Make sure Iorizzo knows he has to behave this time."

Alexia's mind was whirring. Iorizzo—his name was in the file Romy had handed her this morning. He was the hottest soccer player in the world. Wild, Italian, and so famous he only used his last name.

"Yeah, sure, of course."

Tony's eyes darted to Alexia. He was trying to read this scene, but he was having trouble.

Nathan turned his back on them both and went to his desk. They were dismissed.

Alexia shakily picked her bag up from the floor where it had fallen and walked past Tony and out into the corridor, moving as fast as she could without attracting attention, back to the open-plan office where most of the staff worked. But Tony caught up with her.

"Hey…!" He grabbed her arm and hit the spot where Carter had dug his fingers into her and bruised her. She winced and pulled back.

Tony exhaled, showing his frustration. Not having witnessed the morning's scene on the pavement, he thought her wincing was a reaction to him.

"Well, you'll have to find a way to be around me for the next couple of days."

Alexia looked at him. "What do you mean?"

"I'm coming too, didn't Nathan tell you? Seems we'll be together, in a hotel, where there are lots of beds!" He winked at her, then strode away.

Could this day get any worse? thought Alexia. Carter, then Nathan, now Tony! She slumped at her desk. Her mind was whirling. A few weeks ago she was on the run from a brutal relationship. She thought her new life could only be calmer than that, but it had never been so crazy. What on earth was going on? It seemed she had slid headfirst into a whirlpool of confusion and—what? Desire? She felt Nathan's mouth on hers again as she remembered how he'd kissed her just a few moments ago. Was it just a few moments? It seemed like an eternity.

She almost whimpered. She realized that some of the staff were looking at her. She put her head down and pulled the file from her handbag.

The afternoon passed in a blur of phone calls, to the soccer club, the venue, the catering manager, several press contacts. Alexia was grateful for the distraction. But it all felt unreal. Was she really booking a hotel room for herself? Was she really going? She finished her last call, finished typing up itineraries. Sent her last emails, including one to Nathan confirming all the arrangements. Would he reply? What would he say?

She watched her Outlook box, waiting for his name to drop with that telltale two-tone signal. But nothing. She had to make sure he was happy before she left, just in case there was a snag she'd missed. But still nothing. It was nearly 7:00 p.m. She knew he was still in the office, as were a few others. There was nothing for it; she'd have to ask him.

Shakily, she got to her feet. A clenching feeling in her loins made her feel quite unsteady. She walked on trembling legs to his office and stood outside the door. She could hear his voice… On the telephone? The sound of him made her nipples feel exposed despite being tucked away safely under her clothes. She listened to him and could feel them almost pop out at the sound of him.

She realized she was clutching the file to her breasts, half in fear, half trying to rub herself.

Should she knock? She stood there, momentarily frozen, unable to decide. She couldn't disturb him if he was talking, but how long would he be? She couldn't just stand here…

Knock, knock, knock!

She didn't remember deciding to knock, she just realized she was doing it.

"Come!" said the voice inside.

She opened the door. Nathan was on the phone, just as she thought. He looked up. No change of expression on his face. No acknowledgment of her presence, no smile. Nothing.

She took two paces into the room.

"Hang on a sec…" Nathan pulled the phone away from his mouth and looked at her.

"Yes?"

His tone was flat, matter-of-fact. Was it cold or just businesslike? She couldn't tell. The sight of those eyes, those dark blue eyes, so soft earlier, now so cold it made her stomach somersault. She felt a clutching churning in her pussy and she struggled not to squirm.

He breathed out heavily; she was wasting his time, just standing there.

"I sent you an email," she stammered. "Everything's ready for tomorrow. I just wanted to know if…"

"Yes, I've seen it; it's fine. Be here tomorrow at nine o'clock sharp; we have a strategy meeting for the event and you'll need to be here…" He paused, as if checking himself. "Thank you," he added.

She was about to answer, but he'd already gone back to his phone call. Alexia was dismissed. Again.

She mumbled an acknowledgment and crept out, closing the door silently behind her.

She almost ran down the corridor, into the office. She picked up her coat and bag and made for the door. She dashed across the street, straight onto a waiting bus and home.

The shuddering, bumping, and lurching bus took an eternity to deliver her safely home. She had never been so glad to be cocooned in the flat.

She walked in to see Romy going into her bedroom wearing a very sexy negligee and carrying a bottle of sparkling wine. She looked very disheveled, and not at all ill.

"Romy, what are you doing? You're supposed to be in bed!"

"Oh yes. Well…" She held up the champagne just as a very handsome man wearing absolutely nothing sauntered out of the bathroom, his cock semihard, straight past them into Romy's bedroom. "Busted!" she said, by way of explanation.

"What the hell…?"

"Look, I'm fine, clearly. No cold, nothing wrong."

"Then what was this morning all about?"

"Look, I…" Romy looked into the bedroom, smiled at her companion, and shut the door on him. She walked over to Alexia. "I wanted to make sure you and Nathan were, you know, thrown together. So he could see you weren't Tony's tart."

"Oh my God!" Alexia's knees buckled. She slumped into a chair. "What have you done!" she wailed.

"A bloody big favor to you—except you don't realize it yet. And we are a sports agency after all—you'll be his sub."

Alexia's eyes widened.

"His second half substitute!" laughed Romy. She tipped her head and tried to look innocent. "Look, I really think he likes you and I've never seen him notice anyone in the office. He's never asked about a temp before... Never!"

Alexia blinked. Likes me? That can't be true, she thought. But that kiss... She flushed and breathed out hard.

"Hey, you okay? Tony hasn't had another go at you, has he?"

"No," said Alexia. She knew her disheveled state needed an explanation but she wasn't going to mention the kiss. "Carter turned up at the office."

"What? How the hell does he know where you work?" Romy was incredulous.

"I don't know, but he won't be coming back. Nathan came out and punched him."

"Whoa! You're fucking kidding!"

"No, I'm not. God knows what he thinks of me now. He must think I have a string of men."

She was suddenly miserable again. First Tony, then Carter... What would Nathan think now?

"Well I bet he didn't get up again. Nathan was in the army before he started the agency, something in the sneaky-beaky brigade. He can handle himself."

An image of Nathan in uniform crossed in front of Alexia. She felt a huge surge of wanting as she thought of his upright bearing, the hard muscles under his tunic, and his ruthless efficiency in dispatching Carter. She was getting wet again.

"Are you okay?" asked Romy.

"What?... Yes, yes, I am. Carter disappeared; I don't think he'll be coming back." She remembered the guttural sound that came out of him as Nathan's punch landed in kidneys. "It's okay, I'm just tired."

"You sure? Must have been a hell of a shock."

Yes, it was a shock, but not as much of a shock as what happened next, thought Alexia. She realized that, just a few short weeks ago, Carter appearing would have rocked her to her core. But now? Now she didn't care. All she cared about was Nathan and that kiss.

"Look, I'm okay. Just go back to your friend."

Romy smiled sheepishly. "Nicky. Well, his engine is running…"

"Yeah I could see that," said Alexia, remembering the bobbing and stiffening cock that had sailed past her a few moments ago. She felt a pang of jealousy of the sex her friend had clearly just had and was about to have again. Why was it so easy for everyone else?

Romy kissed her on the forehead and skipped back to Nicky. Alexia picked herself up from her chair. She felt so heavy. She shrugged herself out of her work clothes, made herself a simple supper, and poured herself a glass of wine. She finished her food without really tasting it and realized she had polished off three glasses of red.

She poured herself another as Richard walked in.

"Hey, beautiful. You on your own?"

"Hi," whispered Alexia. She still felt sheepish around him after the night before.

"Turns out Romy isn't ill. She just wanted me to go on a trip instead of her." She felt the need to conceal the truth about Nathan from Richard.

"I kinda worked that out," said Richard, sitting down on the sofa next to her. He took the glass of wine from her hand and drained it in one go.

"I got the job!" He smiled.

"Oh, that's brilliant. Well done."

"Yeah, it's pretty good." He shrugged. "Means I'll be working evenings, though."

"That's okay, isn't it?"

"Oh sure, it just means that…"

His gaze swept over her and Alexia felt his intention. She blushed.

"I told you last night I wasn't going to fuck you because I think you're saving that for someone else."

Why was he saying that? Alexia wondered. And then she realized he might be right. Was she saving it? She was no virgin, but she knew she had never truly been made love to or made love in return. She'd never been fucked, really fucked by someone she wanted, truly wanted.

The wine and Richard's nearness made her want to clench her pussy to try and squeeze away the feeling that was uncoiling in her now. That feeling of want, the one that seemed to be running her life at the moment.

Richard held her face in his hand. His mouth was so close to hers.

"But, my lovely, you need to loosen up and you need to feel your own passion. It's all bottled up in there—and it ain't doin' you no good. And I said I'd teach you to uncork it so you're ready for whoever this guy is. So… class is now in session."

He got up off the sofa and took her hand. He pulled her toward her bedroom and she let him take her there. The raging emotions of the day had left her washed out and exhausted, but she needed release from it all. She needed this.

She was wearing light blue sweatpants that hung around her slim hips. Richard stood in front of her and pushed his fingers into the waistband.

The warm touch of his fingers made a small moan fall from Alexia. She breathed out, relieved to feel the human contact. To feel a man's hands on her. He leaned forward and kissed her. She could taste the red wine on his lips; that sweet blackberry darkness she'd been drinking all evening was now mixed with the taste of him.

She curled her arms around his neck, wanting to hang off him and drink in his scent. His tongue circled her lips and he bit her gently as he dug his fingers into her flanks beneath the soft material of her trousers.

Her cunt clenched and unclenched; she wanted him so badly. Nathan's kiss had started a fire this morning that had been there all day. It hadn't gone out, it had only been damped down, to flare again under Richard's hands.

"Hey, tiger!" He laughed and dropped to his knees, taking her sweatpants down to her ankles in one swift swoosh of fabric.

He was face-to-face with her pussy and he saw how his undressing of her had caused a rush of juices. Her pale pink panties were wet and quivering.

Alexia's legs were trembling. She could feel the heat of his breath whispering through the curls beneath the slim strip of satin covering her modesty. He knifed his hand up between her legs and she gasped as the edge of it made contact with her swollen labia.

She shook her feet free of her trousers and stood with her legs parted. She heard Richard moaning, "Good girl! Open up for daddy…"

And she wanted to open up; she wanted badly to open up to him, to feel his cock inside her. But he wasn't going to do that. He'd told her he wasn't.

His fingers pulled the damp satin to one side and she closed her eyes. Her hands rested on his head, her fingers in his soft, disheveled curls, and she felt his head move forward. She felt the warm wetness of his stiffened tongue flick her clit.

She gasped. She waited a moment, wanting to feel it again. Waiting for his tongue to send that sweet jolt of electricity through her. But nothing happened. She waited. And waited.

She was breathing hard, eyes still closed. She realized she could hear sounds floating into the room. She opened her eyes and let the sounds fill her ears.

Moans and gasps came from the other room. Romy and Nicky were fucking, really fucking, and they weren't being quiet about it.

The animal sounds sent another thrill through Alexia. Her friend was getting hammered and Alexia had seen the size of the cock that was hammering her when it was only semihard. Really hard, it must be huge. No wonder Romy was being so vocal.

"Well, isn't that just getting you horny," said Richard from down below.

Alexia looked down to see Richard peeling away her panties. She could still hear the other couple. Moan, moan, moan, fuck, fuck, fuck... On and on they went.

Alexia couldn't stand it; she pushed her hips forward to Richard's mouth, but he laughed and held her hips.

"Take your top off, let me see your tits," he said, his voice low, an insistent command.

Alexia obeyed. She felt her breasts bounce free as she pulled the T-shirt over her head, dropping it to the floor. She looked down and saw Richard's smiling face between her own quivering breasts. Her nipples stood proud.

Richard looked back to her mound and pushed his tongue deep into her slit.

She gasped and pushed her hips forward again. Richard reached up with one hand as he ate her and pinched her left nipple. The jolt from breast to pussy was agonizing. She grabbed her other nipple herself, unable to cope with one being left unloved. She grabbed his head with her other hand and felt the movement back and forth as his stiff tongue worked her clit in time to the screwing couple, whose headboard was now banging the wall.

Alexia felt like she was in a brothel and she didn't care. She just wanted more.

Suddenly, Richard withdrew and Alexia gasped. The cold air on her pussy was like a smack of admonishment after the warmth of his tongue, his mouth, his chin, his face all buried in her. He was covered in her juices. He licked the side of his mouth, tasting her.

"I can't get in deep enough like this," he said.

Deep enough? The words sent another surge through her, as Richard pushed her back onto the bed. Her back hit the mattress and she felt her breasts bounce, sending another shock through her nipples. He dragged off her panties and she lay back, closing her eyes, waiting for his mouth. But it didn't come. ·

She picked up her head to look at him. He was staring at her open, wet cunt. A few days ago this nakedness, this exposure, would have reviled and shocked her. But his gaze was thrilling. And she opened her legs to give him the view he wanted.

He laughed to himself.

"Oh baby!" he said and grabbed her legs, pulling her forward so her bottom was on the end of the bed. The jerk toward him with her legs open almost made her come. She could feel the contractions wanting to start.

He was still kneeling. He lifted her legs and draped them over his shoulders, either side of his head. The feel of her feet dangling down his back, the helplessness of it, was intoxicating. She was desperate for his tongue again as she heard the competing couple speeding up. The sound of the banging headboard interspersed with Nicky's and Romy's animal grunts made this waiting an agony.

Richard pulled up Alexia's hips, and then he did it. He parted her lips with his fingers and plunged his tongue into her. As she rocked with the pleasure, he covered his index finger in her juices and slipped it slowly into the one dark place she thought she'd never want to feel a man. The shock was enough to send her over the edge.

Alexia's hips were almost grinding against his face, covering him in her juices, trying to pull in his tongue and his finger. With his other hand he rubbed her engorged nub with the flat of his thumb. With two hands and his tongue he was stimulating her in ways she'd never thought possible, not altogether. She was so wet, she felt she would drown him.

She heard Nicky's final agonizing, animal shout of orgasm from next door, and she came. Her feet were digging into Richard's back and her hands were curled in his hair as her hips rocked with each contraction. She rolled in her pleasure and let the feel of the orgasm fill her veins, all the way to her toes. Her breathing was hard and ragged. She had arched her back up and now it was coming back down to rest on the mattress. She lay there panting, her legs still dangling over Richard.

He withdrew slowly and dropped her legs down, placing her feet on the floor. She was still breathing hard, her chest rising and falling violently. She looked up and saw Richard.

"Yup, you're a quick study. Definitely an A student!" He laughed softly and stood up. She could see his erection in his pants.

He wiped his face with the back of his hand, then licked it.

"Now get some rest, sister. You'll sleep well tonight."

He turned to leave the room.

"Where are you going?"

Richard laughed to himself. "Oh, I have an appointment with the bathroom," he said, with his hand on his now desperate erection.

Alexia sat up. "But can't I help?"

Richard's mouth curved into a lopsided smile. He was very cute when he was aroused, she thought.

"Oh yeah, but that's tomorrow night's lesson."

And with that he left the room.

Alexia flopped back down onto the bed. The room next door was silent, but her heart was still pumping hard. She crawled under the quilt and cupped her mound with her hand as if to keep the feeling in.

Richard had just brought her to climax, but her mind quickly turned to Nathan and the kiss, that swirling, mind-bending kiss. She cupped herself harder as if protecting herself, her vulnerability. Tomorrow she would see him again. He'd kissed her, but then he'd spurned her. He thought she was Tony's and that was enough to disgust him.

But why had he kissed her if he thought she was just one of Tony's office shags? Maybe the answer would come tomorrow?

Tomorrow she would have to face him again.

Chapter 6

ALEXIA WAS GETTING USED to her daily journey through the London rush hour traffic to the offices of Fallon Sports Agency. But she wasn't getting used to the churning in her gut that accompanied her commute.

Today was going to be torture; not the mild kind, not the "really uncomfortable but I'll put up with it" kind. Today was going to be the "I'd rather chew off my own arm" kind. She would be stuck in a strategy meeting with the man who had kissed her then tossed her aside in the belief she was another man's tart.

But she still couldn't understand why he had kissed her. Was he just feeling sorry for her after Carter's sudden appearance? Men don't do that because they feel sorry for you. But he was comforting her, she was in his arms; perhaps it was just a normal male hormonal reaction to having a woman pressed up against you, nothing more.

The thought that she meant nothing to him, just a casual kiss, made her more miserable than ever. Romy said he didn't sleep around. He didn't mess with women in the office. It was all too confusing.

She noticed that more of the men in the office were looking at her. Why now? Did she look different? The memory of last night, of her total abandon with Richard, flooded back and flushed her cheeks. Just the trace of the memory was enough to swell her pussy. The feel of his mouth on her, holding her thighs either side of his head.

Stop it, she thought. The feel of Richard's tongue was so fresh in her mind she felt that people could see it in her face.

"You look good enough to eat today."

Alexia almost jumped out of her skin. It was Tony, and he was regarding her with hungry eyes. Did he know what she'd been thinking?

"Nathan wants you in his office."

Nathan wants you. The words made Alexia want to squirm, to rub her thighs against each other.

Tony was watching her. "Strategy meeting, it's in fifteen minutes. He needs you first."

He stalked off, Alexia watching as his athletic form mesmerized the secretaries as he went by.

He needs you first, he'd said. If only he did, thought Alexia.

She gathered up the file and paperwork for the soccer press event, a pad, and a pen and walked the long walk to Nathan's office. She had dressed carefully again. Smart skirt and heels and a blouse that wasn't too revealing. It was Romy's, a beautiful dusky pink. But she realized that Romy was a little smaller around the chest and her top button kept sliding open. She checked. It was still fastened. She pulled her chest in and knocked the door. Her heart was hammering.

"Come!" came the now familiar command.

She walked in. Nathan was typing something on his laptop, an earpiece in his ear. He was talking.

"Look, Iorizzo's deal depends on him behaving. We can't have another screw up like last time."

There was silence as he listened. His face was impassive, unimpressed by whatever excuses poured into his ear.

"Look, it's really simple: he wants this deal, he behaves. No more coke, no more high-class hookers. The sponsors want him to look athletic and clean. If he has to get laid by a different girl every week, find him some who are more discreet…"

He looked up, and Alexia thought she saw a flash of disapproval as his gaze swept over her on the word "discreet."

"He'll only be the face of the brand for a year, along with Lopez and Carsten. Then they can do what they like."

He ended the call. Alexia got the feeling that Nathan was in charge of every call he made and every meeting. He was not aggressive, but his quiet authority made people defer to him. Must be the officer training.

There was an awkward silence in the room. He was staring down at his desk, but he didn't seem to be looking at anything in particular. Was he as uncomfortable as her?

He was in a beautiful handmade navy suit, a crisp ivory shirt, and golden tie. His thick, black hair was brushed straight; no pretty-boy gel for Nathan, not like Tony. He was classic. She found she couldn't help but study him. His skin was lightly tanned and his face was strong, his cheekbones were pronounced and ran in line with his jaw. His nose was not straight; perhaps an army scrap? But it lent him the kind of raw masculinity that betrayed his perfectly turned out appearance. There was much more to this man than the cool operator, of that Alexia was sure. But she was sure of nothing else.

She felt that small bundle of nerves deep inside her, her sweet spot, rippling, aching for attention. He broke the silence.

"I'm sorry about yesterday. It was unprofessional and it shouldn't have happened."

Alexia felt winded.

"I just wanted to…" He seemed to be thinking about his words carefully.

Just wanted to what? Alexia's head was swimming. Why didn't he look at her? Look at me, see me!

"Clear the air," he said at length. "We have a lot to do, we need to start now."

She wanted to feel his lips on hers again, but he'd just made it clear that wouldn't happen again, never again.

There was a knock on the door and in came Tony with a couple of other staff. Suddenly the room was filled with chatting and Nathan got up and moved to the large boardroom table he used for meetings. *The* boardroom table. People took their seats. Alexia's legs seemed stuck to the floor.

"Are you joining us?" came a smooth female voice. Phillipa, the commercial director, Tony's fuck buddy.

"Er, sorry… Yes." Alexia put her head down and scuttled to the table. There was only one seat free, between Tony and Nathan. She caught sight of Phillipa's wry amusement at her embarrassment. Did she know anything? Would Tony have told her? Or was she just laughing at Alexia's mousy behavior? She was the type.

Alexia sat down gingerly, trying to make herself as small as possible, almost frightened that if she brushed up against one of the two men she'd burst into flames.

She opened her file and gripped the sides, not wanting even a sheet of paper to stray into their table territory.

Nathan kicked off the proceedings.

"I've spoken to Iorizzo's assistant. He's not going to be easy to control, but he knows if he screws up again he loses the deal."

"And we lose an enormous percentage," said Phillipa archly.

"Quite! Tony, this is your department."

Tony looked pleased with himself. He was only a junior agent, but he had good contacts in the Premier League and he'd managed to get quite close to some influential players.

"Well, I can't keep him chained up," he said.

Nathan didn't allow a longer excuse. "You can contain him, or any damage he might do to us. If he's stupid on this press trip, make sure his stupidity is confined to the rooms where the press don't get to him or his partners in crime, and make sure he is suited and booted for the press conference on time. As you're kindred spirits, you should be able to anticipate any trouble."

Did she detect a barb in those last words? She sneaked a look at Nathan. Impassive, as always. She looked at Phillipa, who was watching Tony. The other two seemed to be watching Tony too.

"So you should be able to keep him on a short lead."

"What about Lopez and Carsten? They're just as bad, just not as big!" countered Phillipa.

"Tony?" Nathan inquired.

"They do run as a bit of a pack. I guess that means I'm baby-sitting."

Alexia had trouble imagining Tony as any kind of babysitter. Nathan was rounding up.

"Okay, everyone, this is an especially big pay day for this company, so we handle it, manage it, and it runs like clockwork, clear?"

Everyone nodded.

They went through the technical arrangements. Tony was clearly bored by the minutiae of the business. As Alexia made notes on her pad she felt a sudden brush against her thigh. She caught her breath. She felt Tony's hand slowly running up her leg. He wasn't using the arm that was next to her; he held his chin in his hand with that one. No, he was using his other hand, so no one could see, crossed over his lap and running his fingers on Alexia's now quivering leg.

She looked up. Nathan was still talking; people were studying their folders. Her nerves were jangling. She was terrified they'd notice, that Nathan would notice. It was such a chaste touch, really, but under the circumstances it was bold and dangerous and it sent a tightening clench through her cunt.

She could hear Nathan's voice, his low, warm voice, as she felt Tony's whispering touch on her leg. If she shut her eyes, she might feel it was Nathan's touch, Nathan's fingers. But they weren't, they were Tony's. She stole a glance at him, but he was looking at his notes as if he had no idea what was happening. How could he do that? How could he be so barefaced?

She gave a small gasp as she felt his foot suddenly curl around her ankle. The others looked up at her. She gave a small, hiccupping cough to hide the giveaway breath.

Her head was swirling. She wanted everyone to leave and then for Nathan to turn to her and kiss her again. Tony's clandestine caresses were stoking her passion. Tony's hand, Tony's foot.

In the distance she heard Nathan wrapping up the meeting. People were stirring, closing files and picking up papers. She snapped back into the room and felt the swift withdrawal of Tony's touch.

She grabbed her own papers and hurried to the door as the others started to leave.

"I need these photocopied." Phillipa's voice. "Four of each, please. It's Alexia, isn't it?"

Alexia turned around. "Yes, yes, it is."

Phillipa wasn't smiling; she wasn't a woman's woman. She clearly regarded all other women as competition.

Alexia took the papers. "I'll bring them to your office."

"Straight away." Phillipa turned away. She'd given her order, she didn't need pleasantries.

Alexia caught Tony looking at her. Phillipa saw it too and she wasn't amused. Alexia rushed out, straight for the safety of the photocopying room.

She still hadn't got used to wearing high heels to work, but it seemed to be the required uniform here at Fallon. All the girls were groomed and dressed to perfection. She felt even more insecure on her heels today. If only she realized that insecurity gave her a Marilyn-style wiggle that was completely at odds with her cool, aloof beauty.

A couple of guys turned to look at her as they passed her in the corridor. She could feel their eyes on her. She got to the photocopying room and shut the door behind her. She breathed out hard and almost collapsed over the giant machine, fearful she would faint.

She clutched the edge of the photocopier to steady herself, her head hanging low, hoping the blood rushing from it would return. She breathed in and out, steadying herself. She stood there, bent over for what felt like an age, unable to stand, waiting for her panicked breathing to calm. Then she heard the door.

"My, my, bending over for the headmaster!" Tony was behind her. Before she had time to straighten up he was on her. He was right behind her, gripping her hips and pressing his already hard cock against her backside. She hated herself for it, but it shot a jolt of pleasure right through her like an arrow.

She released her hands from the photocopier to try and stand, but the force of his pressing on her pushed her hard against it. He shot forward with her, and as she stood jammed against the machine he pressed his entire length against her back. In an instant, his hands were around her, clasping her arms to her side as he cupped her breasts. They heaved and she felt a thrill as his fingers traced the flesh in the valley between them. Damn that button, she thought; it had popped open, revealing the creamy mounds as her tits strained against the fabric.

He thrust his hips and his erection against her backside as he pushed his fingers inside the flimsy gauze of her bra, searching out the pink and quivering nipples that were standing proud, ready for his expert attention.

She let out a startled gasp. She didn't protest, she stood letting him knead and play with her as he rubbed himself into the crack of her buttocks.

He bent and bit the side of her neck, just a nibble, but it sent another shock wave through her. It was the spot where Richard had traced his lips, but Tony's touch was harder, more demanding, hotter.

She couldn't move her arms and she was grateful to be pinned. It was easier to tell herself that she couldn't move. But did she want to move?

Tony slid one foot between her stilettos and shoved her right foot away from her left. She almost toppled, but he held her tight. The feeling of exposure between her thighs caught her unawares, and she moaned.

"God, you're gagging for it!"

He released her suddenly and his strong hands grabbed her and turned her around to face him.

Pulling her to him, he kissed her with a ferociousness that frightened her. The electricity of his tongue was like a surge through her, from mouth to cunt. But this was wrong. It wasn't Tony she wanted. It wasn't his hands she wanted. She pulled away.

"Tony, no… Not…"

"What, not here?"

"No, I…" she protested, but he just took her protest as a sign she was afraid of discovery.

"Yeah, you're right, and the dragon queen wants those copies."

She suddenly remembered Phillipa, waiting for her photocopying. That was one woman Alexia knew it was wise to stay on the right side of. Tony stepped back and adjusted himself. He was wildly turned on, that was clear.

"We can get back to this tomorrow. We'll be in a building with beds, after all."

He clicked his tongue and winked, then turned for the door. He stopped and looked back.

"Gagging for it."

And he was gone.

Oh my God, thought Alexia, what the hell is wrong with you? He's a playboy, and you'd have let him take you over a hot photocopier if he hadn't stopped.

He was right, she must be gagging for it, but she wasn't gagging for him, so why did she respond so strongly to him? Was she so desperate that any man would do? She didn't know anymore. He was undeniably attractive and she had witnessed his prowess in the art of lovemaking, if that's what you could call what he'd done to Phillipa. Nathan had set the real fire, but he'd made it clear he was not about to stoke it. Tony was volunteering.

She turned to the photocopier.

Out loud, she said, "What is it with you men and small office spaces?"

She let out a noise of deep frustration, sexual and personal. She rebuttoned her blouse, then grabbed the pile of papers and set about copying Phillipa's documents. When they were compiled, she made sure her blouse was done up almost to her neck and stroked down her hair.

She was sure she had stained her skirt. The agony of the meeting had made her wet and Tony had opened the tap right up. She twirled her skirt around her hips to check. No, it was fine. That was a miracle.

She took to the corridor at a clip. Phillipa's door was open, and she gave a cursory knock and walked in.

"Your copies, Phillipa."

"Over there," said the older woman, nodding at a collection of documents.

Alexia deposited the copies and turned to leave, but Phillipa wasn't finished.

"Your skirt looks a little squiffy. Run into Tony while you were copying these?"

Alexia almost gasped with shock. She didn't speak. Had Phillipa seen them together or was she fishing?

"I'm sorry, I don't understand," said Alexia. She hoped for once that her ice maiden looks would be a good defense, a cool exterior hiding inner turmoil.

Phillipa regarded her carefully, as though trying to decide whether to believe her. Was she jealous? She looked like the type who didn't care what her conquests did when she wasn't fucking them, but she also looked like she could be vengeful.

"Mmm…" Phillipa made a small noise indicating that she was yet to be convinced. She went back to her work. Alexia left the office, trying not to break into a trot.

Why, she wondered, do I seem to spend every day now leaving the office as fast I can?

─────

Alexia had been home for two hours. She'd been sitting with Romy, but couldn't bear to tell her friend about the ridiculous sexual ping-pong she seemed to have found herself in the middle of.

All Romy was interested in was how she was planning to get Nathan on her side during the press trip.

"Look, all I can do is be professional, and that will have to do!" protested Alexia.

"Oh, come on. You'll be in the hotel with him, and you'll probably have dinner and maybe a drink and…"

"And nothing." She couldn't tell Romy what had passed between her and Nathan and how painfully clear he had made it they would not be repeating the experience. She felt a deep pang of regret.

"Anyway," she continued. "Tony's going to be there too."

"OMG, double hotties! Talk about stuck between a rock and a hard place."

Romy laughed at her own double meaning, but Alexia wasn't amused.

"No Nicky tonight?" she asked, spooning up a little of the ice cream Romy had brought home.

"No, worst luck, and I'm so bloody horny. God, he's good!"

"Yes, I could hear," said Alexia.

"Hmm, well, maybe you'll make some noise with whoever you choose tomorrow night."

"Funny," said Alexia, relieved that Richard's nocturnal visit to her bedroom the night before seemed to have gone undetected.

But then she remembered he'd promised to visit her again that night. With all the turmoil of the day she'd clean forgotten. At the thought of his warm, soft, and oh so intimate attention, Alexia felt a surge of what Romy was feeling.

"Where's Richard tonight?" she asked, trying to sound casual.

"I don't know. Anyway, I'm knackered, didn't get *any* sleep last night." Romy giggled. "And I've taken one of my mum's magic sleeping pills, so in about twenty minutes I'll be so sound asleep that even if Nathan Fallon himself tried to hump me from behind I wouldn't wake up."

The image was suddenly too clear for Alexia. She thought of Nathan, naked, dragging Romy's bare ass backward so he could thrust his cock in her. But in her mental picture, Romy's face had turned into her own.

She rammed some cold ice cream in her mouth.

"Steady. You'll give yourself an ice cream headache," said Romy. "Right, I'm off to bed. You'd better pack, girl; you're off to the country tomorrow with Nathan…"

She sashayed out of the room with a casual "sweet dreams" thrown over her shoulder as she disappeared into her bedroom and into the arms of a dead sleep.

Alexia envied her. She should have asked her for one of those sleeping pills because she was sure she would not be lying in the arms of Hypnos tonight. The Greek god of sleep would not be her companion; she would be wracked with the torture the gods reserve for those who have transgressed. And she felt she had transgressed; she had been bad, very bad.

She went into her room and pulled the clothes she planned to take on the trip from her wardrobe. Romy had lent her quite a few little outfits, before her first paycheck would allow her to reclothe herself in the smart attire her new position demanded.

Smart satin blouses, tight skirts, killer heels, minimal jewelry, and just the right amount of perfume. She picked up pajamas. No, that wasn't right. She reached into a drawer and pulled out a satin nightie. She felt its texture and it slipped through her hands. She imagined what it must feel like to a man as he slid it over a woman's skin, the way Richard had slid hers over her hips as they lay on the bed. A surge of yearning hit her again. First Nathan and then Tony: today had been an agonizing journey toward extreme frustration and need.

She breathed out hard. "Oh, come on, pull yourself together!" she said aloud to herself. She finished packing. Toiletries, her sexiest bra set, and she was packed. She zipped up her roller bag and set it on the floor.

She got ready for bed. On her way back from the bathroom she heard a gentle snoring coming from Romy's room. Those pills must be good.

She picked up the satin nightie that Richard had found her in and slipped it on, feeling it slide down over her breasts. It made her nipples shiver.

But where was Richard? He'd said he would be with her tonight. Suddenly she felt very needy for him; she wanted his hands on her, his mouth wet with her juices as his delicious tongue flicked and licked her to orgasm again.

She got into bed with a gut-wrenching need deep in her pussy. It ached to clench around something hard and male: a cock, fingers, a stiffened tongue.

She lay back and thought about the next couple of days. She'd be close to Nathan all the time. So close and yet so far. But then Tony would be circling, like a vulture waiting for its prey to become weak. Weak. That's what she was, weak. Weak and needy, oh so needy. She hated herself.

She heard the door latch as Richard crept into the flat. She held her breath. She waited for him to open the door. And she waited. It was agonizing. But why couldn't she go out and greet him? Surely they had been intimate enough now? But she couldn't. She needed her nocturnal visitor, her teacher, to come to her, to take her, and not to brook resistance. She needed him to override her natural reticence and show her what she was missing, what she was craving.

The bedroom door opened slowly, a crack of light appearing and framing Richard's silhouette like a halo. He was her angel, her angel of pleasure. She couldn't see his face; in the darkened room all she could see was his outline. It was enough. She found she had parted her legs and her hand had already moved south, cupping her mound.

Richard walked in and closed the door.

"Hey, beautiful."

She heard that low southern drawl and felt moisture reach her hand. He moved to the bedside table.

"Shade your eyes." He clicked on the small lamp that let a gentle glow into the room.

Alexia blinked and looked up.

"Ready to continue our lessons? It'll be the last for a while."

She didn't speak, didn't move; she just looked at him, her blue eyes begging him to start.

He took off his shirt to reveal downy hair on his chest. She had never seen his naked torso or felt it; it had been covered in their encounters. She reached up and ran her fingers over it. Touching his skin made her breathe harder. She sat up in bed, her face level with his fly.

His groin was swollen. His cock looked as if it would burst from its casing, and it was right in front of her.

"Richard…" Her voice was quiet, hesitant.

"Yeah?"

"There's something I don't really know how to do. I know it sounds crazy at my age, but my first boyfriend never asked me to. And Carter, well, he didn't want it; he just liked…"

Her voice trailed off.

"Fucking!" Richard finished her thought.

"Yes… So you see, I don't really…"

She looked at his groin. Richard was shifting slightly and the bulge in his jeans looked painful now. Then she looked up at him.

"Then we can move the curriculum along a little…"

Richard undid his belt and she heard the whisper of the leather as it slid through the belt loops, then the buckle clank as it hit the floor. She had never seen his naked erection, much less touched it.

He peeled the metal buttons open one by one, slowly moving down until his jeans were open. His cotton shorts were tight and gray, like an athlete's. His navel betrayed the fluttering in his stomach as he waited for her to touch him.

She reached up slowly and pulled his jeans to his knees. There was a dot of moisture on his shorts. The sight of it inflamed her. The idea that his cock was weeping for her excited her.

With trembling fingers, she eased his shorts over the tip of his cock and pushed them to join his jeans.

He was rock hard. Right in front of her face, she could smell the salty precome that glistened on the small slit. Circumcised. Romy was right about American men.

"There's nothing to it, really, just like a Popsicle." Richard smoothed her hair. He wasn't grabbing her head, or guiding her in, just reassuring her that it was okay to be nervous.

She put the flat of her hands on the front of his hips, either side of his erection. She breathed hard and felt his muscles flex under her hands as her breath enveloped his balls. She inched forward and gently put her mouth on his tip. She felt him catch his breath.

She ran her tongue over the dab of wetness. Salty. She drew her head back and looked up. He was watching her. It's okay, his eyes said. In your own time, honey.

She opened her mouth, took a couple of inches of him into her mouth, and pulled back, allowing her lips to trace along his length. She felt so decadent, so wanting of him. She was squirming as her cunt nagged at her for attention, but she was focused on him, on his ramrod cock. She moved forward again, sucking him into her mouth then moving back, each time daring to go a little deeper but not daring to take too much. She ran her tongue over him, rolling it around over the hard, pulsing flesh. She could feel him trying not to rock, trying not to push himself into her mouth. He was letting her set the pace.

Her hands had crept around and were holding his buttocks. She could feel his muscles straining to stay still. She wanted him to lose himself this time; she wanted to be the one in control.

She brought one hand around and traced her fingers around his balls. She heard a loud moan escape from him and she repeated the action, tickling then circling, her fingers curling in his hair. She felt more precome hit her tongue. She pushed her finger under his balls and traced the line to the secret hole behind. She heard him make a sound somewhere between a moan and a grunt and she felt his thighs shivering.

"Okay, that's enough!" His voice was heavy.

He pulled back and Alexia looked at him, unsure what she'd done wrong.

"This is about your pleasure too, and I can't fuck you, so before I come all over that beautiful face, we're going to do this together." He pushed her back onto the bed and pulled up her nightie.

"I think it's time we moved our lessons on to math," he continued, "so think of a number somewhere between sixty-eight and seventy."

With a swift movement he was on her. He grabbed a pillow

and put it under her head, propping it quite high. Then he turned completely so he was facing her feet. He was on his knees, his cock bobbing and dangling in front of her mouth.

"Now multiply by two…"

He lowered his hips slowly so that the tip of his cock traced Alexia's lips. She opened and sucked greedily. She clutched his hips to steady him and pulled him deeper into her mouth.

Her pussy was screaming now, screaming to be touched, teased, caressed, invaded.

Richard parted her legs and she felt the nearness of his face as his hot breath surged over her cunt.

She bent her knees and pushed her hips up to meet his eager mouth. His tongue tickled her clit and she almost bit his cock from the shock of the pleasure. The trace of her teeth sent a shiver through him and his teeth nipped her labia in return. Then he bit again, this time harder, sending a wave of pleasure-pain through her.

She was bucking now and he had to hold her hips. He steadied himself on his elbows, then slipped his arms under her thighs to pull them open a little more.

The anticipation was agony. She was sucking hard, hoping her urgent mouth would make him move faster. Suddenly he drove two hard fingers into her. A loud, hard "ah" escaped from her, muffled by his cock in her mouth.

Her wetness let his fingers enter her unhindered and he drove them in, not bothering to curl them against her G-spot. This was straight finger fucking. He had sworn not to use his cock inside her but he was going to make her clutch against the hardness of a man, the hardness of his fingers.

But he was not in control anymore. She was driving him now. She sucked and pumped her mouth on him harder and harder, driving him to fuck her mercilessly with his fingers, to punish her clit with his hardened tongue. Faster and deeper they both pushed and pushed until she felt the rush of warmth as his come hit her mouth. As he came, he rammed his fingers home and she bucked hard. This was no slow, uncoiling orgasm. This was a shuddering explosion in her cunt. She dropped her head back to gasp and the last spurts of him fell on her cheek. Her back was arched and she pushed her hips upward to grip him with her last shuddering contractions.

The waves subsided. It was a short but intense orgasm that was almost painful. Richard pulled his leg back over her and collapsed on his back, breathing hard. Alexia was panting too, exhausted and sated. She couldn't believe the violence of her orgasm. But as her breathing returned to normal and her mind cleared, she realized it wasn't only Richard's ministering that had pulled the reaction from her. Nathan was still in her mind, if not in her pussy. And he wasn't leaving anytime soon.

"I think math could be your best subject!" Richard's voice broke her reverie. He propped himself up on one elbow and wiped his own come from her face. She blushed. Somehow she was shy again, even after her wanton behavior of a moment ago.

He laughed quietly to himself.

"Yeah, it's going to take a while before you're really comfortable with this, in daylight hours anyway, but there's time…"

He leaned over and kissed her gently, almost chastely.

"Romy says you gotta big day tomorrow."

"Yes, yes, I have. A couple of days."

"You packed and ready?"

"I'm packed…."

Richard laughed. "Well, whether you're ready or not, sometimes you just gotta jump, sweetheart. Now get some beauty sleep. I ain't gonna sleep here because there is no way I could stop from fucking you if I do that!"

He kissed her forehead, then stood up. He picked up his

clothes, and with that he was gone, shutting the door gently behind him.

Sometimes you just gotta jump, he'd said.

But how? With Richard she felt safe, he *was* safe. Tony was definitely not; he was a walking trap. And then there was Nathan…

Chapter 7

THE AIR WAS ESPECIALLY cold. Alexia pulled the fur of her coat collar closer around her neck as she stepped off the bus. It was midafternoon, but the day was still wearing the chill it had woken up with. She looked up. An ice blue cloudless sky. She hoped the freezing wind wasn't a sign of a Siberian chill in Nathan's mood.

Alexia looked across the road to see him pulling up outside the office in a dark blue Jaguar, the sporty version. It was a beautiful car, the car of a very successful man. A car she would have to spend the next two hours in. Two hours with Nathan. Every nerve in her body was screaming at her to turn and run, run home, run away, far, far away. But he was climbing out of the car now and he had seen her. Her heart was thumping.

She crossed the road. There was very little traffic in the small London square and the noise of the wheels of her roller bag seemed to bounce off the office façades as they rattled along the pavement. Any hope of sidling up quietly was gone.

"Good morning," said Nathan. He'd barely looked up at her. Professional, stark, cold.

"Good morning." Was her voice shaking? Hard to tell above the rattling wheels. She reached the car, reached Nathan. Now he looked up.

He looked tense, a little tired, as if he was carrying an invisible weight. But he was still immaculate. He was wearing a beautiful jacket with an open shirt, tieless, and his long legs enveloped in chinos.

Alexia tried to push down the handle of her roller bag, but it was a cheap case and the handle was sticking. She desperately wanted to appear in control on this trip; this wasn't a good start.

He reached forward and took the case from her. He pushed the handle down easily with one rasping slide. He pressed his key fob and the trunk opened gracefully with the whisper of expensive engineering. Smooth, sleek, efficient.

"Once we get out of London it shouldn't take us too long. Make yourself comfortable."

Alexia obeyed silently. She walked to the passenger side of the car. Nathan took off his jacket and put it on the backseat. Alexia did the same. It seemed to be an intimate act, putting her coat in the backseat of Nathan's car. How silly was that? But it did.

She climbed into the front seat and sank into the luxurious leather. The car was a cocoon; the outside world sank away as the heavy door clunked shut. Two hours in this tiny space with nothing to do but talk?

She busied herself, stowing her handbag at her feet and pulling the seat belt through its runner to wrap around herself. The click pinned her in; she was strapped into his world. She felt a blast of cold air as he opened the driver door. She looked up to see his long leg and strong flank ease sideways into his seat. He seemed to fill the car. That aftershave. Every time she smelled it she felt that now familiar clutching sensation deep in her pussy. The scent of him, the nearness of him was agonizing.

"Okay, let's go." He pressed the ignition button and a low, rumbling purr emanated from under the hood. He eased the car away from the curb and took them out of the square into the traffic. She watched him drive. People say you can tell what a man will be like in bed by the way he dances, but she thought the way a man drives tells you more about him.

The engine noise barely registered as Nathan slipped the wheel through his long fingers, gliding the car through the traffic with a sureness of touch. He was a man in control, in control of a big, mechanical cat.

"I need to find out what's going on today, if you don't mind." Nathan put the radio on, a sports talk station going over the morning news stories.

"Of course not," said Alexia. Work, she thought.

The babbling of the presenters filled the car. She was glad of their disembodied company; it eased the tension as Nathan drove them expertly through the traffic, taking shortcuts and side roads that brought them to the edge of the city with remarkable speed.

As they hit the freeway, Nathan opened up the accelerator. She could almost feel the flex in his thigh as his foot squeezed down, thrusting them toward the speed limit in a single breath.

The engine purred only slightly louder as the car ate up the distance between London and Cleaver Hall, the country house hotel that was to be their home for the night.

The radio news program finished and Nathan turned the dial. The car was silent again.

What now? Alexia fixed her gaze out of the window, not daring to turn and look at him.

"Are you okay?" he asked.

Alexia's heart leaped, unsure how to answer. "Um…"

"About this evening, I mean. The dinner arrangements for the boys and the sponsors, and the press conference?"

Her heart sank. She was terrified when she thought the question was personal. But now that it was clear it wasn't, she felt a crushing disappointment.

"Um, yes, I think so. Romy's made sure I'm up to speed. And I reconfirmed everything yesterday afternoon. I won't let you down." Alexia hoped it would satisfy him.

"I don't think for a minute you'll let me down, Alexia. I just…" Nathan hesitated.

He'd used her name. She looked at him. She'd never really studied him from this angle. His face was strong, and in profile that ever so slight crookedness in his nose made him look very French. His lashes were long over dark blue eyes. But she couldn't read the expression in them.

"I just don't want you to be nervous," he said.

It wasn't the event that was making her nervous. She wanted to yell at him, scream at him that just being next to him was shredding her nerve endings, spiraling her hormones into free fall. How could he not know? She wasn't that good an actress. Or maybe she was…

Or maybe she was…

"Well I'm here to do whatever you need—I'm your sub," said Alexia.

She thought she felt Nathan catch his breath slightly. "I mean your substitute PA!" she blurted, catching a note of panic in her own voice.

There was silence again. She dared not look at Nathan. Her face was burning.

"You seem tense."

Alexia didn't reply. What could she say?

Nathan shifted in his seat. Even the slight movement of his body unnerved her in this confined and cushioned space. But he seemed to be sharing her discomfort. He breathed out heavily.

"Look, I… The other day in the office, that… I'm sorry, it shouldn't have happened."

Alexia felt her heart in her throat. It shouldn't have happened?

"I… I…" Alexia started to speak but no words would come. She wanted to ask him why it shouldn't have happened, but the words wouldn't come. The silence between them was like a stone wall.

Nathan broke the silence eventually. "That man. Your ex-boyfriend…?" It was a statement, but framed as a question.

"Oh God, I'm so sorry. I'm so sorry he turned up at work."

Alexia was wringing her hands.

"I'm not worried about that. I was worried about *you*," he said.

Silence again. He was waiting.

"Carter, his name is Carter."

Nathan didn't reply; he was letting her fill the gap. He wasn't going to pry but clearly wanted to know more. He pulled into the slow lane.

"I lived with him for a while, after I left college. It wasn't… He wasn't…"

How would she describe him? She couldn't use the same language she'd used with Richard, not here, not now. *Cunt!* Yes, he was, but she felt Nathan might crash the car if she confessed to that.

"He was a bully. He caught me when I was vulnerable and inexperienced and…"

She felt a need to tell him everything, to confess, to apologize for Carter's sudden, unwanted appearance outside the agency. The details were wildly inappropriate, too much, but she desperately wanted to explain.

"I didn't realize it at first but he's nasty. He's the kind of man who strips your confidence. Slowly, so you don't realize it's happening, and before you know it, you're a doormat…" Her voice dropped. "A trapped doormat."

Alexia felt tears stinging behind her eyes. She fought them back, afraid Nathan might hear the telling sadness in her voice.

He turned to look at her for a moment. Then his hand was on hers. The shock of its warmth and tenderness sent a surge of need through her, not erotic need, but a yearning for comfort, for strong and secure arms to hold her. His arms.

He was watching the road but his attention was all on her as she talked about Carter.

"You wonder how you could end up like that, in a situation like that, a relationship like that. You wake up one day and think, how did I get here? But then you don't have the confidence to get out."

She almost hiccupped the last word and fell silent. Afraid her emotions would spill out. She closed her eyes.

Then she heard Nathan's voice, low and soft. "Did he hurt you?"

Alexia froze for a moment. It was hard to breathe. Hard to form words.

"Not... No, not exactly. He didn't hit me, but..." She looked out of the window again, unsure how to answer. How could she tell him about Carter's bedroom cruelties?

But he understood. She felt a soft squeeze of her hand. She felt she would cry if he kept squeezing, kept touching her. She had to move the conversation on.

"You were amazing, really. I've never seen anyone drop someone to the floor like that."

Nathan laughed to himself. "Army," he said. "No more explanation necessary."

"But I'm..." Alexia looked at him. "Thank you."

Her voice was low and soft, and as it trailed away she saw his expression change. The tension had left his jaw, and although his eyes were on the road, she could see they were softer.

He faltered. He looked embarrassed, unsettled. He took his hand from hers; the sudden removal shocked her. She wanted it back.

But he needed it, he was driving, and he clicked the indicator and pulled onto the off-ramp. They had reached the end of their freeway journey. She clasped her hands tightly together, afraid if she left her hand on her thigh it would look like an invitation, a plea for more.

"Not far now, a couple of miles," said Nathan. Their "moment" was over; he had retreated into his professional shell.

They drove through a small market town, past tasteful little shops and restaurants with Tudor fronts, catering for the many ladies who lunch who clearly inhabited this wealthy part of England.

A little bleeping sound emanated from her handbag. Self-consciously, she put it on her lap and fished out her mobile phone from an exterior pocket.

Texts might be private, but in this little space she felt the arrival of the message deserved an explanation. She pressed the button and her heart sank.

"It's from Tony," she said, afraid to look at Nathan. "He's waiting for us in the hotel lounge."

"Okay," said Nathan, his voice now cool and hard.

The rest of the journey passed in silence. Tony had come between them again.

They drew up to the gates of Cleaver Hall and pulled in to a sycamore-lined driveway that swept them up to the house. A stunning seventeenth-century manor house came into view. It was magnificent, refurbished as a luxury hotel and spa, fit for the rich and famous, the only clientele with bank accounts large enough to feed its voracious appetite.

"Only the best for the Premier League," said Nathan, as he uncoiled his long legs and stepped out of the car, handing the keys to a uniformed doorman.

Alexia undid her safety belt and stepped unsteadily out of the Jaguar. She was unaccustomed to such luxury and was glad that Nathan was clearly unfazed by the rapid attention they received from the staff.

She realized that Nathan was waiting for her to walk in before him. Carter had trained her so well to expect nothing that a man being a real gentleman was quite a surprise. She smiled a weak thank you and walked past him.

As they walked through the galleried lobby, Alexia received another text. She thought she saw Nathan's jaw tense. She pressed the button. It was from Romy.

Hi hon, have put a little giftie in your bag, might help keep things under control ;-) xxx

They walked up to where an immaculately turned out young woman was sitting at a large French writing desk.

"Ah, Monsieur Fallon, how good to see you again," she cooed. French desk, French accent. "We 'ave reserved your favorite room." She made a rather indecent Gallic meal of the word "favorite." How can French women pout and talk at the same time? thought Alexia.

"Thank you, Michelle, that's very kind."

He was so smooth and the woman gave him a kittenish smile. Alexia felt a surge of jealousy. Don't be ridiculous, she told herself. It's her job to be charming.

"One of your colleagues 'as already checked in," the receptionist said, checking her paperwork.

They chatted for a moment. Alexia fished in her bag, looking for whatever Romy had put in there to try and distract herself. It was a large bag and it took some rooting, but eventually she put her hands on a pocket vibrator.

She slammed the bag shut and looked up.

"And you must be Miss Alexia Wright…" The receptionist looked at Alexia and gave her a polished hospitality smile.

"Er, yes," said Alexia, aware that the warmth flooding her face must be visible. What was Romy thinking?

The receptionist continued, "Here are you keys, Monsieur Fallon. For you, the Ashbourne suite, and for you, Miss Wright, Room *Soixante-Neuf*."

Alexia gulped and flushed. Was the woman serious? Room 69. She felt as if she'd landed in a French farce, quite literally. She felt a curling in her loins as the memory of Richard's tongue inside her pussy raced back to greet her. She darted a look up, but Nathan's attention was already elsewhere. Tony was striding toward them. The junior agent was in his element, swaggering around in the luxurious surroundings. He was casually dressed in designer jeans and an immaculate shirt, the kind with a patterned collar that says "I may be in a plain shirt, but I've got style."

"Hey, Nathan…" He strode up and looked at Alexia. She flushed again. She turned around to greet him, her key in hand. He saw the number and grinned.

"I asked Michelle to sort our rooms out so we'd be next to each other so we could *coordinate*," said Tony, his words heavy with double meaning. He held up his own key. Number 70. His eyes danced.

Nathan's face darkened. "Well, our soccer players are in the suites, and you'll be spending most of your time babysitting them, Tony, so I'm afraid you won't have a chance to get too comfortable."

He flashed a charming and winning smile at Tony.

"Of course," said Tony, with a very slight bend of his head.

Alexia realized that Nathan was definitely the alpha dog, and he didn't have to say much, or do much, to be the head of the pack. Just his presence, his word, that was enough.

He turned to Alexia. "Okay, well, I'll be having dinner with Tony and the players later. You are welcome to join us, but their company can be a little… colorful."

"Oh, she won't mind that, will you, Alex?" chimed Tony. "She's a game girl."

Shut up, shut up, shut up! Alexia wanted to scream at him. But the damage was done; Nathan's eyes had grown cold and he was picking his mobile phone from his inside pocket. "Okay, see you both at seven." And with that he was striding down the oak-paneled corridor that led to the suites, answering a call.

"We're this way," said Tony.

He moved to take her arm but she was furious.

"I can manage, thank you."

"Okay, okay." He raised his arms in a yielding gesture. "Whatever you say. I'll see you at dinner anyway, and maybe later…"

He winked at her, then disappeared toward the bar.

———

Alexia collapsed into her room and threw herself onto the large bed. It was a stunning bedroom, and normally its taffeta curtains and gorgeous silks would have thrilled her, but its elegant luxury was lost on her today. Nathan had asked about Carter. "Did he hurt you?" His soft words swirled around her head, lilting, caring, caressing. "Did he hurt you?" But hot on their heels was Tony's voice. "She's a game girl."

Romy had wanted to give Nathan the chance to get to know her, but now? How could that happen with Tony hovering, ruining everything? She would have to keep her distance from him, but that wouldn't be easy; he seemed determined to make her his next conquest.

Mortification, jealousy, fear, and lust swirled in her veins in a toxic cocktail of confusion. She clutched her arms around her stomach. Sitting with Nathan in that car for two hours had forced her emotions on a collision course with her hormones. She wanted him to hold her, to kiss again. "Did he hurt you?" Did he care? Why did he care? The touch of his hand on hers, such a small gesture, such a surge of feeling.

Alexia stared at the ceiling. She'd sat on her emotions, her sexuality, for an eternity. She had closed herself down for so long, but now? Pandora's box was no longer shut. Tony's boardroom display had knocked on the lid, Richard had pried off the lock, and Nathan... Would he open it? For a moment she thought there was a chance that he would. But she remembered the legend. When all the evils swarmed out there was one thing left at the bottom of Pandora's box—hope. Not for Alexia. There was no hope, not with Nathan.

She felt that clutching inside her pussy again. Life was easier when she was shut off from herself. The surging in her cunt seemed to be ever-present now and it was ferocious.

Romy's text seemed to betray a psychic insight. Might help keep things under control.

She flung herself across the bed and grabbed her bag, fishing desperately for Romy's secret gift. She couldn't find it. Damn! Where was it?

She turned her bag upside down and the entire contents spilled out—makeup, purse, brush, phone, keys, tissues, umbrella, tampons—all falling onto the bed and clattering onto the floor until... There it was, nestling in its box, winking at her through its plastic display window. A ten-speed bullet vibrator.

She tore it open, and palmed the tiny, sleek missile of sexual deliverance.

Flinging herself back on the bed, she hitched up her skirt and pulled down her panties. Romy had persuaded her to wear thigh highs instead of tights and now she was grateful. She needed to feel open, completely open. She clicked the bullet on; it was so quiet, discreet. As she felt the thrum of it in her hand she also felt wetness flood her pussy and her clit tingle in anticipation.

She parted her legs and closed her eyes. She pictured Nathan, tried to recall the masculine smell of him misted with his aftershave. She had felt the firmness of his body when he'd held her and she longed to feel it again. She tried to imagine him pressing against her as she brought the bullet down to touch her clit.

Her thigh muscles twitched at the sharp shock it gave her. Too high! She had flipped it to max speed in her haste. She turned it down and it found its way back like a homing beacon to the gathering of nerves that longed to feel its angry vibrations.

The buzz went through her from clit to core. She dipped her fingers in her wetness and rubbed the tips gently around her labia as the bullet speeded on. She pushed up the speed, a little more—then a little more.

She pictured Nathan, the way he uncoiled from the car, his long legs, long, strong thighs. She wondered how it would feel to wind her own thighs around his, naked, hot, raw.

She dug her heels into the bed, lifting her knees and arching her back. A little more—a little higher.

She imagined the muscles in his thighs flexing and tensing as he lay on her, looking down at her. Looking into her.

Her eyes flew open; even in her own imagination the sight of his eyes boring into her sent a stomach-rippling surge of shock through her.

She picked up her head and propped herself up on her elbows. She had positioned herself on the bed opposite a long wall mirror. There she was, splayed open, silver toy in her glistening, wet hand, her swollen pink labia, framed by damp blond curls, quivering.

The sight of her own sex shocked her. She stared at it for a moment. This is what Richard saw, she thought. And the memory of his gaze before he plunged his tongue into her sent her fingers searching for the speed button. More, more, more…

Almost before she knew it, the bullet was speeding at maximum again, at first so shocking, but now so thrilling. She rode the waves, desperate for release.

"Oh God, Nathan!" she moaned out loud as a crashing orgasm bucked her hips and she jammed the bullet against herself. The contractions ran through her, each one a small wave hitting a shallow beach, hitting the sand then raking its way back.

She lay back and threw her arms over her head, panting. She snapped the bullet off; it had done its job. It took a while for her breathing to come back to normal. She pulled her legs together and felt the wetness on her thighs.

She stood up and looked at her reflection. Not so pale now. Her face was pink and flushed. Is this my just-been-fucked face? she thought. If only. How would she look if she had really been taken? She didn't know; it had never really happened.

She walked into the bathroom and splashed her face with water. She had rarely felt more fragile than at this moment. She had to find some inner confidence; she had to show Tony that she was not to be toyed with and show Nathan she could do her job. Whatever else he thought of her, she would make sure he could find no fault with her work.

It was 6:15. Only forty-five minutes to get ready for dinner. She had just enough time to shower and get ready to meet the players.

When she was done, she applied her makeup, lining her eyes a little more heavily than usual, a little more smokiness to bring out the blue. She arranged her hair in a loose up-do and pulled on the dress she'd brought with her for the evening. It was another Romy hand-me-down, but it was beautiful. A dark royal blue bodycon dress that skimmed her body and gave her an hourglass silhouette. Just formal enough to appear businesslike, just sexy enough for dinner. She slipped her feet into her heels, applied one more swipe of lip gloss, and grabbed her key and phone. It was 6:55.

Alexia made her way down to the dining room. Guests were milling around, and many cast an admiring look as she passed them. But her focus was completely on staying serene. She was desperate not to look afraid or out of place.

She walked into the dining room and there was Nathan. Her clit still tingled from an hour ago, and the sight of him sent another rush right through her. Was it possible he looked even better than he did earlier? He had changed into a dark suit and was talking to their three Premier League clients, Iorizzo, Lopez, and Carsten, the new faces of the world's sexiest aftershave.

They were typical top-flight soccer players. An Italian, an Argentinian, and a German… Peacocks all. Watches that cost more than Nathan's car and designer suits that hugged their gym-honed bodies. All finished off with hair gel, diamond ear studs, and eyebrows groomed with designer gaps.

But standing next to Nathan they looked like boys, boys who were trying too hard to impress. The body language was clear. He was the alpha in the room. He wasn't much older than them but, despite their fame and the adulation that followed them, they were seeking *his* approval.

She heard a low, quiet whistle behind her, then felt a hand brush up her back. It sent a wave of heat up her spine that almost melted her composure.

"You certainly scrub up nice," said Tony. He walked in front of her, wearing his wolfish grin.

"Stop it!" She almost spat the words at him.

"You're right, of course. This is work, absolutely, although—we might find a convenient closet later!" He flashed his eyebrows, then sauntered off to join Nathan and the players.

Alexia steamed quietly. He was infuriating. She didn't even like Tony; he was arrogant and cocky. But he had a knack for turning her on. She stood in the room, unsure what to do. Should she walk up to them, or should she wait for Nathan? No, that would be ridiculous, he was her boss.

Her turmoil must have been evident, as a beautiful, dark-skinned woman walked up to her and said, "Are you Nathan's new PA?"

Alexia felt a flood of relief that someone had saved her from her very obvious isolation.

"Yes, yes, I am."

"Sonia Varma," said the woman, extending a perfectly manicured hand. "Chief financial officer for the brand."

"Oh! Good to meet you."

Sonia could see Alexia's discomfort and smiled warmly. "Come and sit with me at dinner. The boys will be swapping stories all night. They'll only be interested in us later, when they're a bit more tanked!" she said.

She escorted Alexia to a table and they sat down.

"You been with Nathan long?" asked Sonia.

"No, no, just a couple of weeks, but I'm only on this trip because his PA is ill. I'm just filling in." Alexia realized she'd bitten her lip at the end of the sentence.

"Don't worry. Nathan always makes sure these things run like clockwork. You're just window dressing, really, once all the arrangements are in place. Hotels like these never let anything go wrong."

"Oh good."

Alexia exhaled, relieved to have found a safe companion for the evening. "Do you know Tony as well?" she asked. "He's looking after the players."

Sonia laughed. "Looking after them… Well, yes he is! He's as bad as they are, of course. They all party hard, this lot. But then that's why he makes a good babysitter. He gets them what they want and he joins in, but he keeps it behind closed doors."

"Oh. I don't think Nathan approves."

"Hmm. Well, he doesn't join in, certainly."

Alexia looked at her.

"So many ladies have tried to land the white whale. You know all the women call him that, don't you?"

"I'd heard."

"Mmm. I think it's partly the thrill of wanting what you can't have. He keeps his sex life very quiet, so no one can ever use it against him or play him. Clever guy, cleverer than most. But don't think he's a prude. Look at him, he's all man."

Alexia was silent. She followed Sonia's eyes to Nathan. He was chatting to the soccer players but, as if some unseen thread had twanged between them, he looked up, straight at her. She felt a surge through her cunt and that telltale warmth in her pussy that betrayed approaching wetness.

Sonia was watching Nathan. "But then again, perhaps he likes ash blonds." She smiled as she swept the last word over Alexia.

Alexia flushed, wishing the aching in her loins would subside.

Sonia bent her head low and whispered, "If he *is* interested, are you ready for that tiger in your bed? I don't imagine he's the standard shag."

The sudden intimacy of the conversation with a total stranger made Alexia's head swim. But she didn't correct Sonia. She didn't deny that Nathan had shown interest. She gave the woman a half smile, then looked back at him. But his attention was now elsewhere. Looking in her direction was Tony, who appeared to be pointing her out to the soccer players.

"Oh my God!" said Alexia.

Sonia giggled. "My, my. Well, if you want a fun night, you've certainly got your pick, but be careful"—she tapped Alexia's arm—"unless you like spit roast!"

Waiters appeared behind them, but Alexia was confused. Her eyes settled on the first plate, foie gras, then darted to the menu card. Salmon. What did Sonia mean, spit roast?

The food was exquisite, and Alexia managed to relax a little to enjoy it. The others at their table were from the sponsor's company and the talk was general, and a little boring; about sport, and who was doing a deal with who. Then the conversation turned to who was *doing* who, which was a good deal more interesting, and shocking. In the last few weeks, Alexia had come to learn that she had entered a world where sex was used as a currency, but the frequency of exchange still shocked her.

She stole glances at Nathan but he remained deep in conversation, seemingly oblivious to her presence or proximity. But Tony was very well aware of it. He kept throwing lascivious glances as he swallowed glasses of the rich red wine.

She realized she'd been silent for most of the meal, listening to the gossip, which meant she was drinking her wine a little too quickly. The coffee arrived and she poured a cup and downed it as swiftly as its temperature allowed.

The diners rose to leave.

"Drink at the bar?" asked Sonia.

More alcohol would not be a good idea, but she needed company.

"We won't see much of the boys tonight."

"Won't they be coming to the bar too?" asked Alexia.

"The execs might, but not the soccer boys. They'll have other entertainments planned, almost certainly."

The two women adjourned to the bar and seated themselves on tall stools. Sonia ordered whiskey sours. "They'll help you sleep," she said.

Alexia didn't think she'd need help after the wine.

"I have to say," said Sonia after a large gulp, "you're not the usual type."

"Usual type for what?" asked Alexia, tasting the drink. She'd never had a sour; its tartness played with her tongue.

"For this kind of industry, the sport/showbiz world. You seem too *real*."

"Real? I don't understand." Alexia took another gulp.

"Well, most of the girls who work in agencies like yours are after something. They want to bag themselves a soccer player, or hang with the fast crowd. They're either über-manicured gym bunnies or posh girls who like to ride the men as hard as they ride their horses. They're all ambition—for the men, that is, not a career. But you…" Sonia regarded her. "I like you. You actually might have some substance."

Alexia laughed. She liked Sonia too. She was blunt, but she was funny and kind.

"I can see why Nathan would want you to work for him," she continued.

At the mention of Nathan's name Alexia felt a skip in her stomach. "Why?" she asked, desperate for an answer from someone who seemed to understand him.

"He's a really good guy, which is bloody rare in this business; they're all either peacocks or piranhas. Or both! But Nathan, he's not called the white whale for nothing. I wonder if he knows that's what he's known as?" Sonia laughed to herself. Then she became serious again. "What I'm trying to say is, he must get so tired of the women who flock around him. I'm sure he's had his fun like any guy, but sometimes you know when a man is looking for something more. And if Mr. Fallon was ever a 'flirt, fuck, and go' man, he's certainly grown out of it."

Alexia was hanging on to Sonia's every word. She heard a familiar voice from the archway into the bar. She looked around to see Nathan bidding good night to some of the sponsors. He looked up and caught her eye. Her stomach flipped again and her pussy yielded up that now obligatory drop of moisture that seemed to follow every stolen glance of him. He tipped his head to her and was gone.

Sonia was watching. "If you do want to catch him for yourself, be careful, Alexia. I don't think that big fish will be easily reeled in."

Alexia looked back at her new friend and downed her remaining whiskey.

Chapter 8

ALEXIA HAD JUST REACHED her room when her phone pinged. She looked at her texts. Tony's name leaped out from the screen.

Need you in Clarenden suite ASAP. Problem with arrangements.

At this time of night? She'd been so careful to nail everything down; she'd gone through the list of things that could go wrong over and over. She couldn't believe there was a problem. The last thing she wanted or needed was to be forced to speak to Tony tonight. Clarenden was Iorizzo's suite.

She turned on her heel, went to the wing of the hotel that housed the plush suites, and looked for the name next to the door. She passed Ashbourne. That's where Nathan is, she thought, a pang of regret and wanting flooding her instantly. The carpet was very deep on this side of the hotel; every inch of it screamed luxury and privilege. She kept walking, her feet barely registering a noise on the thick wool. There it was, Clarenden, the word on a small, discreet nameplate to one side of the oak-paneled door.

She cleared her throat, she wasn't sure why; a reflex action. Even the tiny sound seemed too loud for the quiet corridor. She knocked. Nothing. She knocked again. Still nothing. She didn't want to hammer on the door. She looked at the nameplate. She had the right suite, so she texted Tony.

Am outside, you're not answering!

She waited, her foot jiggling with frustration and nerves. Then the door swung open. Tony seemed slightly flushed and there were raucous noises coming from deep within the suite.

"Ah!" he said, and reached forward to grab her arm. Before she had time to object she was pulled into the suite, the door shutting firmly behind her.

"What's going on? You said there was a problem with the arrangements."

The suite was enormous; they appeared to be standing in a small hallway that led into other rooms. She couldn't see the revelers, but it was clear from the cheers that the soccer players were having a good time.

"There was a problem. *You* weren't here, that was the problem!"

"What?"

"Well, you see, there's something I think you should see..."

"Tony?"

He smiled. That worried her.

"Let me put it into context for you."

Alexia knew something was wrong, but she couldn't quite work out what it was. She sensed he was playing a game, and one he was good at.

"Remember how we first met...?"

Tony let the thought hang in the air. He knew he was conjuring up the image of his own thrusting buttocks and Phillipa's flailing legs, the image he knew Alexia was only too well acquainted with.

Alexia was gritting her teeth now. "What about it?"

"Well, as it seemed to put such a flush in your cheeks I thought there was something else you might need to watch..."

He tugged her arm, trying to pull her deeper into the suite, but she resisted and turned away.

"Let me go, Tony, I'm going back to my room."

"I really wouldn't go out there just now if I were you."

Alexia rounded on him. "Why not?"

"Because I saw Nathan go back down to the bar a moment ago. I think he was looking for you."

Surprised, she stared at Tony. He had no idea what had passed between her and Nathan, or had he guessed? Was he telling the truth?

"So?" she demanded, trying to sound as unconcerned as she could.

"Well, as you're here, not there, he'll be coming back any minute, and you don't really want him to see you coming out of this suite, now do you?"

The realization hit her like a slap. Tony had trapped her; she felt the blood drain from her face. He employed his best disarming smile.

"Don't look like that! Like I said, there's something I think you might like to see, then you can go. Won't take long."

Alexia had no real choice. She stood rooted to the spot, but as Tony took her hand to lead her forward, she felt her legs start to move obediently.

The noise and music from deep in the suite grew louder as Tony took her through into a small, dark room. He closed the door behind them. Then she saw it: an internal window looking straight into the master bedroom.

There were Iorizzo and Lopez, either end of a girl who was on all fours on a huge bed. Carsten was sitting on a chaise longue, two more girls draped over him. One was playing with his erection. They were all naked.

"Two-way mirror," Tony explained. "It's one of the reasons the big stars like to party here, and why the hotel can charge criminal sums of money. Good, isn't it?"

Alexia's eyes were fixed on the bed. Iorizzo knelt on it in front of the girl, his erection pointing at her mouth. Lopez was standing behind her, holding her hips, his erection pointing at her pussy.

The girl was about to be skewered from both ends and she clearly couldn't wait.

"Spit roast," whispered Alexia, remembering Sonia's remark at dinner.

"Exactly," said Tony. "Hey, the fun's about to start, so you might as well enjoy the show, seeing as how I know you like to watch."

Alexia barely heard his words. She knew she should make her escape but her feet were fixed to the spot. Tony was close behind her, and she could feel his breath on her neck.

In the bedroom, the girl waited. Iorizzo was holding a glass of champagne to her lips; bubbles and liquid were spilling from the side of her mouth as she tried to drink from the cup on all fours.

Everyone laughed and she threw back her head, her long, bottle-blond hair falling down her back. Alexia saw the girl's breasts jiggle as she tossed her hair, and she felt a tug in her own nipples, trussed up in a bra, now wanting to be free.

The spectators on the couch started chanting. "Spit roast! Spit roast! Spit roast!"

Alexia felt a squirt of wetness hit her panties. She realized to her surprise that she wanted to see it as much as the gallery did.

She felt Tony's hands on her hips, but didn't protest, didn't move. He held her firmly from behind and pressed himself against her back, his erection rubbing her bottom.

His voice was low. "I told you you'd want to see it. Her name's Tanya, she loves to get fucked hard."

Just hearing the word "fucked" whispered into her ear made her want to grab her own pussy.

In the bedroom, Tanya was writhing, waiting for the two stiff cocks to find their way home.

Iorizzo was first. He moved up the bed, the tip of him a millimeter from her mouth. He was southern Italian and was deeply tanned, as was Lopez. The little pale blond in the middle looked like a virgin sacrifice to the god of sex, and he was hungry.

She opened her lips and pulled in Iorizzo's cock. He held up his arms, champagne glass in hand, as if he'd just scored a goal, and everyone cheered. As Tanya started to devour him, Lopez was watching her rhythm, waiting to plunge at the right moment, when the movement was right.

Alexia thought it looked like those playground group skipping games where the enormous rope circles through the air and hits the ground, over and over, round and round, and you wait for your chance to jump in.

Lopez saw his chance as Tanya was about to move forward down Iorizzo's considerable length. He plunged into her cunt, sending her mouth forward onto Iorizzo.

More cheers.

Tony was also busy, but Alexia was transfixed and hadn't registered what he was doing. His hand had found its way inside her dress and he was peeling back one lacy cup of her bra.

Then the weight of him pressed her forward and she slapped a hand against the glass to steady herself as she watched the trio fucking.

Now she felt him. Tony wound his fingers in and grazed them over her straining nipple. It was hard, and the feel of his hands sent a strong shudder through her abdomen right down to her clit.

The trio were in a good rhythm now. Tanya looked like she was suspended by the two hard penises, their dark lengths plunging in and out of her pink lips above and below.

The erotic ballet continued as they all moved in perfect synchrony, like a melting flow of flesh and juices, driven from either end by strong, fit buttocks, piston engines, trained to perfection on the soccer field.

Tony's fingers worked Alexia's nipple, teasing and pinching. She felt her breasts swell, heaving up to meet his hand. She hated him, she loathed him now, but this felt so good she couldn't stop him.

He moved his other hand to find the breast still tucked in her bra and freed it to enjoy the same attention as the other.

Alexia had both hands against the glass now, her chest completely open and free for Tony to play with and punish. It was a strange sensation, seemingly to be so completely visible to the group in the bedroom, to be right in front of the glass, and yet completely unknown to them. It was thrilling. Watching but unwatched. Present but removed.

Tony pushed her forward until her breasts touched the window. The shiver of the cold glass sent another wet surge through her cunt.

She was hard against the window and yet she was still invisible.

She watched the men's backsides as they moved back and forth, pushing and plunging into Tanya, who was struggling now to concentrate on the dick in her mouth.

Alexia was struggling too. She sensed the imminence of Tanya's orgasm and she wanted her own, but Tony's attention stayed on his erection as he rubbed it against Alexia's bottom, pressing her against the window.

He was getting his kicks from making her watch.

Lopez had grabbed Tanya's long hair, like a cowboy tugging the mane of a skittish horse. He pulled her head back slightly, making her teeth rake Iorizzo's cock. The Italian grunted and bared his own white teeth, gritted with the pleasure-pain. He put his hands on either side of her head and pushed his cock forward.

Alexia couldn't believe how the girl managed not to choke.

"Oh, she's good," purred Tony in her ear. "A real sword swallower."

Tanya took Iorizzo so deep into her mouth he shut his eyes tight, his hands clamped to either side of her head as they moved. Then his chest heaved, he gave a deep, guttural, animal grunt, and came in her mouth. He thrust twice then pulled out suddenly, grabbing himself to spray his come all over her face.

The crowd cheered and Iorizzo put up his hand in his goal-scoring salute again as his cock showered her with the white, dribbling liquid.

And then she came. It sounded almost theatrical, but Alexia couldn't imagine the amount of pleasure two men could give. Iorizzo moved to the side to let her have her moment and Lopez gave one huge thrust to push every contraction out of her. Tanya's mouth dropped open as a porn-queen scream filled the air. Then Lopez dropped her hips and she collapsed on the bed. Fucked. Really, really fucked, thought Alexia.

Her own need gnawed fiercely at her now. She watched Tanya's panting afterglow with envy as the two men wiped their dicks. Slowly, the girl climbed off the bed, smiling and wiping her mouth as she joined the others. Iorizzo followed her and sat on the chaise lounge as Carsten got up to replace Lopez, who'd moved himself onto the bed where Iorizzo had been.

Tony growled low in Alexia's ear, "Taking it in turns."

"Who's next?" said Lopez. The chaise lounge was in front of the secret window, and as he faced it, asking for a volunteer, Alexia felt as if he had looked straight at her. Her stomach jolted and her pussy squirted again. She was soaking wet through to the tops of her thighs.

"Fancy it?" said Tony. His hands had crept up to her breasts again and he held them trapped, palms covering each one completely. She could feel her own heavy breathing against his hands as her rib cage rose and fell.

For a fleeting moment, she imagined herself accepting Lopez's invitation; the glass melting between them; being in that room, naked, and climbing onto the bed; placing her knees apart to leave her cunt yawning open for Carsten… Blond, Germanic, and square-jawed Carsten. He had cold features and a ruthless expression. His cock seemed even harder than the others; he'd been drinking less and he was primed to go.

She felt herself falling against the glass and imagined herself tumbling into the room. But the fantasy was short-lived, as a brunette climbed off the sofa and onto the bed. She was curvaceous and a little chubby, but she had large breasts that Lopez eyed appreciatively.

"Yvette," explained Tony, his hands now sliding down Alexia's body.

Yvette was quickly followed by a boyish-looking girl with a pixie cut and small, high breasts that stuck out.

"And Paula. Small tits, but she fucks like a minx," said Tony. Alexia had the feeling Tony knew from experience how she fucked, but she didn't care. She wanted to see more.

The boys may have planned another spit roast, but it seemed the girls had a better idea.

Yvette said, "How about a race?"

They all cheered again. Lopez got off the bed and stood next to Carsten. The girls knelt in front of them.

Yvette explained the rules. "First one to come buys Jimmy Choos for all of us!"

The girls hooted their appreciation.

Iorizzo took on the role of starter.

"On your marks… Get set… Suck!"

The girls greedily grabbed the two men and pushed their lips around them.

Alexia was rocking now and Tony was holding her.

"Do you want it? Do you want it too?" he purred in her ear.

She was moaning. She watched the girls as their heads bobbed, sucking and licking, as their hands searched for the men's dark holes, to push one little finger in and press the accelerator inside, to win the race.

"Do you want it?" repeated Tony, his hand moving down and pressing through her dress onto her pussy.

She gasped.

"Don't worry, Alexia. You'll be in even better shape for tomorrow if you get off tonight."

Tony whirled her around, but his mention of tomorrow had broken her reverie. Images of Nathan flashed before her. She stared at Tony, his eyes heavy with knowing. He knew he had her, knew she needed it. But now Nathan was in her head and he would not leave.

"No!" she moaned and pushed him away. "No!"

"Oh, for fuck's sake…" Tony's composure snapped.

She rushed for the door and ran out, grabbing her dress closed as she went. Tony dashed after her as Iorizzo emerged still naked, looking for more champagne. He saw them and Alexia froze.

"Hey Tony, you frighten your little friend away." His Italian accent was thick and seductive. He addressed Alexia, "Don't worry, pretty lady, if Tony is no good for you, give me few minutes"—he cupped his semierect cock—"and I can run you to the touchline too, eh?"

He laughed, gave his hips a little thrust toward her to show he meant business, and went back to the party. Tony grabbed her arm, but she pulled it free and finished doing up her dress.

"Leave me alone!" She frantically grabbed the door handle, but he stopped her before she could turn it.

"Why are you running? You know you want to." His face was inches from hers. He pressed himself against her and she felt his hardness again, right against her clit, right against the place that need urgent attention.

She was breathing hard. He took her silence as permission, moving in for the kiss. His tongue was warm and demanding, as hard and insistent as all the erections she'd been watching. He wrapped his arms around her, grabbed both ass cheeks in his hands, and dug his fingers in hard as he pulled her pelvis against his own in one sharp tug.

Alexia gasped. The strength of his hands, the pain of his pressing fingers, was exquisite, and the fire in his tongue was more than she could bear.

But Nathan, what about Nathan? She knew she had to break free of Tony. She had to clear her head. She wanted him, yes, but not because of *who* he was but because of *where* she was. She had witnessed an orgy and he was the man who had stood behind her, kneading her breasts, urging her to watch, urging her to feel her own wants.

But Nathan. Oh God, Nathan. She pushed Tony away and ran out of the door, just as Nathan was walking into his own suite. Tony dashed out after Alexia to find the two frozen in the corridor.

Nathan looked at the wide-eyed Alexia and at Tony, hot on her heels. He was clearly trying to work out what the tableau meant, but he was uncertain. The three stood there for what seemed like a heart-stopping eternity. Then Nathan went into this suite and closed the door.

Alexia gasped and ran down the corridor, leaving Tony far behind. Her mind was reeling; tears pricked behind her eyes. Where was she going? She had to cross reception to get to her room.

She dashed through, hoping no one would see her, but as she passed the archway into the bar she saw that Sonia was still there, scrolling through emails on her phone, nursing the last few drops of her drink.

Sonia looked up and caught sight of Alexia. Her expression changed. "What's wrong?" she mouthed.

The bar was almost empty, so Alexia scurried in and threw herself back on the bar stool she'd vacated earlier.

"God, what's happened? Alexia?"

Sonia turned to the barman and motioned with her hands that he should bring another round.

"Are you okay? What's happened?"

Alexia relayed the events that had brought her here. She expected Sonia to look shocked, but she didn't. She just smiled a cynical, knowing smile.

"I thought you knew what a spit roast was? Oh God, I'm so sorry. You really are new to all this, aren't you?"

Alexia nodded.

"Oh dear. Tony obviously knows that, so he tried to take advantage."

Alexia did not divulge how turned on she'd been—she left that bit out—or how she'd first met Tony. She just told her what she'd witnessed and how Tony had chased her out—and, worst of all, how she'd run into Nathan.

She almost wailed his name as Sonia put a fresh drink in her hand.

"Big gulp, throw it back, it helps with shock. Come on…"

She held Alexia's hands around the glass and motioned for her to throw back a shot. Alexia obeyed, coughing as the alcohol hit her throat. But Sonia was right: it jolted her, like slapping a hysterical person. It stopped her wanting to cry.

Sonia looked at her. "Well, Tony is a real player and you're a challenge now. Ignore the soccer players. They're just little boys, you don't have to be alone with them again. You're now a few hours older and a whole lot wiser than you were earlier this evening."

Alexia smiled weakly. "Yeah. I've obviously got a lot to learn."

Sonia returned her smile. She was in her late forties and had been around the block. She liked Alexia. Her voice was low and motherly.

"You really like Nathan, don't you? Not the way everyone else does, not just lust. You really like him."

The honesty of the question surprised Alexia, but she was feeling too vulnerable to pretend. She nodded her head. "He kissed me."

Sonia was surprised. Alexia told her what had passed between them in his office and how he vowed it would not happen again. Sonia was silent. She sat pensive, as Alexia sipped the rest of her drink.

"Look, I know a bit about him. It's not common knowledge, so keep it to yourself. One of his old army friends is a close friend of mine, and Nathan and I know each other socially, a little. They were in the same regiment in Iraq, the Blues and Royals. Nathan got shot—not life threatening, but bad enough to put him in hospital for weeks. Something happened, something awful, and he wasn't the same when he came back. None of them were. I think it happened to a lot of them out there, the things they saw; women and children killed, friends blown up at the side of the road. It can't be easy to readjust."

Alexia was listening intently. Romy had told her Nathan was ex-army. She began to get a glimpse of a very different Nathan. The wounded soldier, the man who could put Carter on the floor with a single blow.

Sonia continued, "He was engaged, but he was difficult to live with when he got back—posttraumatic stress and all that. His girlfriend, she—she didn't support him like the other wives and girlfriends, she dumped him just when he really needed someone. My friend said it really changed him. He doesn't trust women anymore."

"I'm not surprised," said Alexia.

"A friend of his father's was a sports agent and offered him a job when he left the army. The guy retired and Nathan ended up taking over the agency. He was so good at it everyone wanted him, so he renamed it after himself. But he's always been slightly aloof from it all. He loves sport, so he's in his element there, and the players and stars all love him—and the sponsors do too—but he's never been interested in all the glitzy stuff or the hanky-panky that goes with it. I suppose you can see why. Although some men who've been what he's been through would go the other way, sleep with every woman in sight."

Alexia didn't speak; she just looked at Sonia. Nathan was starting to make sense to her now. His cold bearing, his total ease with authority, his bottled-up emotions.

"He made it clear he won't kiss me again. And, worst of all, he thinks Tony and I…"

Alexia crumpled. She needed to talk, she needed to empty out all the emotions that had wracked her since joining the agency. She poured out the story of how her life had brought her to this point, how she'd run from Carter, how he'd turned up at the agency, how she was so confused about who she was and what she wanted. And how it felt utterly wretched to be so badly misunderstood by Nathan. Sonia listened patiently.

"Look," she said when Alexia had finished, "getting a man like that to trust you, to even see you properly, that takes time. You work for him; just be yourself and let him see who you are. I told you at dinner you aren't like the others, and he must see that too. He kissed you, so there's something different going on. He must be attracted to you. Okay, so he's fighting it, or he thinks you're screwing someone else, but he'll soon find out it's not true. Just do your job, and be there for him. Time will take care of the rest."

"Thank you," said Alexia quietly. "I wasn't expecting to find a friend here. You've been amazing."

Sonia smiled. "You remind me of myself at your age."

She got off her stool and gave Alexia a hug. It felt so good to Alexia to have human contact that was safe.

"I think you should go to bed, sleep like a baby, and get up tomorrow ready to face whatever the day brings. Nathan is a good man, and if you two are meant to be together, then a playboy like Tony won't get in the way, and if you're not—well, you'll have learned something."

The idea that they might not be meant for each other sent a hollow lurch through Alexia's stomach, but she knew Sonia was right. She thanked her, bid her good night, and went to her room.

The plate at the side of the door said 69. "Oh please!" said Alexia wearily as she let herself in. She thought of Tony's bedroom, number 70, just next door. There was a connecting door between the rooms; she hadn't noticed it earlier. Had he arranged that? She checked the handle. It was locked. She moved a small table in front of it.

She brushed her teeth and cleansed her face like an automaton, then laid out her clothes for the following day.

Injured in Iraq. His girlfriend left him. She wanted to know more, she wanted to know Nathan, really know him. But that won't happen tonight, she thought. Tonight I have to get to sleep somehow and face him tomorrow.

She took off her dress and caught the heady scent of Tony's aftershave lingering on her collar. It wasn't like Nathan's, soft, expensive, and inviting; this was flashier, more obvious. But its musky notes invaded her nose and the sense memory put her straight back in that darkened room, watching through the two-way mirror.

She felt her pussy clench as it yearned to be invaded, to be ravaged, to be completely filled as Tanya's had been by Lopez. It was agony. She'd stood and watched the orgy, and wanted to be part of it. She had to admit to it; in the darkest region of her, she knew it was true. Perhaps only in fantasy, but that was enough. She wanted it; she wanted the feel of a man's cock inside her. She was standing in her bedroom, but her senses were back in the suite, back at the orgy.

She knew she would get no sleep tonight if the gnawing, clawing want in her pussy was ignored.

She pulled off her clothes and looked for the bullet. She'd washed it and put it back in her bag, discreetly hidden in a deep pocket. She fished it out and buried herself under the pink satin quilt covering the king-sized bed. But she had second thoughts. She didn't want to be tucked away like this; she wanted to feel freer, naked.

She threw off the quilt and got up on all fours, then looked across at the mirror at the foot of the bed, looking at herself in profile. She saw the curve of her back, arched like a cat as she pushed her bottom high. She traced the angle of her breasts as they hung off her chest, the nipples full and proud as the blood followed gravity to engorge them. She clicked on the bullet and set it to five. Halfway to heaven.

She brought her hand to her clit, watching as she did so, and felt the buzz hit that sweet spot. The pleasure of watching herself as the thrumming went through her set her pulse racing faster. She didn't recognize the look in her own face; it was desperate, yearning, like the look on Tanya's face before Iorizzo had plunged his cock in her mouth.

Alexia pressed the bullet harder to her clit and eased up the speed, her pussy rippling with each gear change, climbing with each increment.

She looked again at her mirror and thought of the cold glass that had separated her from the soccer players. *Alexia Through the Looking Glass*. Her back was arching and her hips rocking as she rode the waves. Her eyes were heavy now, begging, begging…

Up again, up to ten. The last furlong. She was riding her way home and she needed to get there, to get there fast. The blood was rushing to her nipples as they hung down and she felt that coursing need in her veins.

She clenched and unclenched the muscles inside her, trying to create the tension that would push her to orgasm. And then she came, pleasure flooding her abdomen. She rocked with it and bucked her hips forward with each contraction. But as she rode the waves she felt no real satisfaction. The release was short-lived, hollow. There was more, she knew it.

She breathed a few soft exhalations, then pressed the bullet to herself again. Her clit responded, not with irritation, the soreness that comes from postorgasmic play. It was still hungry and she fed it. On she pressed, clenching and tensing her leg muscles and rocking. And she came again. This time, the surging was different. No contractions, just swirling, swooshing, shuddering gasps of pleasure that poured all through her, right down her legs. She collapsed onto the bed, just as Tanya had done. She had not been fucked as hard as Tanya, but she had found her release. It was enough for now. It would have to be.

Chapter 9

THE BUZZ IN THE hotel lobby was tangible. Journalists, photographers, and cameramen were arriving, talking on their mobiles, swaggering and strutting as if this was their sole territory. For the next few hours, it was.

The staff were busy, never breaking into a trot or a sweat as they were all too well trained. But they were clearly gearing up for a big event.

The press conference was set for the afternoon. Nathan and Tony had been in a huddle all day, leaving Alexia to fend for herself. She wasn't needed. She'd busied herself as best she could, making sure all the arrangements were in place for the press conference and the drinks reception for the celebrity guests afterward. She'd had to deal with all their publicists on the telephone, confirming they'd make an appearance.

Alexia found the hotel's liaison, a tall, polite, very camp young man called Oliver. He was immaculate. She couldn't imagine anyone with better manicured hands or neater eyebrows.

"All ready for the kickoff. Just call me if you have any questions or you need anything, absolutely anything." Oliver smiled widely, but the smile didn't reach his eyes. He was a pro, polished, stylish, and hard-nosed as hell. "Anything," he repeated.

I'll bet, she thought. Did he order the girls last night, or was that Tony? Perhaps both.

Sonia walked into reception. "Hello, sweetie, how are you feeling today?"

In truth, Alexia's head was a little fuzzy from the wine and the whiskey sours. "A little cloudy, but better for talking to you last night."

Sonia squeezed her arm. "It'll all be okay today. The soccer boys will be too busy looking cool for the cameras to worry about you, and Tony will be too busy looking cool for the soccer boys to worry about you. And Nathan, he'll just be worrying about everything except you. So just stand back, do your job, make sure there are no hitches, and fix them if there are... Then breathe out!"

The two women laughed together, but Alexia's laugh was all gallows humor. Her stomach was churning and it wasn't going to stop anytime soon.

"See you in a bit," said Sonia and left to speak with her colleagues from the fragrance company who were paying a king's ransom to have the three soccer players fronting their brand.

Alexia felt alone and exposed, standing in reception, watching all the movement and hustle, not quite knowing how to fit in. She watched as the journalists disappeared into the press conference room, taking the paraphernalia of television and radio with them. The lobby fell silent again.

"Alexia," said a deep voice behind her.

She turned around to see Nathan. He towered over her, immaculate as always. But she couldn't help noticing he looked as if he hadn't slept well, just a slight darkness under those dark blue eyes.

"Any problems with the publicists or are we all set?"

"Er... No, we're fine. I've just had another chat with Oliver, our liaison at the hotel. It's all under control."

Nathan eyed her for a minute. "No last-minute hitches with Iorizzo or the others?"

He was watching her carefully. It was obvious he was talking about last night. She wanted to tell him, to explain that nothing happened, she wasn't part of the fast crowd, that she'd been tricked, but there was no time. Down the corridor, like a royal procession, came the soccer players and their entourages—and Tony.

"Gentlemen," said Nathan.

"*Buon giorno*," said Iorizzo, shaking Nathan's hand vigorously. He went first in the pecking order; after him came Lopez and Carsten. As they greeted Nathan, Alexia felt a rush of fear as Iorizzo passed in front of her. She remembered his offer to do her next, as he'd stood in front of her, his cock on its way back up to an erection after coming all over Tanya. But he looked straight through her. Did he not remember? Was she so forgettable? Was his life such a procession of girls that he didn't distinguish one from another? Or did she look so different last night, her hair down and disheveled, not the neat PA she was today?

He registered no recognition and waited to be shown where to go by Nathan. A wave of relief swept over Alexia. Tony was hovering and she stood well back, trying to make sure she didn't catch his eye or give him the chance to say anything to her.

"Shall we go? The press are waiting." Nathan gestured the way and the soccer players strutted into the press conference, their entourages following behind.

Tony brought up the rear, trying to catch Alexia, but she tucked herself behind the far side of the group, away from his reach. She thought she saw Nathan notice her moving out of Tony's way, but she couldn't be sure. His concentration was on his charges, surely?

As the doors opened, Alexia heard all the camera shutters go off at once. It was like distant gunfire as the soccer players walked into the room in a blaze of flash bulbs. They were used to the attention, and they reveled in it.

She stood well to the side as Nathan ushered the CEO of the fragrance company onto the stage to join the soccer players. He was a smart man in his late fifties, but he looked gray and corporate next to the preening soccer stars.

Alexia wanted to move to the back of the room, but she knew she must stay close to Nathan in case he needed anything.

The press conference passed in a blur. The journalists fired a barrage of inane questions at the stars: why this aftershave, why this brand, did they actually wear it, did their girlfriends like it…?

They tried a few sneaky questions about the England manager and the players' private lives, but Nathan was having none of it. He stepped forward and firmly told them how pleased the boys were to be associated with such a prestigious brand. He was good, Alexia thought, he was very good. He drew the Q&A to a swift close and offered the photographers staged shots.

The boys and the snappers quickly got into their positions. They'd all done this before.

She looked at Nathan. He was so in control, so deft, so practiced, his authority unquestionable. But as she watched him, she couldn't stop thinking about the other side, the private side; the side she had glimpsed all too briefly, the softer side. It wasn't on show today, and she found it hard to bring it clearly to mind.

He saw her. She was staring, and his eyes had moved across the room and fallen on hers. Her stomach lurched and instinctively she dropped her head and looked at the floor. She kicked herself. Why couldn't she face him? She forced herself to look up again, but his gaze had traveled on, to a photographer who was being difficult.

She wanted him so much it hurt. To see him in this room, so close and yet so far. She ached to feel his arms around her again. Sonia had said he'd been dumped by his girlfriend. How could any woman dump him? Alexia couldn't imagine ever leaving a man like Nathan.

She looked over at Tony, who was chatting to some journalists. What a difference, she thought. He loved this. He loved every minute of being associated with these people, of being the gatekeeper the journalists would have to try and get through to get to the stars.

Lopez walked past and slapped Tony's arm. "My man!" he said, and sauntered on despite a couple of the journalists trying to speak to him. Tony's chest swelled almost visibly. And his ego, thought Alexia.

Tony looked up at Alexia and she saw him make a tiny thrust of his hips toward her. No one else would have seen it, but she did; it was meant for her.

She wanted to slap him, but he still managed to turn her on. She felt a squirt in her panties. She stepped away, turning to look at the rest of the room. Why did he still turn her on? Everything seemed to turn her on at the moment. Why? She knew why. She needed sex. Real sex. Real, honest to goodness, pin you down, tear your clothes off, fuck you till your ears rattle sex. Watching the spit roast last night had unleashed not just a yearning for lovemaking but a yearning to be taken. She felt as if the tension in her vagina was almost visible; it was agonizing.

The photographing was over and Nathan was ushering the soccer stars into the reception room where celebrities and hangers-on were already gathered to celebrate the union of soccer and fragrance. It was all completely fake, but this deal was worth a huge amount of money to the agency, Alexia knew that.

The crowd was liberally sprinkled with some very well-known faces and a few that Alexia recognized only vaguely, the C-listers who turned up to these events just to get their pictures in the *About Town* sections of the tabloids.

She saw Sonia talking to a soap actor. He was looking over her shoulder the whole time, to see if anyone more "interesting" was coming into the room. Sonia looked up and saw Alexia; it was her cue to get away.

She sauntered over, grabbing an extra glass of champagne from a waiter on the way. "Well, it's all gone very well," she said, handing a glass to Alexia.

"I'm working," said Alexia.

"Just sip it. No one will fire you for that. Not Nathan, anyway."

"Please stop talking about Nathan," she said, and took a large gulp of the sparkling wine.

Alexia was trying to keep her now rampaging desire dampened down, tucked away in a closet where it was safe. Just the mention of Nathan's name ensured it burst out of its captivity and danced a jig in her vagina.

To make matters worse, he suddenly appeared close by. It wasn't an opportunity Sonia was going to miss. She called him over.

"Nathan! Good event, my company is very pleased. It'll be great for the brand," she cooed.

Nathan smiled. "Thank you, Sonia, we do our best. And it's good to see you here, some sanity."

He didn't look at Alexia. But Sonia was on a mission.

"I've been talking to your new PA here. You really do hire very good people, you know. I might steal her away from you!"

Alexia was mortified. What was Sonia doing?

"Well, thank you." He was thrown by Sonia's remark, but only for the briefest second before full composure was restored. Sonia wasn't fooled. She moved in for the kill.

"I'd hang on to her very tightly if I were you." She smiled.

Nathan was unsure whether she was being straight or playing with him. Alexia could feel his hesitation.

"I intend to," he said.

Sonia smiled at them both. Nathan still didn't look at Alexia.

"If you'll excuse me, ladies, there's something I have to see to."

"Of course," said Sonia smoothly.

And with that he walked away. Alexia breathed out hard and took an enormous gulp of champagne.

Sonia smiled a wicked smile. "He 'intends to.' Hmm!"

"What was that for?" hissed Alexia.

"Shhh, someone will hear you." Sonia giggled.

Alexia moaned with distress.

"Hey, listen, it was only three words, but it was a very loaded answer, don't you think?"

Alexia thought. "I—I don't know. What else could he say?"

"That guy likes you. He may not like the *fact* that he likes you, but he likes you. And trust me, darling, I've known him a long time and I've never seen that before."

Alexia was silent. Could it be true? She daren't hope. Her eyes searched Nathan out. He was talking to a group of actors. He looked animated, engaged; they hung on his every word. In this room full of money and glamour, this former cavalry officer stood head and shoulders above them all, physically and in every other way.

"If you want him," said Sonia, "then you have to take a risk. You may lose, you may get your heart broken, but you may never get another chance at a man like him, Alexia. They don't come along every day."

Sonia squeezed her arm and moved on to mingle with the other guests, leaving Alexia alone with her glass of champagne.

They don't come along every day, Sonia had said, and she knew it was true. But what if she did get her heart broken? If it was broken by Nathan, she couldn't imagine it would ever mend.

She wasn't alone for long; she'd avoided him all day, but, with an inevitability that seemed to cling to all her dealings with Tony, there he was, at her side, his hand on the small of her back as he leaned in a little too close to talk to her.

"You really should have stayed last night."

"Stop it!" hissed Alexia. She couldn't make a fuss; the room was too crowded and she was on show, part of the Fallon team. She was trapped again. Trapped with Tony.

"It's a nice game, this cat and mouse thing. It'll be a lot of fun when Tom eventually gets Jerry…"

He lowered his hand to circle around her hip and pulled her ever so slightly to him. He could get away with it, he knew; in a room full of celebrities, tactile conversations were the norm.

She hated herself for feeling it, but the warmth of his hand on her gave a small thrill of pleasure.

"I'm not a mouse," she said quietly.

"Oh no, not you. *I'm* the mouse…"

Alexia looked at him, puzzled. His eyes were wicked as always. That slightly cruel twist in his mouth made the angelic aura his soft blond curls gave him even more seductive.

"Yes, that poor little mouse is me. You're definitely the hunting pussy." He rolled his lips around the word *pussy*, making sure its double meaning wasn't lost on Alexia. "Like those cats who get a mouse then let it get away, pretending they're not interested, then grab it back again, before they start the game all over again, torturing the poor little thing. That's you, my little minx."

Tony put on a pathetic face as if he were the tortured mouse, all hurt and wide-eyed.

"Stop being ridiculous," protested Alexia.

"It's true." His voice was low and his eyes twinkled again. "Fuck me, don't fuck me, fuck me, don't fuck me… Isn't that the game you've been playing?"

"No, it isn't!"

Tony gave an indulgent laugh. "Oh baby, don't deny it, why else would you get so hot?"

He breathed the word *hot* into her ear as if to press the point home, and her cunt flared at the feel of his breath, just as he knew it would.

"And why else do those gorgeous little nipples of yours stand to attention every time Uncle Tony wants to play with them?"

As if obeying his orders, she felt her nipples do just that. Alexia knew she had no control. He knew how to press her buttons, and he was pressing them now.

She looked around, terrified people could hear, but the guests were all deep in their own conversations. The only eyes that strayed were those rubbernecking, looking for someone more famous to talk to. Their gaze never rested on Alexia and Tony.

"Last night you'd have let those guys fuck you blind if that window hadn't been there."

Alexia's stomach lurched. She wanted to slap him, but she knew it was true—well, perhaps almost true. She might not have let them, but she had certainly fantasized about it. How was Tony in her head?

"I bet you're wet right now, aren't you?" asked Tony, rubbing his fingers in little circles on her bottom, his hand out of sight of the crowd.

Alexia couldn't deny it. She could feel the telltale dampness, the warmth in her crotch.

"We're still booked into the hotel tonight, and the boys will be having another little… barbecue. Why don't you join me in our observatory and we can finish what we started?"

Alexia wanted to run, but the thought of watching another of the soccer players' orgies excited her. The thought must have showed on her face, and Tony seized on it.

"You see, that's more like it," he said.

But Alexia sensed there was something wrong. She could feel eyes on her, she could feel Nathan. She looked up and, sure enough, he was watching her with Tony, and he didn't look pleased.

Oh, why does this keep happening? thought Alexia. Why can't I keep Tony away from me, and why can't I stop…?

She knew it was pointless, Nathan would never see her as she really was. But then, who was she? The good little girl who liked watching other people have sex? The good little girl who claimed to hate the office lothario but who succumbed whenever he put his hands on her?

She twisted herself free from Tony and walked out. She went

straight into the ladies' to get her balance back, to try and regain her composure. She had been there only a minute or so when Sonia walked in.

"You okay? You shot out of there like your ass was on fire."

"I can't do this."

"Do what?"

"Work for Nathan and Tony."

"You don't work for Tony…"

"Yes, but he's always around, and Nathan thinks…"

"Stop panicking, Nathan's not a fool. He knows what Tony's like. He knows he's predatory. Just keep calm and be nice." Sonia smoothed Alexia's hair. "Now put some more lip gloss on and get out there and circulate."

Alexia bit her lip, reluctant to leave the sanctuary of the ladies'.

"I've got to go back in and rescue my boss," said Sonia. "He's getting drunk and he's a bit loose-lipped when he's had a few."

She patted Alexia's arm and left. Alexia looked at herself in the mirror. Could he really like me? she wondered. A man like that? She heard the door swing again, but it wasn't Sonia returning, it was a tall, leggy blond. The woman was almost Amazonian she was so tall, with endless legs, visible through a long slit in her skirt. Alexia didn't recognize her. A wife, a girlfriend, a supermodel? She looked like a model, the tall, runway type. The newcomer looked at Alexia but didn't smile.

"You're Nathan Fallon's PA, aren't you?"

"Yes, I am," said Alexia, surprised to hear his name.

The woman pulled a red lipstick out of her bag and started reapplying, admiring herself as she leaned forward, mouth open.

"I'm only a temp, though," continued Alexia, not sure why she felt the need to explain.

Blondie twisted the lipstick back into its tube with her red-taloned fingers as she rubbed her lips together.

"I'll bet you are," she said coldly, running her gaze over Alexia's petite frame. Then she walked out, like a flamingo, all legs and hair.

Alexia stood baffled by the exchange. She didn't even know the woman but she had taken an instant dislike to her, and it seemed the feeling was mutual. How did she know Nathan?

She slipped on some clear lip gloss, bland and timid compared to the scarlet welt Blondie had painted on her face, but it would have to do. She opened the door and went back into the reception.

Several of the guests were now sitting in the booths around the edge of the room. The lights had been turned down. The champagne had flowed very freely all evening and many people were looking even more tactile than they had earlier. There were no journalists present here, only invited guests, and they were taking the chance to let their hair down. This room was now for famous people only, no civilians, and that meant boozing and flirting.

Alexia looked for Tony so she could avoid him, but he was nowhere in sight. A woman walked up to her and introduced herself. She was an older woman, and slightly drunk.

It was clear the woman was bored and being ignored by most of the men on the hunt for younger quarry—of which there was plenty, and very willing. The woman's husband was around somewhere, but she'd lost him. Alexia listened to her ramble as she saw Blondie from the toilet glide through the room to a booth in the far corner, out of the way of prying eyes. But Alexia couldn't see who else was in it. She edged sideways toward the wall so she could get a look at the woman's companion. The woman sidled with her, still talking. Blondie curled herself into the booth behind the table to sit with—Nathan!

Alexia was floored. She watched as the woman flirted and teased him. He was sitting impassively, watching, but didn't stop her.

The woman demanded some attention. She was asking questions now, something about the agency and whether it would represent a bunch of soccer players' wives who wanted to do a charity record.

Alexia mumbled that she'd ask someone. She looked back at Nathan. Did Blondie have her hand under the table? She was moving it, she was… rubbing? Nathan was sitting still and he seemed not to be joining in, but was he…? Alexia couldn't see his expression properly; was he enjoying it?

Blondie leaned over, her mouth inches from Nathan's, and whispered something as her hand continued to work his crotch.

Alexia couldn't breathe. She could hear the woman still chattering away, but she was barely concentrating. She soothed her with occasional "mmm" noises to pretend she was listening, but she tried to keep her eyes fixed on Nathan.

She watched as he moved his hand and brushed Blondie's hair from her face. Then she watched in horror as Blondie leaned in and planted a soft kiss on his mouth.

No! Alexia wanted to scream, she wanted to run over to the booth, drag the woman out, and tell Nathan he was kissing the wrong girl. Why was he doing this? He didn't play around, everyone knew that; he wasn't a bed hopper. What was he doing?

"So you think Nathan will go for it?" asked the woman.

"What?" Alexia whirled around and almost spat out the word.

The woman was startled and started stammering. "The charity single? Do you think he'll go for it? Nathan?"

Alexia realized her mistake. "Oh yes, sorry… I…"

"Are you feeling okay? You look a bit flushed."

"No, I'm fine, really. It's just noisy in here and I didn't catch what you said… Really… I'll—I'll ask him."

The woman looked over to where Alexia's attention had been fixed and saw Nathan.

"Ah, there he is. I've been trying to find him. No time like the present!"

To Alexia's horror, the woman took off across the room toward Nathan. Alexia froze for a moment in complete panic, then dashed after her without thinking.

The woman was now quite drunk and she was oblivious to Blondie and her secret tryst with Nathan.

"Nathan, lovely to see you... Brilliant event, really brilliant. Just wondering... Am getting some of the wives together... Charity single for menin—meningit..."

She was slurring and struggling with any word of more than two syllables. She took another run at it.

"Men-in-git-is! We need you. Everybody needs you, don't they...?" The woman laughed and looked at Blondie, completely oblivious to the cozy tête-à-tête she was breaking up.

Blondie looked thunderous and glared at Alexia for not protecting Nathan from this unwanted approach. Nathan took a deep breath. Was Blondie getting him hard? Was he trying to steady his voice? "Sandrine, of course. Let's chat... Make an appointment with my..."

He looked at Alexia. She was sure he'd seen her notice what Blondie was up to, but he seemed not to care. Was he enjoying it? Was he enjoying her misery? Alexia's head was swimming.

"With my PA, as I see you've already met."

He held Alexia's gaze. Blondie could sense the tension between them and she wasn't amused. She curled her arm around his and did her best to drape herself alluringly.

The woman chattered on. "Oh, brilliant, that would be great, such a good cause, be lovely to get together..." On and on she went. Alexia thought she would never stop. The woman didn't even notice that Nathan wasn't looking at her, he was looking at Alexia. But then he turned to her; she might have been drunk, but he wasn't going to be rude, he was too smart for that.

"Alexia will set it up for you now."

He was dismissing them both. He smiled graciously at the woman.

"Oh, of course, of course. Well, see you soon then… Er…"

Her words dribbled away as Alexia took her arm and led her off. Nathan had already turned his attention back to Blondie.

Alexia promised to ring the woman once she returned to the office and managed to find her husband and deposit her safely in his care. Then she dashed out of the room as soon as she could. She couldn't breathe, she was gasping, falling, crashing, drowning… She had to get away, far away from Nathan and Blondie.

Hotel staff tried not to look startled as she raced through reception all the way to her room. The key in her hand wouldn't fit in the lock. Her fingers were shaking. She grabbed the fob with both hands and shoved the sliver of metal into the lock. She pushed open the door, almost ran toward the bed, and flung herself on it.

She knew she didn't have the right to be angry but she was. Hot tears ran down her cheeks as she tried to squeeze away the memory of his face as he'd looked at her coolly, as Blondie kept her hand on his knee.

She broke into sobs, wracking sobs that convulsed her whole body. She curled herself into a little ball, curled herself as tightly as she could. She lay there for almost an hour until the tears subsided and emotional exhaustion overtook her.

She was numb. She had cried out the anger and all that was left was the hurt, the swirling, black, and inky hurt. She closed her eyes and prayed for sleep but it wouldn't come.

Her mobile rang. She lifted her head groggily, finding it hard to register where the noise was coming from. *Ring ring, ring ring.* She sat up, puzzled, and realized she was lying on her phone. She picked it up and saw Richard's name blinking at her. Richard! In all of the craziness of the past two days, she had almost forgotten him.

"Hello," she said.

The soft American drawl came through the ether like warm honey. "Hey, that's a small voice. What's up, kid?"

"Oh, it's just been a long day… I'm just exhausted."

"Sounds like more than that to me."

Alexia thought about pouring it all out, of telling Richard how wretched she was, but she couldn't bring herself to speak the words.

"I'm okay, really. Just been a really crazy day and I'm wiped."

"You poor thing… Sounds like you could use a bath and a neck rub. Wish I was there to help."

His voice was comforting and Alexia lay back on the bed, the mobile to her ear. "I wish you were too."

And she did. She wished he would walk in and take her in his arms and hold her. Hold her, safe and warm.

"Well, sugar, I can't be there in person, but I can be there in other ways…"

"How do you mean?"

"Go to the bathroom and run the bath."

"Richard, I…"

"Don't argue; you sound beat, and you sound like you need some Richard magic, so do as I say."

Alexia didn't argue. "Okay."

She walked into the sumptuous bathroom, her feet barely clearing the floor as she dragged each in front of the other. She walked like a small child, climbing the stairs for bed, almost asleep in motion. She turned the taps.

"How's the hotel?" asked Richard.

"Oh, it's gorgeous. I've never been in a place like this in my life."

"So I bet they have all kinds of lotions and potions for the bath?"

Alexia surveyed the row of beautiful little glass bottles. "They do." She ran her finger across the bottles. "Bergamot, lavender, white musk, and—" She blinked. "They have one called sensual massage! It's an oil."

"Whoo-hoo, doll, that's what we'll go for. Put some of the musk in the bath, then get those clothes off and I'll give you a massage."

"*You'll* give me a massage? How are you going to do that?"

"Well, that's easy. I'll be using your hands…"

Alexia understood, but she felt so miserable she didn't think that anything could make her feel sexual again. She started to protest, but Richard was having none of it.

"Listen, hon, I can tell by your voice that things are going a little south over there, so listen to me. We are going to relax and take your mind off whatever ails ya. And I am not taking no for an answer."

Alexia smiled.

"I can hear you smiling…"

"Oh, stop it." Alexia laughed softly.

"That's better, much better. Okay, now what are you wearing?"

"Blouse, skirt…"

"Undo your buttons."

Alexia started to obey, but Richard hadn't finished.

"Look in the mirror while you're doin' it."

She stood up and put the phone on speaker, then laid it on the countertop and started to unbutton. Richard's voice on the speaker sounded raw and husky.

"What do you see?"

"Breasts," said Alexia as she peeled off the blouse and let it drop to the floor.

"Take off your skirt…"

She unzipped it slowly, having turned so the sound of the zip would echo down the phone line. She heard an appreciative moan.

She shook off her skirt and kicked it away. The water was bubbling into the bath. She picked up the bottle of musk and poured the thick, white liquid into the bath. It dropped from the bottle very slowly into the bath, in perfect round globules, foaming as the rushing tap water reached it.

"You got bubbles yet?"

"Yes, lots of bubbles."

"Good. Now, back to the mirror. What color are your panties and your bra?"

"Black, lacy…" Alexia ran her fingers over the cup of her bra; it was thin, gauzy, and she could see her nipples through the mesh.

"Pull down the cups, look at your tits."

Alexia obeyed and freed her breasts from their halter. She gave a little moan, to assure Richard she had obeyed. But she didn't have to act; it was a relief to feel naked with him. She trusted him and she needed distraction.

"God, you have beautiful tits. Imagine my tongue is on them, right now…"

Alexia traced her fingers along her nipples as she listened to Richard's instructions. She'd never attempted phone sex, she had always thought it sounded so dry, but she was amazed how the addition of Richard's voice gave her fingers the power to thrill.

"Can you feel me?"

"Yes," said Alexia. She stroked her nipples and sighed with the pleasure that spread through her breasts.

"I want to bite you," said Richard.

Alexia pinched her nipples and gave a little gasp of pleasure. She felt the nip send that lightning bolt straight down her abdomen to her pussy. She watched the triangle of gauze and wondered if she would see the moisture she could feel escaping into it.

"You getting wet, honey?"

"Yes… Yes, I am."

"Good. You get so wet. So, so wet…"

Alexia was biting her lip, she realized. She watched herself in the mirror and she could see the color flush her cheeks and her lips; she could see her nipples harden as she flicked and pinched them one at a time.

"Take your bra off."

She reached around and unhooked it, and it slid to the floor with barely a whisper.

"Are your breasts free?"

"Yes." She obeyed him without question.

"How do your breasts feel?"

Alexia ran her palms around herself.

"Round, soft—warm."

She could hear Richard's small moans of appreciation.

"What are you feeling?" he asked.

"What do you think?" replied Alexia, playfully.

"I'm asking you…"

Alexia was silent.

"Say it!" Richard was not asking, he was commanding.

Alexia hesitated.

"Say it…"

"Your cock."

Voicing the word to a speakerphone in this luxurious bathroom felt brazen to Alexia, but also a little liberating.

"Oh baby, I knew you'd make me want to come if you talked dirty…" Richard's voice was low and sensual.

Alexia felt daring. "It's hard."

"Rock hard, baby, and it's straining to feel your hot, wet pussy…"

Alexia reached down and put her hands into her panties. "I can guide you down there. Let me take you down."

"Wait," said Richard. But Alexia didn't want to wait, she wanted to touch herself. Her clit was pumped with blood and the nerves were tingling.

"No, I don't want to…"

"Wait."

She stood motionless. Her need surged. Why did waiting always make you want it more?

"Go to the oil bottle and oil your hands."

The sensual oil. She'd forgotten about it. She turned and picked up the slim glass bottle and pulled out the stopper. She poured the golden liquid into her palm.

"Rub it on your breasts."

Alexia did so and felt its slippery warmth as she circled her tits.

"I'm putting it on my cock…"

She heard a plastic bottle top snap on the other end of the phone and realized Richard was oiling himself. It'll feel like me, she thought; if his cock is slippery, it'll feel like he's inside me.

She wanted desperately to touch herself now.

"Okay, baby, let's go to Mexico. Down we go…"

Alexia slid her middle finger down her flat stomach, leaving a trail of the warm, scented oil as she went. She ran her hand into her panties and down into the smooth slit at the front of her pussy, passing over the nub that quivered anxiously. She didn't feel a jolt of electricity this time, rather the long, sensuous unwinding of pleasure deep inside her as she slid her finger very slowly up and down, the oil mingling with her juices to make her hand warm and slippery.

"Can you feel me?" she asked.

"Yes. You're soaking, and hot…" Richard's voice was husky and low.

She pushed her finger inside herself and felt the velvety smoothness inside.

"You're inside now… I can feel you…"

She could hear Richard rubbing his erection. He must have put his phone on speaker too, and he must be wanking next to the earpiece. The mental picture gave her a thrill. She remembered how she had taken him in her mouth, the smooth head; she wondered if it was speckled with precome.

"Stroke that little spot for me," he demanded.

Alexia curled her middle finger and felt the gorgeous ache as she stroked. She saw her face in the mirror; her mouth had fallen open with the pleasure of it. A moan escaped her lips.

"You're stroking it?"

"Yes"

"It's *my* finger inside you. I'm running *my* finger right up inside you."

"Yes."

Alexia kept stroking and stroking. She wriggled free of her panties with her other hand and let them fall to her feet. She kicked them off so that she could open her legs wider.

The bathwater was still running. Alexia could hear it bubbling, the foaming water sending the smell of the white musk all around the room.

The mirror was starting to steam, making her reflection hazy. She looked as if she were melting. Her finger curled and stroked. She brought her other hand to her pussy and eased her oiled finger over her clit. She moaned again, louder this time.

"You're getting close…"

"Yes. Yes, I am," panted Alexia.

"Take your finger out…"

"No, I don't want to…"

"Take it out." Richard's voice was low but insistent.

Alexia obeyed.

"How wet are you? Are you dripping?"

"Yes. Yes, I am." Her need was urgent.

"Three fingers, stiff, hard…"

Alexia jammed her fingers together.

"That's my cock. It's real hard, and it wants to be inside you… Put my cock inside you… Let me fuck you…"

Alexia rammed her fingers in and groaned with the roughness of her own action. She heard Richard wanking harder, the telltale slapping sound as his hand hit his abdomen on each down stroke.

"That's it. Oh yes… Right up to the hilt… Keep me fucking you… Come on baby, that's it. Keep fucking, keep fucking…"

She rammed her fingers in over and over as she rubbed her clit with her thumb; she climbed and climbed and Richard heard her gasp as she climaxed. She clamped her hands to her pussy. Pressing hard, she squeezed out every last gorgeous drop of the oozing, swooshing orgasm. The slapping noises from the speakerphone grew frantic until she heard a deep, animal moan and the slapping stopped.

She sank down onto the edge of the bath, her hand and wet fingers resting on her leg. She looked in the mirror, her reflection now a blur in the steam, foggy and soft.

The speakerphone crackled, and she heard a slightly breathless Richard. "Hey, you're gettin' real good at this, sweet pea."

Alexia gave a weak laugh. "I had help."

Richard laughed. "Now that bath must be about full, I reckon."

The bath! She'd almost forgotten about it. She turned and shut off the taps. It was just coming up to full. She dipped her hand, still soaked in her juices, into the water.

"Perfect temperature," she said.

"Then go ahead. Slip in, beautiful, slip that beautiful body into those bubbles and wash all your cares away…"

Alexia was serious for a moment. "Thanks, Richard."

There was a long pause. "Hey, what friends are for, right?"

"Friends?" Alexia laughed.

"The Brazilians have a phrase for it. It translates roughly as 'colored friends'…"

"What does that mean?"

"Friends who fuck, with none of the complications of a relationship. I like the Brazilians; they have the right attitude to life. Now good night, little girl, sleep tight and sweet dreams."

"Okay. See you when I get home."

"Mmm, maybe…"

"Maybe?" asked Alexia. "Will you be gone?"
"Well, I may have moved to Rio…"
She laughed and slipped into the bath.

Chapter 10

ALEXIA PACKED HER BAG and sorted out her work file, ready to leave the hotel and head back to the office. Another long drive with Nathan. She wasn't sure she could bear it. Richard had soothed her last night, taken her out of herself enough to sleep, but it had been a fitful sleep.

Her dreams were tortured and twisted. She didn't dream of Nathan, but of a man trying to catch her, trying to trap her. Tony or Carter? She didn't know and didn't care; there was only one man who really mattered to her, and he had made it quite clear his attentions were focused elsewhere.

Her mobile rang. The office. She picked it up and took a deep breath to steady her voice.

"Alexia here."

"It's Phillipa… I can't get hold of Nathan, he's not answering his mobile or his room phone. Have you seen him?"

"I… No, I haven't, but I haven't left my room yet." Alexia checked her watch. Seven thirty. "He might be having breakfast."

"He'd have his mobile with him. Get him, please, I need to speak to him."

Phillipa hung up. Get him, she'd said. Alexia already felt pretty low; being treated as a servant didn't lighten her mood.

Then the implication set in. Get him? How? She didn't know where he was. The room swam. She didn't even want to face him, and now she had to track him down.

Alexia swiped her key from the table, picked up her phone, and went to reception. Had anyone seen Nathan today? They all knew who he was. No, they hadn't seen him. Would she like them to try his room? No reply. She went to the dining room, then the spa—still no luck.

There was nothing else she could do. She'd have to put a note under his door. She walked toward the suites. The plush carpet under her feet, hushing her steps, took her straight back to the night of the orgy. She looked down the corridor to the room Iorizzo occupied.

She still couldn't get that night out of her mind, how Tanya had waited—no, begged—to be fucked by the two soccer players and how they had obliged her, in style. She felt Tony's hands on her again as she walked down the corridor, playing with her, teasing her, his fingers on her breasts, his voice in her ear. "Do you want it? Do you want it, too?"

She tried to shake the image from her mind, as she'd reached Nathan's suite. She realized she'd arrived without a pen and paper to write a note. She thought of knocking, but what was the point? Reception had already tried. She knew she should try again, but she couldn't bear the thought he might answer the door. She was turning to leave when the door opened. Blondie stood in the doorway, wearing that split-to-the-ears dress she'd had on last night, exposing her runway model legs. She was barefaced, but she was still striking, even without the lipstick.

Alexia felt that familiar sick tumbling in her stomach. Blondie eyed her coolly and walked out of the suite, leaving the door wide open. She carried her slingback heels by the straps, slung over her shoulder. Even barefoot, she towered over Alexia.

How can she be so brazen? Blondie sashayed down the corridor, heels in hand, an almost defiant morning-after walk of shame. She was proud of her conquest. She was the right height for Nathan, thought Alexia with a pang of agonizing jealousy.

Alexia couldn't help herself. She stepped slowly into the suite, but there was no sign of life. Where was Nathan? She moved through the rooms in turn. It wasn't vast, like Iorizzo's suite, but it was certainly a lot bigger than her room, as was the bed. It was huge—and the bedclothes were a mess. Not a bed where a lot of sleeping had taken place, she thought, and felt that stabbing pain of jealousy again.

She heard the shower and realized the bathroom door was wide open. Slowly, almost automatically, she moved to stand where she could see straight into the bathroom. There was no steam in the room, so he had clearly just gone in. And there he was, standing with his back to her in the shower, naked.

Her eyes swept over him. Long legs, with dark hair curling on his taut muscles. His thighs were strong and his buttocks were high and exceptionally toned. He could have given the soccer players a run for their money. But then her eyes moved to his back and on his side she saw a large, messy scar, round, about the size of an orange.

He turned in the shower. Alexia's stomach lurched as she saw his chest, covered in downy black hair, come into view. And his cock. She had seen her fair share in the past week or so, but not Nathan's. It was relaxed, long and thick. Circumcised too, the helmet smooth and shiny. She looked up. She was standing so still he hadn't seen her. He was washing himself, lathering the shower gel. She watched his long muscular arms as he moved his hands, soaping the dark hair on his chest. Then he moved lower, and lower, finally covering himself and washing between his legs, taking himself in hand. The sight of him soaping himself made Alexia want to moan. She felt a yearning pull deep inside her and felt her own sex moisten at the sight of his dripping wet cock, his tight balls, and the soft black hair that framed them.

But then he looked up. He saw her. They both froze. Alexia thought her heart would stop. She felt herself holding her breath as embarrassment and mortification swept over her. She turned on her heels and made for the door, but Nathan was swiftly after her. She heard the shower door clang open and soft footfalls behind her.

A jutting side table slowed her progress and she cannoned off the wall and furniture trying to get out, like a small animal trapped in a complicated cage. Then she felt a strong hand pull her arm and she reeled around to face him.

He was right in front of her, hair soaking, every inch of him dripping. He was breathing hard. She daren't look down, but she could see in her peripheral vision that he was clutching a white towel to his front.

His eyes bored into her, fierce and blue. Was he angry? Embarrassed? She couldn't tell. She stammered.

"I'm so sorry. It's just that Phillipa called. She's—she's been trying to get hold of you and…"

He was standing close, still holding her arm. No aftershave this time, but the smell of the shower gel, the sweet, clean smell of fresh skin, so close, so very close. She could feel his breath on her.

"It's just you're not answering your mobile or your"—she hesitated, picturing the rumpled bed—"room phone."

The phrase hung in the air. They both knew what it meant.

They stood frozen, silent again. Alexia bit her lip. She wanted to reach out, to touch his wet skin. She wanted to kiss him, touch him, to rip the towel away and take him in her mouth the way Richard had shown her. She wanted to press herself against him and feel the dripping shower water soak through her blouse onto her own skin.

But he must be sated. Blondie would have seen to that. Blondie would have caressed his beautiful cock with those red-painted lips. She would have tasted him and pleasured him. Alexia felt miserable. So close to him, so agonizingly close, but miles apart.

He dropped his hand from her arm. He pulled the sides of the towel and wrapped it around himself, tucking one corner in to secure it in place. He was getting erect. She could see the lump under the towel. For her?

He stepped back, turning into the professional again, her boss. How could he manage that, dressed in a towel? But he could.

"Okay. We have to leave soon, be ready in reception in an hour…"

He was going to make no mention of his nakedness, of the fact she had seen him, or of Blondie. Did he know she had seen her? Did he care?

"Right." Alexia's voice was small, subdued.

He realized he'd been curt. "Thank you," he added, softly.

Alexia couldn't meet his eye. She was looking at another scar, on his front this time.

"A through and through," said Nathan.

Alexia didn't understand.

"It's where a bullet goes right through you," he said by way of explanation. He sounded so matter of fact. Just a bullet, straight through, that's all.

She felt her jaw moving but no sound came out.

"It's okay. It didn't kill me, clearly."

Alexia smiled weakly. "I—er—I'll tell Phillipa you'll call her and get ready to go."

"Good." Nathan nodded. "Now, if you don't mind…" He pointed at the shower.

Alexia gasped with embarrassment. "No, of course. Sorry…"

She was still stammering as she dashed out of the suite. She almost ran all the way back to her room. She didn't see Tony standing in the lounge as she tore past, or hear him follow her to Room 69.

She crashed into her room and went straight into the bathroom. She held on to the sink and fought back the tears. She couldn't cry, not now; she needed to get ready to leave. She went back into the room and texted Phillipa.

She couldn't face speaking to the woman, her voice wouldn't hold. Found Nathan, he'll call you shortly. Alexia. She dropped the phone on the bed. Her hands were shaking.

Then she remembered how Sonia had stopped her from crying by forcing her to throw back a whiskey. She grabbed the fridge door and yanked it open, hearing the telltale clinking of the little bottles of golden booze in the door. She grabbed one. It opened with a tiny cracking sound as she twisted the aluminum cap. She closed her eyes, hurled her head back, and heard the tiny *glug-glug* sound as the whiskey escaped through the miniature bottle neck and hit the back of her throat.

It stung. She breathed out, her eyes still shut tight. She could feel the shock of the alcohol stilling her, but she could also feel the gnawing, throbbing ache in her cunt. Nathan's wet body, his bright blue gaze sweeping over her…

"A little early, isn't it?"

Her eyes snapped open to see Tony standing in front of her, the adjoining door to their two rooms wide open.

"How did—?"

"Oh, an obliging maid," said Tony as he stepped slowly toward her. "So what's brought this on? It's still early and you're already hitting the hard stuff."

Alexia stammered, "I've just had a shock, that's all. It's nothing."

"It's not nothing. I think there are lot of things about you you're hiding, Alexia, but secret drinking isn't one of them."

He was very close to her now, disturbingly close.

"It's personal!" she snapped. "Now, we have to check out, so can you just leave me alone? I have to get ready." She rushed into the bathroom; it was all she could think to do to put space between them, but he was soon after her.

"Well, we do seem to like our little secret rooms, don't we? Small spaces, very intimate…"

He moved toward her. His eyes were pure lust.

"Tony, please…"

The next word would have been no, if she'd managed to utter it, but Tony moved in.

"Tony, please?" He repeated her words but turned the word *please* into a begging entreaty. "Please what? Please fuck me?"

Her denial was muffled as his mouth covered hers. He had grabbed her so fast, enveloping her in strong arms, his tongue possessing her mouth. She wanted to scream but she couldn't. She was so needy, so raw. She shut her eyes and let him kiss her.

He pressed her back against the sink. She felt the hard porcelain rim dig into her back and gave a small yelp into his mouth. He mistook it for pleasure and pressed harder.

She moaned harder and he released her mouth. He pulled her back toward him and grabbed her buttocks as he had in Iorizzo's suite. His fingers were hard and cruel and they thrilled her. He pulled her hips into his, his granite-hard erection pressing against her clit. He watched her open mouth as she panted slightly. He knew he had her, and he vocalized her thoughts. "Yes, fuck me…"

His voice was low, sensual, then, without warning, he whirled her around to face away from him and held her by her shoulders with a viselike grip. He did it so fast that she almost lost her footing.

Tony stood behind her, his face to one side of hers as he looked at her in the vanity mirror. His blond hair was gelled, turning his curls into hard, wet-look coils. He didn't look angelic today; he looked anything but. That cruel mouth was smiling. No more cajoling, no more soft words in her ear; he was going to fuck her—and she was going to let him. She didn't know why, but she knew she didn't want lovemaking; she wanted something rougher, harder, unforgiving. She wanted his cruelty, she wanted to feel punished.

"Yes?" he asked, showing his teeth like an animal that's about to strike.

She couldn't say the words, but she couldn't stand the gnawing, raw need any longer. She needed to feel a man inside her, hard and demanding. She needed to feel his unrelenting thrusts over and over.

Tony reached around her and yanked open her blouse. She felt the air sweep over her breasts as the buttons popped and ricocheted around the room, ripped away from the tiny strands of cotton that had held them in place.

He grabbed the lace that covered her breasts and pulled it down. No teasing nipple play today. He took both pink mounds in his hands and pinched them hard. Alexia gasped, pain/pleasure ripping through her.

"You want it nasty, don't you?" Tony growled.

Alexia could only pant as he twisted and pinched her nipples, each pinch harder than the last, until finally she gasped in pain.

"Oh yes, you want me to hurt you a little, don't you? You want me to"—he waited, to make sure she was listening—"you want me to *make* you, don't you?"

He knew, he knew exactly. She did want to be made to do it, to be forced to throw away her inhibitions, to throw away the little good girl and let a man take her—to take her with no pity, no feeling, to ram himself into her, to invade her and not to stop until he was finished.

She closed her eyes as her mouth dropped open with the pleasure of his torturer's fingers.

"Yes, you want me to make you. You want me to really smack that sweet little cunt of yours…"

With that, he pulled his hands from her breasts and grabbed the zip of her skirt. With one rasping yank it was undone and he pulled her skirt down to the floor.

She stepped out of it, obeying his silent instruction.

He stayed low, kneeling on the floor, running his hands up the backs of her legs. Alexia felt a delicious shiver as they reached the top.

Suddenly, he pulled her legs apart with one sharp tug. He was making the rules; if he was gentle, he reserved the right to be rough, no warning.

He curled his fingers inside the crotch of her panties and pulled the fabric away from her body.

Alexia felt his fingers, snaking through her hair, her pussy giving up an obliging drop of wetness.

"There are some things you can't hide, no matter how hard you try, little Ice Queen."

Tony ran his finger along the front of her sex, up toward her clit. He was still crouching behind her and he curled his finger over her nub and stroked it.

Alexia grabbed the rim of the sink to steady herself as the pleasure seared its way through the little cluster of nerves. It didn't radiate through her abdomen this time; it stayed contained, as she was fingered by an unseen hand.

She rocked with the stroking, sighing with the pleasure of the motion, falling into the rhythm when, suddenly, he rammed two hard fingers into her cunt.

She gasped. There was no warning, just a forceful thrust and his fingers were deep inside her. He thrust them again and again. His other hand was gripping her ankle, his fingers digging into the bone.

She felt pinned. Her foot was held to the floor as he pushed up inside her, making her want to reach up and away from his hand and its hard probing.

He pulled out his fingers and yanked down her panties, grabbing her foot so he could pull them off and toss them to the corner. He opened her legs again. She knew he was on the floor looking up at her, looking into her, looking straight in her cunt.

Nothing happened. She breathed hard, waiting for his next move. She looked at herself in the mirror. She could feel his eyes on her, how they must be examining her from his vantage point on the floor, her labia, her wetness.

"Nice," came his low voice from beneath her, "very nice."

She felt his hands on the back of her legs; his fingers were wet. His strong hands gripped her thighs.

"Bend over," came the instruction, hard, demanding.

She didn't move. She couldn't.

She heard it before she felt it. The hard *slap* sound as the flat of his hand hit her ass. She caught her breath as the sting ripped through her. Again, a whipping crack and the stinging, harder this time, followed by a wave of pleasure.

"I said"—*crack*, another smack—"*bend over!*"

Alexia obeyed, moving her hands so her arms rested on the sink. Bent right over it, she could still see herself in the mirror.

She felt her pussy yawning open behind her and knew he was looking at it. She felt a huge, involuntary squirt. She was so wet the tops of her thighs were soaking.

Slowly, Tony moved his hands over her buttocks, each one covering a cheek. She could feel his breath on her; she felt it move, whispering from front to back, first on her bottom, then on the space between, then on her labia.

Then another smack, this time between her legs, hitting her clit. She caught her breath so hard she had to shut her eyes. She gave a stifled whimper, then felt the tip of his tongue trace its way along her slit. He was licking her, lapping her up. He flicked his tongue back and forth in her slit, not reaching her clit, which was still stinging. He was teasing her at the entrance to her sex.

Her legs were trembling. She arched her back, to make herself more accessible to his tongue. All control had left her; all she could do was let her body take over, let it do what it wanted to get its fill.

"Now, now, daddy decides when…"

Smack! Another blow, this time on the other cheek. She felt the imprint of his hand and knew it would leave a welt. Tony was in control, and he wasn't going to let her forget it.

The agony was wonderful.

Then she felt his tongue again. This time he pushed it out so it was hard. Its tip landed right on her engorged nub, and he raked it all the way back, all the way down her slit straight back to the forbidden hole at the back.

Alexia almost shrieked. She had never felt a tongue there. All the surrounding nerve endings were zinging. He rolled his tongue around it.

The pleasure almost made her come; she could feel the tension inside her like a pressure cooker.

His tongue circled, then *smack!* And again. *Smack!*

Alexia felt as if her knees would buckle. She was standing open-legged, bent over, and a man she hated was fingering her, licking her, smacking her, looking right into her most intimate places. And she was letting him.

He stood up, but kept her down, holding her back flat with the heavy palm of one hand. She craned her head up to look in the mirror to see him.

His face was hard and cruel. "You want to see me, do you?"

He reached forward, grabbed her pony tail, and tugged it, as if restraining a misbehaving horse. Alexia felt her pussy almost rippling with anticipation.

"Take a good look…"

He held her head there and, with his free hand, he very slowly unzipped his trousers. She panted; she could hear the teeth of the zip giving up one by one. She imagined what lay behind them. This was it, he was going to fuck her, he was going to fuck her now!

She felt him pull out his cock and rub it against her bottom. She could feel the hot, marble smoothness of the tip and she ached to feel it inside her.

"Oh yes, you want this, don't you, my little Ice Queen? I told you spring was coming. Meeeelting season…" He stretched out the word as he rubbed himself up her slit, coating himself in her juices, sending a ripple through her cunt. She desperately wanted to move, wanted to push herself backward. But he yanked her hair again.

"But spring isn't here just yet." He let go of her hair and pulled his cock away.

She moaned with the sudden absence from her pussy. She looked at his face. His eyes weren't on her, they were on something higher up. Something above her head…

"Well, well, what have we here?" said Tony, his voice dancing with amusement.

He reached up and Alexia remembered with a horrible lurch what she had left on the glass shelf on the wall. She saw his hand move in front of his face, holding the small, silver object as if he was examining a diamond.

She heard him flick the switch and the telltale buzzing filled the small room.

"Such a little toy. Let's see how big a kick it's got, shall we?"

He held her gaze as he moved his hand down and pushed the object up against her clit. It was cold and she gave an involuntary shiver. He didn't take his eyes off hers; he was watching her, watching for her reaction. Then he flicked it on…

A thousand angry bees came to life and her nub was ravaged with the pleasure of their attention. She gave a series of short, shuddering intakes of breath, almost as if there was no time to breathe out between each gulp of air.

He turned up the speed. The bees got louder. Alexia was biting her lip hard; she feared she would draw blood, but she was afraid if she stopped she would scream.

Tony pressed the bullet harder and rocked it against her so the pleasure would hit her in waves.

She heaved. She would come, and very soon. But Tony did not want to let her off so easily. She should have known, the way he'd made Phillipa wait, made her beg, when he'd fucked her on the boardroom table. Sex wasn't about pleasure for him; it was about control.

He watched her closely as he pulled his hand toward himself, pulling the bullet along her, right up to the back.

He laughed as he caught the flash of shock in her eyes. Then he pushed the buzzer up to ten and pushed the tip of it inside her bottom.

Alexia had to grit her teeth. Someone was shaking the hornets' next, and shaking it in a place she never knew could be so good. She let out a string of loud gasps, clutching the sides of the sink to steady herself. Tony was watching and loving it, loving her pleasure-pain.

He was teasing the bullet back and forth, the merest fraction at a time, but the tiny movements were exquisite, as her muscles gripped the warming metal. She came hard, her hips bucking. He clamped his free hand on her backside and stopped her rocking. He was holding her in a vice, keeping her still, forcing her to feel every tiny, rippling contraction.

This was a new orgasm for her; this didn't come just from the jumping cluster of nerves underneath her clit, it was altogether different. It was searing, but it subsided quickly. It wasn't enough.

She looked up at Tony. She heard a click and the buzzing was silenced. He pulled his hand away and slowly, deliberately put the bullet back on the shelf.

"I think spring is here, don't you?" he said, as he took his cock in his hand and rubbed it against her juices. He teased her opening.

It was going to be now; he was going to fuck her!

Alexia's legs were quivering, and the anticipation was almost unbearable.

"Beg me," said Tony.

Alexia stood frozen, watching his face.

"Beg me," he said, harder this time, rubbing himself against her.

But the words wouldn't come. She wanted it, oh how she wanted it, but she couldn't bring herself to say it. If she said it, it was true.

She looked at him. He was waiting. Sooner or later, he knew she would relent and he would just wait. They stood silent, motionless; Alexia didn't know how long. Just like Phillipa and Tony, each waiting for the other, but there was no fight for supremacy here. It was just a matter of time before she gave in.

She wanted to push backward; she wanted his cock inside her. She didn't care how much she hated him, she just needed it, needed it very badly. She hated herself for her need, but she couldn't deny it.

If she could just push back she'd envelop him. She could clutch her muscles around him and he would start thrusting. Pushing her into the sink. Fucking her. The ache inside her was unbearable. She tried to inch back, but Tony moved with her, backward, still holding his tip against her, tantalizingly close, tormenting her with the nearness of him. If her cunt could scream it would have howled with need.

"Alexia!" The shout seemed to come from far away. "Alexia!" At first it didn't register. "Alexia!" Louder this time. It wasn't Tony, it was outside. "Anyone here?"

It was coming from the bedroom. It was Nathan's voice!

Alexia clamped a hand to her mouth to stop the gasp of shock escaping. She stood up and whirled around. Tony's eyes weren't so sure now. The confidence had evaporated. Nathan sounded very close.

Alexia shouted instinctively, "Nathan. Sorry, I'm—" It was hard to speak. "I'm in the bathroom. I won't be a minute…"

"I need you. I have to sort some documents out and it can't wait."

Tony was watching the door. He'd turned from hunter to hunted. It was clear he didn't want to get caught.

"I'll be right there."

Nathan's voice was retreating. "I'll be in the lobby," and he was gone.

There was a moment's hesitation, then Alexia grabbed a towel and covered herself as she rushed into the bedroom. Tony followed her.

"You have to go. You have to go now!" She stood by the connecting door. With horror, she realized that Nathan must have come in through it. Tony's room was open, and a maid was stripping the bed. What would Nathan think? That the door had been open the whole time? Panic flooded her.

"We haven't finished," growled Tony.

"Oh yes, we have. We have definitely finished."

He moved toward her, about to take her back into his control, but he saw the maid next door and discretion got the better of him.

His jaw was clenched. He was breathing hard. He'd tucked himself back into his trousers, but his clothing was disheveled and only half done up. He zipped his fly and stomped back into his own room, sending the maid scurrying out.

Alexia slammed the connecting door behind him and turned the key with a loud clunk. She stood with her back against the door, breathing hard. She could hear Tony stomping around angrily, through the door.

She dashed into the bathroom to pick up her clothes. Her blouse was useless; half the buttons had been ripped off. She rushed back to her case to find another top and dressed hurriedly. She wiped herself, as she was so wet she feared she would leave a mark on her skirt. She threw everything in her bag, except the bullet. She picked it up and dropped it into the rubbish bin in the bathroom. Time Tony was gone, she thought. Then she gathered her stuff, picked up her room key, and made her way to reception without a backward glance. She hoped Tony wasn't following her.

She walked up to the beautiful reception desk to check out.

The same French girl who had checked her in was there again. Michelle.

"Ah, Miss Wright! Did you enjoy your stay wiz us?"

Alexia really couldn't form an answer. She smiled weakly and nodded her head.

The woman's Parisian accent was thick and seductive. "Your boss 'as all ze invoices, so zere is nothing to fill out."

She smiled, nodded a thank-you, and wheeled her bag into the lobby where Nathan was sitting waiting for her. He was casually dressed, but he still looked better than most men look in a three-piece suit, thought Alexia.

Her stomach was churning.

"Sorry, I was—" Alexia started.

"It's okay. I need you to check these over before we leave."

No chitchat, straight to business.

She sat gingerly on the edge of a large, plump chair. She picked up the invoices he'd handed her.

"I just need you to check that they haven't stiffed us for anything we didn't order or didn't get. It's a smart hotel, but they have been known to be a little creative with the bills."

"Oh—of course…" stammered Alexia.

She looked through the list. It was hard to read; the items and the figures were swimming in front of her eyes.

Concentrate, she told herself. She went down the list slowly and said finally, "That all looks in order. I think we're fine."

"Good!" said Nathan curtly. He stood up. "Right, let's get going, I have to be back before twelve."

Alexia jumped up quickly to follow him. He stopped, as if checking himself, then he took a step back and picked up her roller bag and motioned for her to go first.

And there he was again, the gentleman. He was so confusing. Alexia's head swam.

"My stuff's in the car," he explained.

"Oh! Okay, thank you," muttered Alexia and walked out of the lobby.

As they reached the entrance, an immaculately dressed doorman opened the great oak door. She felt a wave of cold air hit her. Back to reality, she thought.

"*Bon voyage!*" chirruped Michelle from reception. "Enjoy your trip home!"

Alexia's stomach somersaulted. Trip home? Two hours with Nathan.

Chapter 11

THE JAGUAR PULLED UP in front of them as Nathan handed a bellhop Alexia's bag. The trunk opened with an expensive whisper and a valet stepped out from behind the wheel, handing the keys to Nathan as her bag was safely stored.

Alexia saw Nathan palm some money into the two men's hands. He did it with ease and practice; they smiled appreciatively. He was smooth, very smooth, every inch the gentleman.

She went to the door but the valet was there before her, opening it and smiling. She wasn't used to such attention.

"May I take your coat, *madame*?" Another French accent. He took it from her and laid it gently on the backseat.

"*Au revoir, madame*." He shut both doors. She was cocooned again.

He'd called her *madame*. Do they think I'm his wife? wondered Alexia. The idea sent a thrill through her as Nathan got in. She tried not to look as his long leg stepped in before he slid his body into the soft leather seat. She was still turned on, and now she was near the real object of her affection, and the need was worse, much worse.

As they buckled up, a red Maserati raced past them and roared away down the tree-lined avenue that led to the road. Alexia saw a familiar head of blond curls behind the wheel.

"Is that Tony?" Alexia spoke without thinking.

"Daddy's money. Some people get things handed to them on a plate."

Alexia flushed. She'd very nearly handed herself to him on a plate. But Nathan had rescued her. And he didn't even know it. Nathan stared down the drive after the red sports car. He didn't look impressed.

"You don't like him, do you?" Alexia surprised herself with the boldness of her question.

Nathan turned his head and looked at her for a moment. Those blue eyes sent a jolt through her again. Her pussy was still wet, and getting wetter.

He turned his head back to look through the windshield. "No," he said coldly, as he fired the car into life, releasing the handbrake and pulling away.

They reached the road and pulled into the traffic. Nathan was silent. They traveled for a few miles and joined the freeway, speeding up to cruise their way back to London. The car seemed to settle in; this was its natural home.

Alexia couldn't live without knowing what lay behind the simple "no" Nathan used to answer her question. She needed to understand; there was something between Nathan and Tony.

"Why did you hire him if you don't like him?"

Nathan thought for a moment.

"You're curious about him?"

She didn't like the implication. Sonia's words floated back. She'd told her that to get a man like Nathan you have to take a risk, that men like him don't come along every day.

"No... I'm curious about you."

She thought he caught his breath slightly. She looked at his face; it gave nothing away. Had she gone too far?

"His father was my colonel in the army. My mentor, really. Rich family, but he didn't take his privilege for granted. Unlike his son. I gave Tony a job because his father asked me if I could use him. He loved sports, he was personable—or so his father thought. I guess parents are blind. They don't see their kids as anything but kids.

They don't see who they are, who they really are, out in the world. He's disappointed his father over and over again. He's not a man who deserves that."

Alexia could sense a deep bond that must have formed between the two men. Brothers in arms, she thought. There are few bonds stronger. Nathan's sadness for the disappointment of his friend in his son was obvious.

"But Tony is charming. He can manipulate pretty much anyone," added Nathan.

Alexia flushed again, ashamed at how easily she'd been manipulated by him. Nathan hadn't finished.

"It's the perfect skill for this job, really, but he's on his final warning now. I can't put up with him much longer, I'm running a business."

"What's he done?" asked Alexia.

Nathan took a deep breath. "He likes to play the big 'I am,' but doesn't put the work in. Some of the stars like him, because he's just like them—cocky, vain. But…" He hesitated.

Here it comes, thought Alexia.

"It's the way he behaves with women."

She knew it. Nathan might have seemed aloof but he was no fool.

"I'm not really blaming the women… Well, some of them"—he hesitated again—"but Tony should know better."

She had to speak, this might be her only chance. She had to tell him. Speak now, Alexia! She was shouting at herself in her head. Speak, girl, for God's sake!

"You mean like when you caught him having sex in your boardroom the night of the party?"

Nathan didn't move, didn't speak. She could see the little muscles in his neck; he was working hard to stay stoic.

"It wasn't me!" Alexia blurted.

He hesitated for a moment. She held her breath.

"What?"

"It wasn't me. In the boardroom…"

"But… I saw you," said Nathan, struggling to keep his composure.

"Yes, but it wasn't me. I mean, it was, but it wasn't…"

Nathan was confused. She saw his eyebrows knit and his mouth open slightly. No words came out. But then she wasn't really making much sense.

"I'd only been with you a couple of days; I didn't know anyone in the party. I sneaked into your bathroom because the one down-stairs—" She stopped, not wanting to get the coke-snorting staff into trouble. "It was full. So I sneaked in—to your bathroom, that is—but once I got in there Tony came in. He didn't know I was there and he was with…" She stopped again.

What could she say? She couldn't tell on Phillipa. She didn't know the dynamic in the office; Phillipa was very senior. Nathan might not believe her.

"Someone," Alexia continued. "He was with someone and they"—she swallowed—"on your table!" She hoped the meaning was clear enough.

Nathan's jaw dropped, only slightly, but he was clearly having trouble getting his head around this one. She watched him, desperate for any clue about his reaction. Did he believe her?

"It wasn't you." His voice was almost a whisper, the intonation making it a question. *"It wasn't—you?"*

"No, it wasn't me. But then she—the woman, that is—left." Alexia was gabbling now. "And he found me. And you came in and then…" Her voice trailed away.

"And then I accused you and threw you out." His voice sounded flat, realization hitting him.

Alexia almost collapsed with relief. "Yes. Yes! I wanted to say something but how could I…? I mean, I hardly know you. And I really didn't know you then, I'd never met you before. And you're my boss, and…"

His hand reached over and held hers. Her panicky breathing almost turned to a sob as she felt his fingers close over hers.

"It's okay…" His voice was warm and reassuring.

They sat for a moment. His hand was so comforting she wanted him to pull the car over, to take her in his arms, to kiss her.

"It's okay," he repeated.

There. She'd said it, it was out. And he believed her. Joy flooded her, and she looked down at his hand, his long, elegant, strong hand, covering hers.

But he pulled his hand away and put it back on the steering wheel. She looked at him; he was unreadable again. Damn him! Was it just a professional touch, the way he'd held her hand; was he comforting a hysterical employee or was it more? She still didn't know. This was agony.

"And the supply closet?" asked Nathan.

Alexia's stomach took a dip on the roller coaster. No sooner did she think she'd got to the top than she was plunging straight down again.

"He followed me in, he keeps following me. He keeps…" Alexia faltered. What could she say?

Nathan's voice was low. "I thought you two were…"

"No!" protested Alexia vehemently. "It's not *him* I want!"

She realized too late what she had said, and its implication. *It's not* him *I want.* That meant there was someone else she *did* want.

The sentence hung in the air between them. They both stared straight ahead, at the morning traffic cluttering the freeway. Alexia jammed her eyes shut. How could she have said that? How could she have been so stupid?

After what seemed like an eternity, Nathan spoke.

"If he's harassing you, then you must make a formal complaint."

He was her boss again, personal curiosity tucked safely away, back in its box.

Make a complaint? Against Tony? How could she? Only an hour ago he'd been raking his tongue over her clit. How could she make a complaint against him? A complaint about what? That he made her wait too long before he fucked her so she went without?

"No, I don't… I'd rather not… I don't want to make a fuss."

"Look, Alexia, this is quite serious. In a previous life, if my staff weren't doing their job and looking after each other properly, people died. And I still take the well-being of my people very seriously."

Alexia was panicking. "I—I know. But please, I just really don't want to…"

She couldn't finish her sentence.

Nathan sighed. "Okay, okay. I understand." He looked over at Alexia; he could see her distress. "Sorry, I didn't mean to bully you. Of course if you're uncomfortable, you don't have to do anything. It's okay, really." His voice was tender and low. "Really."

He looked at her again, to make sure she knew he was sincere. He turned back to the road. "But I won't tolerate bad behavior. He's done enough to be on a final warning. I'll be watching him closely from now on."

Alexia felt a flood of relief. She breathed out heavily and they settled into silence.

The car ate up the miles and Alexia thought about her encounter with Nathan that morning, about Blondie. Their conversation in the car was difficult but it was honest, most of it. But how could she ask about the model? She was just a casual hookup, that was clear, but why? Did he play around after all? Perhaps he was just better at hiding it than most. But he wasn't hiding it all that well last night in the booth at the reception. And had he realized she'd seen Blondie this morning? Would he care?

She was subconsciously biting her lip as the questions churned inside her. Nathan had turned to look at her. She had been too absorbed in her misery to notice.

"Alexia?"

His voice jolted her.

"Are you okay?"

"Oh, I'm sorry… I was just thinking…"

"About this morning? In my suite?"

She was stunned. He'd been thinking the same thing. Had he been wondering whether she'd seen the model leaving his suite? Or was he thinking about the shower, how she'd stood there looking at him, admiring his naked body.

"Um…" Alexia struggled, desperate for something to say that didn't involve his complete nakedness, or his previous night's conquest. "I was just… Your scars…"

Nathan blew out. It was old news to him.

"Yeah," he said, resigned. "Iraq. Sniper."

"Oh my God!" Alexia gasped at the idea that someone could have aimed at Nathan, could have tried with singular determination to take his life.

"Don't worry, he wasn't very good."

"He wasn't?" asked Alexia.

Nathan gave a snort, his face cracked into a cynical smile. "Well, I imagine he was aiming at my head!"

Alexia realized her mistake and laughed a nervous little hiccup of a laugh.

"Oh yes… I see what you mean."

They fell into silence again. He concentrated on the road. This conversation—this journey—was agonizing, like a stop/start dance. One step forward, two steps back. She had to keep it going.

"I'm glad he missed—your head, that is. He obviously didn't miss you completely… But, you know…"

Nathan looked at her and smiled. "Yeah, I know…"

"That was… It must have been hard…"

Nathan was pensive. "All war is hard, for everyone."

"It must have been difficult to—you know—adjust when you came back?"

She knew she was in dangerous territory, but she had to push. Nathan's face darkened.

"Well, not everyone understands. Some people can't—won't—understand."

The deliberate change of word demonstrated his anger was still near the surface. He was still hurt by his girlfriend's betrayal, the way she'd abandoned him. She understood his mistrust of women. How could he trust?

They fell silent again. Alexia looked up to see they were coming into London. Nathan concentrated on negotiating the traffic. It was easier not to speak now; he had reason to be silent.

After a while, she realized they weren't going to the office. She looked around. Nathan sensed her confusion.

"I'm taking you home," he said.

"But... Why aren't we going to the office?"

"You've worked hard over the last couple of days, so I think you should relax and come in tomorrow. If Romy is still ill, then I'll need you at the tennis event. It's only a day thing, in Wimbledon. You don't really have to do much, just be there."

"The tennis event?"

"Yes, just to make sure anyone who approaches Jim Brooker comes through me."

Jim Brooker was the rising British tennis star, only nineteen, but already hitting the magazine covers.

"Oh yes... Okay..."

Alexia thought for a moment. "But you don't know where I live."

Nathan was silent for a moment as he navigated a busy junction. "I know where you live," he said quietly, and moved into the next street.

Alexia kept completely quiet for the next twenty minutes. He knows where I live, she thought. This trip had given her as many questions as it had answers.

She sat with her hands in her lap, adrenaline and tension flooding her body. Nathan turned the car into her street and pulled up right outside the door. She had never seen a parking space free before. But for him everything seemed to be easy. Even the traffic seemed to part for him.

He turned off the engine. She was about to thank him for the lift when he got out, pressing the trunk button on his fob. She climbed out of the car, retrieving her coat, and watched him as he pulled her bag out of the trunk.

He slammed it shut. "Which door is it?" he asked.

"Er—the red one," said Alexia, watching him as he strode toward the entrance.

He put down the bag on the step and she caught up with him, fiddling with her key. "Well, thanks again, you did well," said Nathan.

Alexia smiled and looked down shyly, pretending she was searching for her key on the ring. There were only two keys; it was quite a performance.

"Romy has some competition," he joked, the humor strained. They both knew this was difficult.

"Let me help you with that." Nathan took the key ring from her and looked at the two keys. He picked one and put it in the lock. It turned. Right the first time—of course, thought Alexia.

He handed her the key ring; as she took it, their fingers touched. She felt it. Did he feel it too? The electricity? The undeniable jolt?

She looked up into his face. Unreadable again. He seemed troubled, but what…? She couldn't tell. He was so close to her; again so, so close. For a moment, for one heart-stopping moment, she thought he leaned toward her… He *was* leaning toward her. She looked in his eyes. Did she see wanting there? Was it her own want she saw in his eyes?

He was inches from her, his head bent. She thought he might—just might… Then he stopped.

"I'll see you tomorrow, Alexia. Enjoy the rest of your day."

Back down the roller coaster! She was dismissed, yet again.

He turned away and walked back to his car. Alexia stood and watched as he got in and pulled away down the street. He didn't look back.

In the flat, Alexia almost deflated onto her bed. She had dropped her case in the hall and dragged herself into her room. It was only midday and she was exhausted. The strain of the last few days had wiped her out and she lay back and closed her eyes.

The memory of Nathan in the car clung to her, like the smell of his aftershave.

She went over their conversation. "It's not *him* I want!" she'd blurted. Did he know what she meant? She felt her need for him was so clear, so transparent, how could he *not* know?

"I know where you live," he'd said. Did he know because he knew where Romy lived and, by extension, her? Had he looked it up because of the trip? Or did he just wonder where she lived? She could only hope.

She had a few answers after their journey, but so many more questions.

She lay back on the bed, still holding her coat. She was clinging to it like a teddy bear. She had taken a step toward him by being so bold in the car. But had it gotten her anywhere? Did she know any more about the man, really know? About how he felt, what he felt about her? Did he feel anything? He'd kissed her, and today, just now, she thought he might kiss her again. But then the memory of Blondie crashed in on her fantasy. She remembered the rumpled bed. Blondie had gotten a lot more than a kiss.

She let out a small, frustrated scream and pulled her coat over her head, covering her face as if that would blot out the swirling memories.

She lay there, for how long she didn't know. But she must have fallen asleep as the next thing she remembered was being shaken gently and a faraway voice.

"Alexia... Alexia, hey... You with us?"

She opened her eyes to see Romy sitting on the bed.

She mumbled then lifted her head, blinking to try and clear her blurry vision.

"Well, hello. Welcome home. What the hell did you get up to that you're sleeping in the middle of the day—or shouldn't I ask?"

Alexia sat up, completely disorientated.

"What time is it?"

"Six thirty. So—what happened?"

Alexia was groggy.

"Oh... Give me a minute..." She swung her feet over the edge of the bed. She felt as if she had slept for a year.

"Okay, well, I'll make you a cup of tea. That should help..." Romy went to the door. "But then I want to hear *all* about it!"

She disappeared into the kitchen and Alexia heard her fill the kettle.

Alexia changed out of her clothes and put on a long nightie and a thin dressing gown. She was so tired she couldn't bear to wear anything tight. She padded into the living room to find a hot, steaming cup of tea waiting for her.

Romy shouted from the kitchen, "I've made some casserole, just rice with it."

"Great," said Alexia, as the realization hit her that she hadn't eaten all day.

She took a long swig of the hot tea and felt it bring her slowly back to life as it made its way down.

"I'll just have a quick bath before dinner if that's okay?"

Alexia went into the bathroom and ran the water. The cure for all ills, she thought, remembering how Richard had made her ready for the tub last night.

She spent half an hour in the bath hoping the hot water would shake off the cloak of sleep that hung on her. Sleeping during the day left her feeling drugged. But the lapping of the warm water on her skin made her dream of Nathan even more. She pressed her hand to herself to try and still the ache. She cupped her pussy and squeezed her legs, hoping it would silence the demanding hunger. But she found herself rubbing and tracing her fingers against her clit. "Oh, stop it!" she said out loud, and stood up with such speed, she spilled half the bathwater onto the floor. She breathed a heavy, desperate sigh of frustration and anger and grabbed a towel to wipe up the mess. She trudged into the living room.

Another heavy sigh escaped her as Romy came into the room with two large bowls of steaming beef casserole with two forks.

"There you go," said Romy, handing her a bowl and cutlery.

They sat on the sofa, and Alexia started to eat. The casserole was delicious as always; Romy was a good cook, her Italian mother had seen to that. But Alexia felt as if she were trying to put rocks in her stomach. She was so tense, so miserable, she could barely swallow.

"Now I know something's wrong," said Romy. "You always like my *spezzatino di manzo!*"

Romy put down her bowl, picked up Alexia's teacup, and walked out. Alexia loved the way her friend's North London accent would suddenly morph into Neapolitan whenever she broke into her mother's native Italian. She returned seconds later with a bottle of wine and two glasses. She poured and gave Alexia a huge glass.

"Drink!" It was an order, which Alexia dutifully obeyed.

"Can we watch some TV, just for a while?" she asked.

Romy was about to protest—she was still waiting to hear about the trip—but Alexia shot her a pleading glance. She needed to blank out for a bit longer.

Romy picked up the remote and reluctantly switched on the television. They watched a succession of dreary soaps. Alexia wasn't really concentrating, letting the parade of arguing actors pass in front of her, one program running into another.

After an hour and a half Romy could wait no longer. She snapped the TV off and sat facing Alexia, her arms folded. She raised an eyebrow. "Well?" Alexia had helped her demolish a bottle of wine and they had started on a second.

Slowly, Alexia relayed most of the events of the weekend to Romy, neglecting to tell her how turned on she'd been at the orgy, or what had passed between her and Tony that morning. That was too painful, and Romy didn't need to know.

"Bloody hell! I've been on those trips, but I've never seen that— well—never been invited… God, the tabloids would have a field day with all that!"

"You're telling me!" said Alexia.

"So did Tony organize it—the girls—or did he just let them get on with it…?"

"I don't know."

"Surprised he didn't join in!"

Alexia flushed. She hadn't told Romy what Tony had done to her as they watched.

"Alex?"

"Well, he did try it on…"

"I bet he did. Weren't you tempted, even just a little?"

Alexia didn't know how to answer. "It—all happened so fast…" She took a large gulp of wine.

Romy studied Alexia for a moment. "And what about Nathan?"

Alexia stopped drinking.

"What happened with him? Anything?"

Alexia thought for a moment. "I—I don't know. It's hard to tell…"

"Mmm. Well, something happened."

"In the car, on the way home… I managed to tell him about the party—the bathroom."

"God, you didn't tell him Tony was with Phillipa, did you? She'll kill you!"

"No! I didn't tell him who it was, just that it wasn't me."

"Well, that must have been a relief. At least he knows now, knows you aren't Tony's bit."

Alexia looked at her friend. "Yes," she said weakly, "he knows now."

Not Tony's, thought Alexia. She very nearly was, so very nearly. She still couldn't get him out of her head. She could still see his eyes in the mirror, feel him pulling her hair, feel the desperate, exquisite pleasure of him smacking her, him playing with her, looking at her intimately, playing with her until he could finally…

"Yeah, now you might get to fuck him!"

"What?" Alexia was shocked.

"Nathan. You might actually—you know, get off with him."

Nathan! Of course, they were talking about Nathan. For a horrible moment, she thought Romy was reading her mind. Alexia shivered. Nathan. She needed to be near Nathan.

"He said if you weren't well enough to go to work tomorrow then I'd have to go to the tennis bash with him, the one with Jim Brooker," she said, desperately hoping her friend would oblige again with a sudden cold.

"And you would like me to be poorly again?" asked Romy.

Alexia blushed. Romy laughed.

"Oh, you are so funny… Look at you, you're as red as a tomato!"

Having Romy point out her tendency to give herself away with maidenly blushes really didn't help.

"Okay, why not? All in a good cause." Romy gave a little fake cough. "I think I can feel a relapse coming on... I think I should go to bed..."

Alexia laughed. Romy was a good friend; infuriating at times, but definitely a good friend.

"Right, well, I definitely am off to bed. I was up most of the night with Nicky. God, he can go like a train... I need a night off!" She leaned over and kissed Alexia's cheek. "You better bag that white whale, Captain Ahab, and quick. I can't keep taking time off."

She got up.

"Where's Richard?" asked Alexia, not anxious to be left alone.

"Oh, he'll be back soon. He's been working at the bar tonight. See you in the morning,"

"Night!" shouted Alexia as Romy disappeared into her room.

She put on the TV again and watched some American crime drama. She wasn't really sure which one; they all merged into each other. At least it's not *Moby Dick*, she thought.

An hour later, she heard the key in the door and Richard came in.

"Well, hello, little lady!"

She was so pleased to see him. Warm, cuddly, safe Richard. She marveled at how safe she felt with him. They had been so intimate, and yet he still seemed like just a friend.

He walked up to her and put his arms around her, planting a huge kiss on her mouth. "You look beat," he said.

"You could say that," Alexia replied, and exhaled.

"Wanna talk about it?" he asked.

She shook her head.

"Okay then, no talking..."

"There's food in the kitchen," said Alexia.

"Nah, just ate—but I'll have a glass of that if there's any left."

Richard walked into the kitchen and she followed him,

nursing her own glass. He poured himself a generous serving. He drank appreciatively.

The light in the kitchen was dim; only the undercupboard lights were on, and they cast an intimate glow in the small space. There was a lamp on the table and it lit up Alexia's face as she sat down.

Richard looked at her.

"Well, who switched the light on?"

"What? Oh, I think Romy must have…" She looked at the lamp.

"Not that," said Richard. "You!"

Alexia blinked. She didn't understand him.

"I don't know what happened on that trip, or maybe I should say I don't know *who* happened, but somebody turned a light on inside of you that wasn't there before."

Alexia was shocked. Did she look so different? And if she did, why? Because of who? Nathan? Tony? Or the soccer players and their Bacchanalian orgy? Perhaps all of them. Perhaps the trip had changed her, woken up the sexual being inside her.

"Whatever it was, whoever it was, I like it," said Richard. "Come here."

He took her by the hand and pulled her to standing. He moved her around so her back was against the units and he could look at her with the light behind her, framing her.

"Yes sirree," he said. "I sure do like it."

She felt his hands on her shoulders as he looked deep into her eyes.

"Not sure you're gonna need any more lessons."

Alexia looked at him. He was probably right. She felt a pang of regret.

She moved her hand to his groin and felt he was hard.

"Well, perhaps just one more?" she said.

Richard smiled. "Sure thing, ma'am."

He dropped to his knees and pulled up her nightgown. The

familiar blond triangle greeted him, the quivering pink lips nestling, waiting for his attention.

"I think maybe some revision…"

She heard Richard's voice, thick and low. She parted her legs for him and felt the heat of her own wetness as she exposed her pussy to the air.

This feeling of nakedness, of openness, was something she needed. Only weeks ago she would never have dreamt she could be so wanting, so free; now she craved it.

He puckered his lips into a perfect O, then he blew very gently into her curls. She felt the breath dancing on her clit and a delicious tingle ran through the nerves.

"That tickles!" She laughed. He laughed with her.

"Just checking for cobwebs—but it doesn't look like they've had a chance to gather over the past couple o' days!"

She slapped him gently on the side of the head and heard him laugh.

"No, my beautiful little pussy," he continued, "she's been getting some attention."

Alexia's thoughts flashed back to that morning, of bending over the sink, of Tony's fingers ramming into her, of him pushing the bullet against her, making her come, then getting ready to fuck her…

Then Nathan. Nathan's voice in the background. What if he had walked in on them? The thought made her head swirl and she gave a little moan.

"My, my. It must have been good," said Richard, unaware that the moan concealed a painful memory, not a pleasurable one.

"Stop talking, Richard," said Alexia, "just…"

"Yes, ma'am," he said. And his mouth was on her. She moaned with the pleasure. She needed his warm tongue, his soft, safe attention. She needed it to block out the morning, to replace it with a happy memory, the way he had done last night on the speakerphone when he'd brought her to orgasm with his voice and her own hands.

He pushed his tongue over her clit and flicked and stroked it. She moaned loudly. Then quickly put a hand over her mouth. She didn't want to wake Romy. Her flatmate had no idea about their nocturnal classroom.

Richard continued to work her with his tongue. It was so different from Tony. This was warm and comforting; the pleasure was not as acute but it was all-enveloping. She felt the tendrils of it reaching around her abdomen as he gently tugged at her nub with his teeth and lapped at her with his tongue.

She ran her fingers through his hair and held his head to her hips as he moved his chin up and down with his tongue, running it along her slit.

He placed his left hand flat on her lower stomach and pulled up, stretching the skin away from her cunt, exposing her clit even more and making it pop out. He flicked it with his tongue and this time she felt an electric jolt.

He ran his other hand up her thigh and wiggled his fingers in her lips, like an anemone fluttering against her.

She felt her juices coating his fingers. Then he slipped two fingers gently inside her, curling them forward against her G-spot.

"Ahhhhh!" The sound of soft pleasure escaped from Alexia as if her lungs were deflating with relief. She was losing herself in the delicious feel of Richard's tongue. It was a soft, curling, uncoiling road to orgasm, not a steep, agonizing climb as it had been with Tony. She had been close all day, ever since Tony had left her hanging. She felt as if she had been on the brink since she'd fled that bathroom.

Richard curled and stroked, his fingers working inside as his tongue worked on the opposite bundle of nerves on the outside.

The exquisite sensation filled Alexia completely, and she held his head with both hands now, holding his tongue firmly against her.

She was close; she didn't want him to stop. Tony had kept stopping, making her wait, but Richard would not be so cruel. Richard was warm and tender and he was working for her pleasure.

He stroked and stroked and Alexia felt it, the encroaching flood of pleasure. She gripped his head and Richard felt the tension in her legs, felt her internal muscles grip his fingers as the contractions started.

She moaned a long, soft moan as the orgasm unwound in her, a slow uncoiling that turned her veins to liquid mercury.

She stood against the cabinets, panting. It amazed her how despite making no movements, no effort, an orgasm could leave her so breathless, even if just for a moment.

Richard stood up, wiping his chin and lips, covered in her, covered in her wet passion.

"Well, I don't think you need any more revision. I think you have that one down pat!" Richard chucked her chin. "I don't think I've ever made a woman come that quick, someone must have set your motor running before I arrived…"

Alexia kissed him. She wanted to silence him. She wanted no reminder of earlier attentions, only Richard's. She could taste herself on his lips.

"What about you?" she said, running her hand along his erection. It was still tucked in his trousers, but it wanted to be free.

She undid his fly and took him in her hand. He breathed in hard, holding his breath for a second as he adjusted to the pleasure of being in her hands.

She started to bend her knees, to go down, but he stopped her.

"Use your hands," he said. "I want you to look in my eyes when you see me come. You need to know how to tell when a man is really close. That way you can…"

"Control him?" Alexia finished his sentence.

"Top of the class!" he said.

He gripped Alexia's hand and guided her on his cock, showing her the pressure, the speed. She was shocked by how hard he wanted her to hold it, to run her grip over him.

She worked hard, and she watched his face as she pulled and clasped him.

She watched his face as his pleasure mounted, never moving her eyes from his. His eyes became cloudier, his breathing more rapid.

She worked harder, moving her fingers in a rippling rhythm to draw out an orgasm, to milk it from him.

His breathing was rasping now, the air coming from deep in his lungs. On she went, the muscles in her forearm tensing and tiring, but she never looked away; she wouldn't show him her tiredness. She was going to bring him to climax.

"You're going to come," she said, and it wasn't a question. He had made no sounds, no moaning, tried to give her no clues, but she knew.

She gripped harder and wanked him as forcefully as she could.

"Come for me!"

"Ahhhhh!" Richard exploded. She felt hot come spurt all over her hand, her nightgown; it seemed never-ending as it spilled out of him. He convulsed and his hips thrust forward, making her struggle to hold onto him. He shuddered as the last drops left him. Then he stopped, breathing very hard. Her eyes never left his. It was an extraordinary intimacy.

His hands were either side of her, gripping the counter top. He sucked in hard, trying to bring his breathing back to normal. He stood back and grabbed a tea towel.

"Don't tell Romy!" He laughed as he wiped Alexia's hands.

They both giggled, then he wiped himself and threw the towel into the washing machine.

He leaned forward and kissed her deeply.

"I think my little chick is ready to go into the world," he said.

Alexia smiled. She hoped he was right.

Chapter 12

THE ALARM CLOCK SHOOK Alexia out of her slumber. She reached an arm out and hit the Snooze button. Ten more minutes. She turned over.

She'd set the alarm early to make sure she'd have enough time to dress well and perfect her makeup. She'd be on show again today, at Wimbledon—with Nathan.

Which Nathan would she get today? she wondered. The cool professional or the gentle, concerned boss? He could switch so suddenly from one to the other. Jekyll and Hyde? No, that was Carter. Nathan was a mystery but she didn't sense a dark side. Troubled perhaps, but not dark.

Her head was thumping. She had slept very deeply, and the wine had dehydrated her. She reached over and opened her bedside cabinet, fishing around with her hand to find her painkillers, when her hands fell on something unfamiliar. She pulled out a long box.

She blinked, trying to adjust her eyes to the semidarkness. She read the dark lettering. *Rampant Rabbit.*

She sat bolt upright. On the front of the box was a shocking pink Post-it note with a smiley face on it and one word. Romy! Followed by a large X.

"Unbelievable," said Alexia out loud. Was the whole world trying to turn her into a sex addict?

She looked at the box again. She'd never owned a rabbit, though she'd certainly heard of them. Who hadn't? She pulled the cardboard open at one end and the clear plastic tray that contained her new toy slid out with a scrape. *Her* new toy! The idea sent a small, illicit thrill through her. What was it about vibrators? Why did they seem so—well, naughty? Such an old-fashioned word, but it fit.

The rabbit was the same color as the Post-it. Typical Romy. Even her sex toys had to be beautiful.

At the base was a slightly bulbous part in clear plastic filled with little colored beads. Decoration? It sheath was long and thick, but not as thick as Nathan, thought Alexia, and she'd only seen him relaxed.

She felt a curling sensation in her sex. How could just the thought of him naked do that? She thought of his body, how the water had run down his torso, down around his long cock as he'd stood in the shower. Her fingers curled around the vibrator. Nathan.

She wished suddenly that Romy had warned her about the toy, told her to buy the batteries that would bring it to life. She slapped it down on the bed in frustration.

Alexia looked at the clock. Still plenty of time. She reached down to the floor and picked up her laptop. She flicked it on and surfed quickly to the pictures of Nathan she'd found before.

A new picture emerged. Nathan with Iorizzo, Lopez, and Carsten. All smiling for the camera. Alexia felt a strange tug of pride. Days ago she'd looked at his image and seen a stranger, but now… She was there, she was right there, standing just behind the photographer!

She reached down and touched her pussy, but it was too soon; she wasn't ready. She looked at the rabbit with its delicious pink ears, its soft jelly that could hum and wiggle to coax even the most reluctant clit.

Damn it! she thought. She looked at the useless lump of rubber and plastic. It's no use like this! But as she stared at it, a slow realization brought a cautious smile to her lips. Romy was a PA. And a good PA takes care of everything, leaving nothing to chance, nothing left undone. Every little detail…

Alexia picked up her rabbit and clicked. *Buzzzzzzzzzz.*

She giggled. "You think of everything, don't you?" she said as if Romy had been in the room.

The pink beads swirled and jiggled around and around in their casing, as the head rotated. So that's what they were for. She imagined the stimulation they would give, colliding against each other as they jostled in their casing, around and around.

Alexia breathed out and closed her eyes. She lay back and pulled her nightie up to expose her body. She was still covered by her quilt; she kicked it to the end of the bed.

She stretched out her legs and brought the lightly humming rabbit ears up to her nipples. She looked across the bed at Nathan; he stared straight at her.

The ears dusted the tip of her breast. A small sound escaped on her out breath. She let the vibrating jelly bring her nipples up to standing and breathed through the gentle pleasure as it warmed her body.

The rabbit was noisier than the bullet, and the colliding beads added a layer of sound to its motion. But she didn't care. Romy and Richard would still be fast asleep at this hour. She was alone, this was private.

She moved her hand to stroke her now dampening curls, sliding her fingers along the tops of her inner thighs, just below the tips of her inner lips.

She looked at Nathan and imagined his fingers, those long, strong fingers she had studied when they covered her hand in the car. They were elegant fingers; they would be gentle at first, she thought, teasing and sensual. She moved her fingers in little circles as the rabbit's attention was fixed on her nipples. Nathan's mouth on her breasts? She looked into his eyes, at his lips, strong, smooth lips. She remembered the taste of him as she brought her fingers closer to herself. She felt her wetness increase.

His eyes looked into her, urging her on.

She moved the rabbit down, tracing the jiggling ears along her stomach. Nathan's hands, Nathan's fingers, running down; a straight line down the middle, down to the secret place she longed for him to touch.

She fixed on his eyes again. She could almost imagine the fire in them, watching her pleasure, the pleasure that came from his touch.

The ears whispered through her downy hair as they settled either side of her now straining nub. She felt the surge, a small gasp. Nathan, look what you do to me. Look at what I want you to do to me…

The rabbit ears were vibrating against her clit now, teasing it from either side, a flurry of buzzing and fluttering, filling her pussy with want.

She pinched her nipple with her free hand. Nathan's teeth. Gentle nipping as the pressure intensified.

She rubbed her heels on the bed, lifting her knees to open herself. The bullet had pleasured her but her delicious little friend had been replaced by a better one, a pink and rampant one that had so much more to offer.

She turned the rabbit so the tip faced her now yawning cunt. She felt it rotate and coat itself in her juices, ready to plunder her, to slide into her.

She looked at Nathan. Why can't this be you? This morning it *is* you, this morning I *will* have you, this morning you're mine…

She pushed the base and felt the head as it swooshed inside her. Her breath halted. She paused and breathed out, relaxing herself to let the rabbit make its way in, all the way in. Round and round it went as it inched its way up, sweeping over her secret spot. She gasped.

She closed her eyes and felt the urgent motion curling inside her, against her G-spot, over and over. It swirled and curled and she felt herself gripping it. Without thinking, she pinched her nipple hard. She was long past thought—this was instinct now, a primeval, driving need, and she knew how to feed it.

The rabbit was up to the hilt, the beads circling faster as she turned up the dial. She bit her lip as she looked at Nathan. What would she look like to him? If he was looking down at her now, driving his cock into her now, what would he see? Would he see how she felt, how she needed him?

She rode the waves and closed her eyes. She had his face fixed in her mind, his eyes boring into her. The pulsating in her cunt grew stronger; she turned the dial again. Now the rabbit was racing, racing to the finish line. The head rotated against her G-spot as the ears trembled against her clit. A pincer movement of exquisite torture.

"Nathan! Nathan!" She voiced her need now, not caring who would hear. She grabbed the end of the vibrator and held it jammed into her with both hands. Two final circles and she came. She pushed her head back into the pillows as the first contraction rocketed through her pelvis. Then another and another, jerking, bucking contractions, followed by a flooding of warmth and peace.

She lay flat. She dropped her knees, her legs lying limply. Spent, exhausted, sated.

She opened her eyes and looked across at his face and felt a pang of regret. "But you weren't really here!" she said quietly. "It wasn't really you."

—◦—

An hour and half later she arrived at the office, dressed as usual in tight skirt, beautiful blouse, and heels. Her morning's fantasy was still fresh in her mind.

It was still very early, and there were only two staff in the office. She made her usual hellos and found that they paid her a little more attention than usual. She was the boss's right-hand woman now, even if only temporarily, and she was getting noticed.

She looked at her computer and saw a message blinking on the internal network.

Message: Nathan Fallon—Come and see me when you get in.
Message Sent: 6:45 a.m.

She felt her heart skip a beat. She knew she would see him today, they had to go to Wimbledon together, and yet a simple message could make her lose her composure. And why was he here so early?

Her hands were perspiring and her mouth was dry. She got up and smoothed down her skirt. This was crazy: if she couldn't control the way she reacted to him, pretty soon her nerves would be in shreds.

As she moved through the office, she tried to breathe some calmness into herself. She went into the small kitchen. She would take Nathan a coffee; that's what personal assistants do, she would anticipate his needs.

A quick examination of the shiny, complicated coffee machine made her doubt her ability to anticipate anything. No instant here; fresh ground, only the best. She'd only ever made herself tea; she had no idea how to work it. She picked up a cup. Where to start?

"Need any help?" Tony was standing in the doorway.

"You always seem to turn up, don't you—" said Alexia coolly.

"When I'm needed?" He finished the sentence.

She didn't respond. He was still very handsome, damn him. He stepped forward and took charge of the machine.

"How do you take it?" he said, his eyes dancing. His double meaning was obvious. Alexia fumed.

"It's not for me," she said. "It's for Nathan."

"Ah, the boss man. Well, we'd better make sure he gets it just the way he wants it."

Alexia couldn't help but wonder what "the way he wants it" would mean. She pushed the thought from her head.

"Strong and blaaaack," said Tony, exaggerating every syllable.

The coffee machine hissed into life under his expert hand. He took the cup from her hand and poured the aromatic, dark coffee into it. He put the cup on a saucer and handed them to her.

She took them without thanking him and turned to leave. He stopped her, holding her arm.

"We still have unfinished business, you and I. Don't pretend like we don't. You weren't running yesterday morning, not until Nathan showed up. You were loving it, you were about to beg me for it—and you know it!"

He had moved very close to her. She could smell his sweet after-shave, smell the fresh toothpaste on his breath. She wanted to slap him, to run out the room, but she was holding a cup of scalding hot liquid and she didn't dare spill it.

He was right and she knew it. The memory of his cock tickling her pussy, the realization that she'd been seconds away from begging him to fuck her, gave her a sickening feeling deep in her stomach. She thought about throwing the coffee in his face. But she realized too that she wasn't feeling turned on by the nearness of him, not anymore.

She wriggled free of him, mumbling an excuse that Nathan was waiting for her, and left the kitchen. But he'd unnerved her. Last night, Richard had helped her forget, but the memory was fresh again, disturbing. She had nearly begged him; she had certainly silently begged him. There was no doubt of that. She knew it—and he knew it. No blushing denials would work here. She longed for Nathan, but he had given his attention to another woman, and she had run for solace elsewhere. Solace? Is that what it was? Or just a need to disentangle herself from the "frigid" label that had hung around her neck for too long now?

Nathan's door. She'd arrived all too quickly. She knocked gently, but heard no answer. She took a deep breath and opened the door, trying not to let the cup rattle as she steadied her nerves. She stepped in to find the room empty. She was putting the cup and saucer on the table when she heard his voice.

"You're early!"

She turned around to see him in his little bathroom, *that* bathroom.

He wasn't wearing a shirt. He appeared to have been washing, and his chest was damp. The wet black curls clung to his skin. She wanted to bury her head in them. Had he been here all night? She watched as he toweled himself dry.

She stammered, "I just wanted to make sure everything was okay—for Wimbledon—and I brought you some coffee…"

He looked at her, studying her. She blushed. "Thank you," he said quietly.

They regarded each other, neither moving nor speaking. She looked into his eyes, the same eyes that had stared out at her from her laptop this morning as she'd fucked herself, when she'd imagined his hands and his cock pleasuring her.

She wasn't quite sure how it happened, or if she'd made a conscious decision. But she found herself walking straight toward him, straight up to him.

She put her hands on his chest and looked up into his face. His mouth had fallen open; he was caught off guard.

His hands moved cautiously onto her shoulders, then something seemed to shift inside him, seemed to snap, and suddenly he was enveloping her, wrapping his arms around her. She felt a surge go through her abdomen and then his mouth was on hers.

She melted against him as his lips pressed against hers. She tasted him again, drank in the warm, masculine smell of him. He pulled her up to meet his mouth, as her heels came off the floor and she strained on tiptoes to accept his lips.

The kiss was endless, searching, tasting, probing. She felt his hand move up her side, tracing up her rib cage to settle on her breast.

She felt him pressed against her, felt his erection harden with the contact.

They staggered back until she was pressed against the wall. She felt the withdrawal of his lips. Not too far, just a few inches, just far enough to let him look at her, look into her face. His eyes were on fire now, on fire for her. He was breathing hard; she felt his chest as he pulled in gasps of air.

She felt him press his cock against her, his hips forward as he bent his head over her. She moaned and he demanded her mouth again. He kissed her hard and she felt herself moisten in readiness for him. His mouth moved down to her throat, to the little pulsing vein in her neck, and he nipped it. Then he withdrew and stood back. She was shocked. Had she done anything wrong?

But he was looking at her again, really studying her. He moved backward, pulling her toward him, and he sat back onto a low sill that ran along the bathroom wall. He was so tall, it made his head level with hers. He pulled her forward, and opened his legs so she could stand right up against him.

He kissed her again and she felt his hand unbutton her blouse. She moaned in his mouth as she felt the warmth of his fingers trace the top of her breast.

Then his mouth was moving down. His fingers pulled aside the lace of her bra and she felt his tongue run over her nipple. She gasped. Only that morning she'd been fantasizing about his lips on her breast, and now here he was. This time it was real. Her fantasy had been a pale imitation of the pleasure his mouth was bringing. His hand palmed the other cup as his tongue worked its way around the straining tip of her breast. She wound her fingers into his thick, black hair and held his head to her chest.

His legs pinned her own together as he held her in front of him.

She longed to free herself, to hitch up her tight skirt and sit astride him, to feel his erection right up against her cunt.

"God, Alexia, I want you," he exclaimed.

Alexia thought the rush of juices would flood her flimsy panties. He had no idea how badly she'd wanted to hear those words. Was it real? Was this really happening? It had been so fast.

She looked down at his face, watching his tongue circle her nipple as his hand held the mound of her other breast. She watched the strong brow, the line of his dark eyebrows, the dark pink of his tongue as it flexed and flicked. She ran her hands over the sweep of his naked shoulders. His skin was warm and soft. She pushed her hips forward. Her need for him was agonizing.

He lifted his head. His eyes were cloudy now, heavy with desire. His hands ran down her and around behind her, settling on her bottom and pulling her hard to him.

"Oh God, Nathan!" she moaned. "I…"

But she couldn't finish. She was afraid of the words that would come out, afraid that she might confess her love for him. Love? She loved him. As she looked down at him and felt his breath on her, she knew she loved him.

She heard a knocking from outside. They both froze. Someone was looking for Nathan. Another knock. They waited—and waited. Silence. Whoever it was had gone away, but it had broken the spell. They had got lost in each other, in their desire, but life had intruded sharply. They were at work. They were always at work.

Nathan looked up at her. "I don't think it would be a good idea to get caught in here," he said.

Alexia laughed nervously. "No, not like last time."

She bit her lip. She hadn't meant to say it; the words just tumbled out of her mouth.

His eyes darkened.

She stammered to explain, to retract, retrace.

"When I was stuck in here… When Tony and…"

Nathan breathed out. He was retreating now, still wrapped around her but moving away, emotionally.

"When he was in here before…"

He pushed her away from him slightly so he could look at her, but he kept his hands on her.

"I have to know, Alexia. I have to know about you and Tony."

She flushed. "There's nothing between us, nothing," she said. "He keeps trying to come on to me…" Her words trailed away to nothing.

"And that's it?" demanded Nathan. He looked at her. "You've never encouraged him or—?"

He didn't elaborate, he didn't have to. She knew what he meant. *Or let him push his tongue into your cunt and then almost fuck you?*

She wanted to scream no. She had never encouraged him, or worse… But how could she? She couldn't lie, she felt so raw, so open; she couldn't bring herself to tell a blatant untruth. His eyes were fixed on her. She felt he could see into her, see right through her.

He registered her silence. His jaw set hard. He stood up suddenly and moved her away from him.

"This shouldn't have happened!" His voice was cold and hard.

She started to protest. "You don't understand."

But he would have none of it. "Oh, I understand, I understand very well. I shouldn't be surprised. Not many women are immune to his charms, why should you be any different?"

The words rang through her like a rapier, straight to the heart. *Why should you be any different?*

A moment ago she *was* different; she was someone Nathan desired. But now? Now, in a matter of seconds, she'd become just another notch on Tony's bedpost.

"I'm going to Wimbledon early. Order a car and be there for two."

And with that, he grabbed his shirt and left. She heard him exit the outer office. He was gone.

She heaved a huge, wracking sob. She sat against the sill as her head swirled. She could still feel him on her breast, feel the wetness inside her. But a chill enveloped her now, a Siberian chill that made her shiver and shake.

She buttoned up her blouse and looked in the mirror. She was disheveled. With shaking hands, she tidied up her hair and smoothed down her clothes. She took a huge, deep breath and left the bathroom. On her way to the door she saw his coffee cup. The coffee was cold.

The rest of the staff were arriving as Alexia got to her desk. She batted off morning greetings and inquiries about the trip with the best smile she could muster.

She willed herself to concentrate on her work. It was agonizing. She combed through the details of the event at Wimbledon. A presentation about something or other; she wasn't really interested. She just needed to work out where and what time they were going. Jim Brooker, the young tennis star and their latest client, was a guest, and he would surely be getting attention from various other guests. Nathan was his chaperone, and he would need his PA in tow. He would need *her* in tow.

Her heart sank as she realized there was really nothing for her to do, just stand around. She'd know no one. Talking to Nathan wouldn't be an option. She closed her eyes and wondered how she could have so quickly made a mess of the opportunity life had given her, the opportunity Romy had created for her. Her new job, her new life was in tatters.

She'd done what Sonia told her to do; she'd taken a risk, a risk on love, on the man she wanted. But she'd lost. So close, but now further away than ever.

Alexia looked through the guest list. She knew there was little point. She was unlikely to find a name that would make any difference to her. They would all be strangers. Her eyes passed over a name and she stopped. Sonia Varma. Sonia was going to be there! Relief swept over her. Her newest friend and, strangely, her greatest confidante.

If only she could speak to her now; she needed to hear her soft voice, her gentle reassurances, her motherly advice.

She'd taken Sonia's card at the hotel bar; it was in her bag somewhere. She grabbed her bag and fished around for it. There it was nestled in a pocket, a little piece of cardboard but a huge piece of comfort. She took it from her bag along with her mobile and went into one of the empty meeting rooms.

It's only 8:45, she thought. But she was desperate. She tapped in the number.

"Sonia Varma," said the familiar voice.

"Sonia? It's Alexia!"

"Alexia, darling," she started in a cheery tone, but stopped. "What is it? What's happened?"

"Oh, Sonia, I've messed it all up!"

Alexia recounted the whole story, even telling Sonia about how Tony had caught her when she was vulnerable, how he'd turned her on but she'd always batted him away, how Nathan had almost caught them. It all came pouring out.

"Tony?" Sonia sounded surprised.

"Oh, don't! I know what it sounds like, but it isn't like that, it really isn't…"

"It's okay. Look, believe it or not, Alexia, I think I understand how you've ended up here."

"You do?" Alexia couldn't believe anyone understood. She could barely understand herself.

"Yes, I think I do. I told you in the hotel, you remind me a lot of me when I was your age. You're still finding your feet, in more ways than one. Tony sniffs out prey; he knows when he can get his own way, and he doesn't show mercy. That would be pretty hard to resist when you're low, when you're confused, and—forgive me, Alexia—when you're young."

Alexia closed her eyes. Someone understands. The relief was like a giant exhalation. She felt the knot of tension in her stomach loosen a little.

"Thank you, Sonia, thank you so much. You don't know how much it means."

"Shhh now, don't fret."

"But Nathan…"

"Nathan nothing. We can sort that out. Are you going to be in Wimbledon later?"

"Yes, yes, I am. With Nathan."

"Okay, I'll see you there. And please don't worry. These are growing pains, my dear, that's all. We all go through them; it's just that you seem to be having several growing spurts at once!"

Alexia laughed softly. Sonia was so kind, her humor so gentle.

"I know. It's exhausting."

"I bet it is." Sonia laughed too. "I'll see you later. Just go and have a big mug of tea and keep yourself busy."

"I will."

"And stay away from Tony!"

Alexia laughed again.

"Oh, don't worry. I'm going to be standing as far away from him as I can get."

"Bye, darling, see you later."

Alexia put down her phone and breathed out again. She looked through the glass wall into the office. No one was paying any attention to her call.

The door opened silently as she stepped out of the meeting room and went back to her desk. Almost 9:00 a.m. Five hours till the car arrived. She sat down and opened her emails. She would bury herself in her work till it was time to go.

Chapter 13

THE BUILDING WAS so familiar. The green exterior of the All England Lawn Tennis and Croquet Club, Wimbledon to most people, came into view.

Alexia's driver had dropped her outside the gates, and she'd jostled her way up to the famous building amid the arriving guests. There were quite a few famous faces, some current and past British players and the usual tennis hangers-on from the world of show business.

The iconic ivy hanging from the façade fluttered in the cold winter breeze. Alexia put her head down and battled through to the door. Her name was on the list and she was ushered straight through. She looked at the announcement board: a presentation for services to tennis for a long-past British hopeful who'd raised the nation's expectations for a brief period, then dashed them again in the face of crushing Continental superiority.

The champagne was already flowing. She wondered how Nathan ever kept his head bouncing from event to event on a sea of bubbly. But then he didn't always keep his head. He hadn't this morning. He had well and truly lost it this morning—for a while.

She felt a pang of fear and pain. Had she blown it, was it over? He'd wanted her. He'd said so: "God, Alexia, I want you…"

She shook herself. She had to be breezy, in control—but her mind had other ideas; it was on spin cycle. Was it just because she'd thrown herself at him? Any man would respond to that, wouldn't he? It wouldn't mean anything, wouldn't mean she was special. The permutations fought and festered in her mind, pinning her down on the emotional roller coaster she seemed to have been chained to for weeks now.

She wandered through the crowd, trying her best to smile. Men watched her go by, admiring the cool beauty, but she was oblivious to their attention.

There was a gaggle at one end of the room, clucking and cooing around a person she couldn't see. She moved around to get a better look. Jim Brooker, their client. The new British hopeful, still only nineteen. He was young and fit but no pinup. His skin was still slightly spotty; he hadn't entirely left his teenage hormones behind. His body was toned, long-limbed, and just starting to grow into the serious masculinity of a top-flight sportsman.

But without his tennis fame, he would never have attracted the type of attention he was reveling in now. Several good-looking girls, probably a few years older than him, were openly vying for his favor. And, to one side, was Nathan. He wasn't with Jim, but she knew that he was keeping a discreet eye on his young charge.

He was talking to Sonia. The one person Alexia was relying on to keep her company and away from Nathan, and here she was, with him!

Sonia spotted her and waved her over. "Alexia!"

The ground seemed to sag beneath her, as if it had turned to rubber. Or was it her legs that were failing to support her?

Nathan didn't turn. He should have turned; that's what most people do when their companion spots a friend and beckons that friend to join them. He merely sipped his champagne. Alexia walked over to meet them and Sonia scooped her up and kissed her like a long-lost friend.

"Darling, you look prettier than ever."

Alexia murmured a thank you.

"We were just discussing young Jim over there. With any luck he's going to be a sensation in a few years. You a tennis fan?"

Sonia was a trooper. She was keeping the conversation light and fresh.

"Yes, yes, I am…"

"Good, I need some decent company at the Wimbledon championships this year. I normally get stuck with some hideous corporate tennis bore because I have to use the corporate tickets *you* give me."

She poked Nathan playfully. He smiled, but it didn't reach his eyes. Sonia regarded him coolly. "I told you I might steal her away from you, Nathan—well, you can't begrudge me her company for a few days in June, can you?" She giggled.

Nathan smiled again, his professional smile.

"Sonia, you know I always try and give you what you want…"

He still wasn't looking at Alexia; he was looking everywhere but at her. He was obviously desperate to get away, to be far from her company.

"Ladies, you obviously have things to talk about, and women's conversations are usually hampered by the presence of a man, so I will tactfully withdraw and leave you to you feminine diversions."

He gave an almost imperceptible bow of the head and moved away.

Alexia waited till she was sure he was out of earshot. "See, I told you he hates me now."

"No, he doesn't." Sonia smiled knowingly; she looked at Nathan's retreating figure. "I'd say quite the opposite."

Sonia took her arm and turned her to face the crowd.

"Look at these people, Alexia; these are the people he has to spend his days with now. Hangers-on, sports bores, corporate junket lovers, and jumped-up playground heroes who earn too much money and think the world should worship them for their talent.

"Not forgetting the women who are only interested in one thing, of course—getting into the beds of the rich and famous or, failing that, getting into the beds of the *people* who can get them into the beds of the rich and famous. This isn't Nathan. He's good at it, yes—he knows how to play this world—but he's an army officer at heart. He's a proper gentleman. And a proper gentleman needs a proper lady…"

Alexia looked at her. "Well, I'm not one of those anymore, am I? Not after the way I've behaved."

Sonia let out a laugh so loud she startled all the people standing close to them. Alexia blushed.

Lowering her voice, Sonia said, "Are you mad? So some playboy got you hot and bothered. So what? We've all done that—doesn't make us the same as all these star-hunting bimbos!"

Alexia looked at Sonia. She wanted to believe her.

"Sweetie, you're a gorgeous girl, and you're young. You should be able to feel sexual with whomsoever you want. That doesn't make you easy; it makes you a woman. What matters to a man like Nathan is that you're real—and that you're honest. God knows he's not an angel; he's had his fair share, I'm sure. Look at him, how could he not?"

Alexia looked at him. Ramrod straight, tall, masculine, in control, with just a hint of imperfection in that slightly crooked nose. She tried not to imagine him with other women, but that was difficult, after the hotel. She told Sonia about Blondie.

"Well, that doesn't surprise me," said the older woman. "You wind him up and then he has nowhere to put all that pent-up lust. He is a man, not a saint."

She spoke so much sense, Alexia wanted to believe her; she wanted desperately to believe her.

"Oh God!" exclaimed Sonia, suddenly.

"What?" Alexia looked up and saw Tony's blond head just above some of the other guests. "What's he doing here? I didn't know he was coming."

"Well, he's here. If I were you, I'd avoid him at all costs, especially if Nathan can see you."

"Oh bloody hell, you're right. I'm going to the bathroom. I'll come back and find you when I think it's safe."

"Okay. If I think he's heading your way I'll rugby-tackle him."

"Thank you," said Alexia and kissed Sonia's cheek. "You're a doll!"

Alexia sneaked behind a large group of people and found her way out of the room and down a maze of corridors, looking for the ladies'. She turned a corner into an empty corridor. She thought she had wandered too far and was about to turn back, when she heard some strange noises coming from one of the offices.

The door was ajar; she moved toward it and pushed it open. She found herself in a long room cluttered with temporary partitions stacked randomly at one end. It was obviously some kind of function room. She could hear the muffled noises from behind the partitions. She walked silently up to them and looked through the gap between two sections.

She could see stacks of chairs, the ubiquitous steel-framed variety used for conferences and weddings. One chair had been taken down and someone was sitting on it. It was Jim Brooker, and he wasn't alone. One of the girls who'd been trying to attract his attention earlier was with him, a miniskirted redhead, and she was kneeling on the floor.

Alexia had to suppress a laugh. She clasped her hand to her face to stop the noise exploding out of her.

Jim was sitting back in his chair, his legs splayed open with his trousers unzipped and his cock sticking up, stiff and waiting. He'd looked too young back in the other room, young and innocent. But clearly he wasn't either.

The tennis player was no oil painting, but the redhead eyed his erection appreciatively. If she's faking it, thought Alexia, she's doing a really good job.

The girl moved forward on all fours like a hunting cat, keeping her eyes on his face the whole time. His expression was lascivious. Alexia stood rooted to the spot as the girl took him in her mouth, all the way in.

"Yesssss!" exclaimed Jim. "Oh fuck!"

He watched the girl's head as she bobbed on his dick, licking and sucking for all she was worth. He was grinning; he already knew his fame would grant him special privileges, and this was one of them.

"Play with your cunt!" he ordered.

Alexia was stunned. Was he really only nineteen?

The girl put her hand up her short skirt and stuffed it into her panties. The two continued in this fashion; she sucking and rubbing, he sitting back, hands laced behind his head, watching as she pleasured him. He was loving the attention, and the power, but after a few minutes he got bored.

"Get up!" he demanded.

The girl pulled away from his crotch and put her finger in her mouth. She pouted artfully, as if he had taken away her favorite lollipop.

He patted his thighs as an instruction for her to sit on him. The girl giggled and smiled. She stood up and pulled down her panties. Alexia could see her well groomed pussy, just a tiny little red-haired landing strip. She'd come prepared. She pulled out a condom from somewhere and quickly used it to cover the glistening erection. Very prepared, thought Alexia. The redhead straddled Jim and watched his face as she lowered herself onto his cock.

"Oh baby!" she moaned.

Oh please! thought Alexia. How corny was that? Was he really fooled?

He had hold of her buttocks and he was sitting back like an Arab sheikh, enjoying one of his harem girls. The couple gasped and moaned in unison as she fucked him playfully.

"I want to see your tits!" he demanded.

The girl opened her blouse and undid her bra, which fastened at the front. She had clearly dressed with a plan. Her breasts jumped free and bounced like excited, pink-nosed puppies as she rose and fell on his lap with ever-increasing speed. The sight was almost comical, cartoon strip fucking.

Alexia wanted to leave but found she was rooted to the spot. How did this keep happening to her? She had turned into a voyeur, and not by design. This was the third time in as many weeks she'd watched other people having sex. Romy had told her the world she'd be entering if she took the job at the Fallon agency would be one she'd have to get used to. "They're a fast crowd!" she'd warned. Alexia had no idea how fast, until now. She felt a pang of jealousy. Why did the whole world seem able to have uncomplicated sex? Everyone except her!

She watched the girl as she bounced on Jim's cock. She felt herself getting turned on. It was a comical performance, true, but it was sex, and it was what Alexia needed, needed very badly. She couldn't believe it, but she was getting wet as she watched the redhead grinding away.

The couple were close to coming. The girl seemed to be matching Jim's groaning, to be reaching climax with him. Perfect timing or perfect playacting?

And then they came. Him with a grunting, snorting, teeth-baring thrust, her with a girlie "oh you're such an incredible lover I just can't help myself." *Ahhhhh…*

What a performance, thought Alexia. He's not falling for that, is he? But why should he care? He was nineteen and a random gorgeous redhead had just bounced on his cock with barely an introduction. And now she'd ridden her tennis pro with gusto, she'd either be trying to make sure she'd be seen about town with him, or she'd be kissing and telling the tabloids.

The tabloids! Alexia panicked. Was this the kind of thing they were supposed to be protecting him against? How could they? The agency couldn't stop him having sex. She thought about telling Nathan, but how could she?

The girl was getting off Jim's lap and he was doing himself up. Alexia knew she had to get out quickly or be discovered, and she didn't want *that* happening again.

She stole out of the room and shut the door quietly behind her. She was making her way back to the function room when she saw a horribly familiar figure coming toward her.

"Avoiding me?" asked Tony.

He was walking toward her and there was nowhere for her to go.

"As it happens, yes!" she said defiantly.

He caught up with her. "Now, that's not very friendly, is it?"

She sighed wearily and shook her head. Behind her she heard the young tennis player talking quite loudly. She turned to see Jim and his redhead walking back to the presentation. Her lipstick was smudged and some of her hair was out of place. He looked perfectly calm. They walked past. Alexia could smell the sex.

Tony looked at her. "My God, you've a taste for it, haven't you? Watching other people screw!"

"Get lost, Tony." Alexia wanted to leave, but he had moved in front of her.

He kept his voice low. "Where were they fucking? Down there?" He nodded in the direction the two had come from. "Well, it's obviously a good spot. Why don't *we* pick up where we left off?"

He moved in on her, trying to move her backward. Alexia hissed at him, trying to free herself without raising her voice. The corridor was empty but they weren't far from the reception.

"I said, leave me alone, Tony. Don't you get it? I'm not interested!"

"Come on, I know what you like."

"Stop it. I told you I don't want you."

"Oh yes, you do, you know you do. Stop being such a prick tease."

"Tony, no…" She was trying to push him away, but he gripped her arm. Then she saw him fall away backward as if he was on a long string that had suddenly been yanked. Nathan towered over him.

"Get off her!" Nathan growled.

Tony was shocked. He stared at his boss for a moment, then shook himself free of his grasp.

"Stay out of this, Nathan. This is between me and her."

Nathan grabbed the lapels of Tony's jacket. His face was cold, emotionless.

"No it isn't. It's between me and you. Now, leave her alone, leave this building—and leave the firm."

His voice was low, no anger, just a cold instruction and an implied threat. He was well trained.

Tony breathed hard. "You don't give me orders; this isn't the army…"

"Want to test me on that?" said Nathan.

Tony was no fool. Nathan was a trained soldier, a trained fighter; he was no match for him and he knew it. He stepped back and moved as if to leave. But he looked at Alexia. "Bitch!" He spat out the word.

Something inside Nathan snapped. With a hollow crack, a right hook connected with Tony's jaw.

Alexia gasped as he fell to the ground.

"Don't test me, Tony. Just get up and leave—now!"

Nathan was a man accustomed to giving orders, and accustomed to having them followed. Tony picked himself up off the floor, holding his jaw.

"I won't tell your father about this," said Nathan, "and neither, I suspect, will you."

It was a standoff. The two men eyeballed each other. Tony's eyes were simmering with fury, but he knew he'd been beaten. He skulked down the corridor and through the door.

Alexia breathed out hard. Nathan put his hands on her shoulders. "Are you all right?"

She nodded dumbly.

"Look, I'm sorry, but they're doing the presentation. I have to go back in. Are you sure you're all right?"

"Yes, yes, I'm fine. Go. I'll be okay…"

He looked at her, concern filling his eyes.

"Really, go," she said, and smiled to assure him she would manage.

He nodded, reluctantly, and let her go.

"Come back in when you're ready, okay?"

She nodded again and watched as he strode back to the reception. Shakily, she followed him in a moment later. People were gathering for the formal presentation and she saw Nathan take the stage. There were speeches, stories, polite laughter, lots of clapping and back-slapping. Alexia wasn't really paying attention.

Her legs threatened to give way under her. She felt as if the past three weeks were about to catch up with her, quickly and violently. She felt like the cartoon character who's been running away from an anvil she's attached to on a long piece of elastic. It's fine as long as you keep running, but the moment you stop, you get hit on the back of the head, hard.

She stood as far back from the action as she could; she'd grabbed a champagne glass on the way and drained it. She took another.

The recipient of the presentation was winding up his speech. More clapping, more back-slapping. The sound of chatter soon filled the room again. She wandered through the throng, drinking her champagne. She couldn't find Sonia; it seemed much more crowded than before. Then she saw her, talking to Nathan again. Really talking.

They seemed to be having a very intense conversation, and Nathan was doing most of the listening. Sonia looked up and saw Alexia across the crowded room. She said something to Nathan, who also looked up. Sonia was still talking as Nathan stared at Alexia. What were they saying? Were they talking about her?

She heard the bark of a man's laugh behind her. It was Jim Brooker, chatting up a brunette. At his age, thought Alexia, it wouldn't take him long to get up and running again if he fancied taking his latest friend for a knee-trembler behind the partitions. She had to tell Nathan.

She moved forward to talk to him. His face looked strange. He was wearing an expression she hadn't seen before; she couldn't read him.

"Are you okay?" he asked.

"Yes, yes, I'm okay. It's just…" She faltered.

"Just what?"

"Well, apart from what just happened, in the corridor, I need to tell you about Jim Brooker."

"Jim?" Nathan looked puzzled, "What about him?"

Alexia relayed what she'd seen, leaving out the juicier details, and explained that he might be gearing up to make another woman a member of his temporary harem right under their noses.

Nathan closed his eyes. "Give me strength! Can't any of these guys keep it in their trousers, at least until they're in a building with no journalists in it?"

He strode away. Alexia saw him flash Jim a charming smile as he took his arm and gently shooed away his female admirer. Jim's face darkened at having his fun spoiled. Nathan took him to one side and, without taking the smile off his face once or looking remotely concerned, proceeded to give him what Alexia presumed was a bit of a dressing down. Jim looked suitably bashful. Nathan was so smooth. No one in the vicinity would have had any idea of the conversation from his manner or expression.

"I told you he was quite an operator," said Sonia.

"He certainly is," agreed Alexia.

"The friend we have in common dropped large hints to me that

Nathan wasn't your average soldier, he was in army intelligence. It explains how he always seems to be able to stay one step ahead and get people to do what he wants."

And never show what he's feeling, thought Alexia. It made perfect sense.

She looked again at Nathan. "Yes, it does explain a lot," she said, almost to herself.

Sonia was watching her. "You know, I think it's time you two talked properly."

Alexia was puzzled. "What do you mean?"

"You have to tell him how you feel, Alexia, show him who you are."

"How can I…?"

"Well, he dispatched Tony pretty swiftly. I think he's worked out you don't want that little rat. And do you really think he'd have hit him if he hadn't called you a bitch?"

"Sonia, you weren't there. How do you know what Tony said? How do you know Nathan hit him?"

Sonia took a deep breath. "Losing control like that is not Nathan. It's not how he does things. So he was pretty angry with himself when he came back in. But… Look, Alexia, why do you think he lost control? It wasn't because Tony deserves to be fired, or because Nathan is disappointed in him. That was all true this morning, and yesterday and the day before. He hit him because he insulted you. It was instinct, protective instinct. And who do men protect?"

Alexia stared dumbly at her.

A huge sigh signaled Sonia's exasperation. "Darling, they protect the people they care about! Otherwise he'd just have told him to go back to the office to try his charm on the security guard packing up his desk.

"Men protect the people—or should I say, *women*—they care about. He may not have it quite straight in his head yet, but you're more than an employee to him. How much more? Well, you two will have to work that one out between you."

Alexia looked back at Nathan. He was chatting to some people, although she couldn't really see them; she couldn't see anything, just him. It was like a movie effect, all the foreground, the background, the people, everything in soft focus with him in the middle, in vivid Technicolor. She wanted him so badly. She was still turned on by that stupid encounter with Jim and the redhead. She wanted to walk up to him and tell him how desperate she was for his touch, his kiss, but most of all to feel his weight on her, that hot, heavy, masculine weight that nothing compares to. She wanted to feel his erection drive into her, to take her, to own her completely. She wanted to be naked and raw and needy. She wanted to bury her head in the hair on his chest and run her tongue down his stomach and wrap her lips around his cock. She'd never seen it erect, but she wanted to. She knew it was beautiful and she knew it would be big and hard enough to rock her world.

She imagined his dark blue eyes looking at her. She wanted to sit astride him the way the redhead had done with Jim. She wanted to feel his hardness as she lowered herself onto him and watch his face as he felt her muscles clench around him.

Alexia stood in the middle of that crowded room and felt her pussy give up more moisture. Her body was ready for him, ready for him now.

Sonia was right: she could waste no more time. He'd been hurt, badly hurt, but so had she. Her friend seemed to be reading her thoughts.

"I know you've been hurt, just like him," said Sonia. "But men aren't like us. They don't come back for more after love has bitten them and left them for dead. They stay wounded. They don't get up and dust themselves off to try again. They hide away; they put their hearts in a little locked box and throw away the key.

"Most of them find a second-best girl to marry because it's safe. A few of them just stand back from the game. I know it's a man's job to pursue a woman, but sometimes she has to show him how to be brave. Facing an enemy who's got a gun trained on you is nowhere near as scary as facing another broken heart."

"How did you get so wise?" asked Alexia. She realized she knew nothing about Sonia. Was the woman married, divorced, single?

"I met a man much like Nathan. I was brave, and"—Sonia laughed—"I still get breakfast in bed made for me on Sunday mornings!"

The women laughed together.

"Sounds perfect," said Alexia quietly.

"Nothing's perfect. But he's perfect for me."

"Do you think Nathan and I are perfect for each other?"

Sonia smiled. "Only you two can find that out."

Chapter 14

IT WAS NOW OR never. Not exactly the place to pour your heart out, but Alexia was afraid if she waited she would lose her nerve. It was so crowded, it felt as if she would never be able to weave her way through the chattering guests, but finally she was standing behind Nathan. He had his back to her and didn't see her until one of the group he was talking to nodded his head in Alexia's direction.

Nathan turned, in slow motion it seemed to her. First the back of the head, then a twist of the broad shoulders, his profile, those razor cheekbones, then his face and then—those dark blue eyes. Heart-stopping.

"Nathan," started Alexia, "I'm so sorry to interrupt but I really need to speak to you for a moment."

A moment's pause. Alexia's stomach churned as she waited for his response.

"Of course." Nathan turned to his companions. "Do please excuse me. This is my PA, Alexia Wright." They nodded in unison. "We'll be happy to accommodate you at the Grand Prix; my office will be in touch. Good to meet you." More nodding, thank-yous. Nathan extricated himself. He was standing right in front of her now.

"What's wrong? I've sorted Jim out. He's on his way home in a car..."

"No, no, it's nothing like that. It's..." Alexia hesitated. "It's personal."

Her heart was hammering against her chest.

"Here?" he asked. "Not really the place for it."

"It can't wait!" A couple of twitched eyebrows around them signaled that Alexia had blurted out her protest a little too vehemently. This wasn't going well.

Nathan took a deep breath. She felt like a child whose father was at the end of his considerable patience.

"Come with me," he said. He led them through the guests, but so many people wanted to talk to him, to say hello, it seemed to take forever. He was smooth, polite; he couldn't rush. Then, finally, they were out into a corridor. They walked through an anteroom of Palladian columns and murals into the members' changing room. The room had clearly housed some of the tennis greats. It looked and felt like the most luxurious spa: polished parquet floors, individual bathrooms, and rich, dark wood. He knew his way around.

"This is the ladies' changing room," said Alexia, her jealousy and suspicion rising rapidly.

Nathan raised an eyebrow. "Not all my clients are men, you know."

Of course, she thought. Why was she so quick to jump to conclusions? She knew why. Because she couldn't believe a man like Nathan could ever really be interested in her. He must have a million women. But Sonia had made it clear he hadn't.

He stood in silence and waited for her to speak.

"Nathan, I…" Where to start? She shook her head, unable to think.

He helped her out. "I'm sorry about Tony, about the way he behaved. That's… unacceptable."

Tony! She'd almost forgotten about him. It was only an hour ago, but he'd been pushed out of her mind. Her focus was all on Nathan. Everything had zeroed down to this. It was time to come clean.

"Nathan. You asked me, when we were in"—she took a huge gulp of air—"when we were in your bathroom…"

She saw Nathan's face change. He shut his eyes momentarily, then nodded his head.

She had to plow on, "You asked me if there was anything between us—me and Tony."

His blue eyes were fixed on her now; she had his total attention. What she said next could finish it, finish any chance of there being a relationship between them. But Sonia was right: Nathan wanted someone real, someone honest. She had to be honest.

"Before I came to the Fallon agency, my life was very difficult... I left college, and I met someone, someone I thought would be kind to me, someone who I could be with."

This was torture, but she knew there was no turning back. He needed to know all of it; she had to tell him everything.

"At college, most of the girls—well, you know what college is like. They have a good time, they go out with lots of guys, but I didn't. I just went out with one and he was very sweet, but..."

It was so hard to find the words. Talking to Richard had been easy; this was like swallowing barbed wire.

"He wasn't very interested in the physical side of a relation-ship..."

Nathan sat on the arm of a chair. This was not going to be a short explanation and he clearly thought he'd need to be here for a while. He looked confused. Not surprising, thought Alexia, he thinks I'm going to talk about Tony and now he gets a history lesson about my boyfriend in college. He's going to think I'm a psycho. But she had to get her story out, make him understand.

"So when I left, I met someone else—like I said—and I thought it would be okay. I had nowhere to live and he—" She thought about her next sentence. In a way, it was the first time she'd really owned up to herself about what had happened between her and Carter.

"He *made* me move in. I thought that it was my decision but actually it wasn't. I was very naïve. He..."

Alexia found she was pacing, walking up and down trying to find the words, trying not to look at Nathan. He was completely silent. Was he being kind? Letting her speak in her own time? Or was he just completely mystified? She wouldn't know till she'd finished.

"It was Carter, the man who came to the office. The man you... stopped."

She looked at Nathan. She still couldn't read him. Nothing, no clues. On she went.

"Being with him... It was okay at first but he wore me down, drip by drip. He sucked all the confidence out of me. No, that's not right. He knocked it out of me..."

"He hit you?" Nathan asked.

Alexia was shocked by the interruption.

"No. No, he didn't hit me, but—"

She was breathing hard now. She was about to lay herself bare. Talk about things only the closest friends, the closest of partners ever discuss.

"The sex..." There, it was out. She'd said the words, and she hadn't burst into flames.

"It was—he liked to control me. He wasn't interested in me, or what I wanted, he was a bully. He..."

She had to start pacing again, to face away from Nathan, to escape from his gaze.

"He had other women, so at least he left me alone a lot of the time, but when he didn't—" The memories were still raw. Alexia swallowed hard.

"Then I ran. I ran away... You've no idea how hard that was."

She bit her lip, remembering the agonizing decision as she walked out, to close or not to close the door. To bottle out, or run.

"I had nowhere to go; my parents live up north now and I couldn't go home. Then I bumped into Romy. We were at school together; she moved me into the flat. It was like a miracle. She saved me! Then she got me the job with you, a flat and a job. I couldn't believe it, but she warned me. She said it was a world I wasn't used to—a fast crowd, she called it."

She heard a cynical laugh from Nathan. She looked at him.

"Well, you've seen for yourself that she wasn't wrong," he said.

"No, she wasn't, but I wasn't really prepared for—" This was it, this was the heart of the problem. "I wasn't prepared for the effect it would have on me, the people would have on me."

Did he realize that he was one of those people? She searched his face. Still no clues.

"You asked me about Tony," she said, finally. Nathan's face darkened. "You asked if there was anything between us, and I said there wasn't, and it was true, emotionally. But…"

How would he ever believe what was coming next? She could hardly believe it herself.

"He just—I don't know. I don't know what happened but he made me feel things… Made me feel like…"

Nathan's jaw was tightening.

"But we didn't… It never happened."

Alexia blurted out the truth.

"It's all because of you!"

"Me?" said Nathan, now utterly confused.

"Yes, you! It's because… Don't you understand? I wanted you, from that first night. I…"

She was gabbling now, ranting, almost sobbing.

"But you were so cold, I didn't understand. And Tony, he just— he caught me when I was vulnerable and feeling lonely, and everyone seemed to find sex so exciting and so easy. I just thought, why can't I be like that? But I can't—I thought I could, but…"

Nathan was on his feet now, and she felt his hands on her shoulders, holding her square to him.

"You didn't sleep with him."

Alexia looked up at him. He was all she wanted. And now she wanted to tell him everything, no matter what. He might walk away, he might stay. She had no way of knowing, but she had to roll the dice.

"Nearly," she confessed.

"What stopped you?"

"You. Literally. The day in the hotel when you came looking for me in my room. I was in the bathroom. So was he."

Nathan looked as if he'd been winded. He stepped back.

"Ask yourself why, Nathan. Why did I let it go so far?"

"Why?"

"I came to find you in your suite, because Phillipa needed you and you weren't answering your phone. Why weren't you answering your phone, Nathan?"

His eyes glimmered. He turned away from her and took a deep breath.

Alexia pressed on. "What was her name—or doesn't it matter?"

"That's not fair!" Nathan was facing her now, his face a mask of restrained anger.

"You save me from Carter, then you kiss me in your office. Then you toss me to one side…"

"Because you were Tony's!"

"No, I wasn't!"

"How was I to know?"

The exchange was fast, bruising. They both stopped to take in what the other had said.

Alexia spoke first.

"I'm not very good at this, Nathan, I haven't had much practice. I didn't know if you had any feelings for me or whether you just found yourself with a woman in your arms, and—well, you're a man. I didn't know why you'd kissed me. You're impossible to read."

Nathan shook his head and laughed to himself. "You're not the first person to say that." He fell silent, reliving some old agony. It seemed to be hours before he spoke again. "I saw you leaving Iorizzo's suite, remember? Tony was following you."

"He sent me a text saying there was a problem. I didn't know..."

She stopped short. He must have had an idea of what his charges got up to, away from the spotlight. He must have known why the hotel was so popular with the stars.

"I didn't know what was going on in the room."

Nathan didn't speak. He knew, he knew very well.

"I didn't know what I'd be walking into," said Alexia, "and Tony, he came on to me. I—I've never seen anything like that before. It was—it excited me..."

Alexia looked at her feet. She had confessed something she never thought she'd tell a living soul and now she was telling Nathan.

"I suppose you don't think very highly of me just now."

"I think you're human—like the rest of us," said Nathan. "I suppose it's a pretty heady cocktail, especially when it's all new to you." He moved toward her. "I just couldn't bear the thought that you and Tony—or, worse still, you and one of the soccer players..."

"What? No!" Alexia was horrified. She had fantasized about it, yes, but would she have taken part? She wasn't sure. She felt it best not to speculate out loud. She feared the answer would be yes.

Nathan was very close to her now. "I noticed you the first time I saw you in the office."

Alexia groaned. "Oh God, Nathan, how could you not? You thought I'd just had sex with Tony on the boardroom table!"

Nathan looked puzzled. "What?"

"When you walked in and I was there with Tony."

Realization dawned. Nathan laughed heartily. Alexia was confused.

Nathan looked at her intently. "Tell me, who was he screwing?"

Alexia bit her lip.

"Alexia, I am not going to sack whoever it was, but I need to know. I need to know because—because of us."

Us? Alexia's heart leaped in her chest. There was an "us"?

"I don't want to get her into trouble…"

"You won't. You have my word."

His word, thought Alexia, the word of an officer and a gentleman.

"It was—Phillipa."

Nathan's eyed widened, then he roared with laughter. Alexia was confused.

"Phillipa?" he said. "God, he's brave. I'm surprised she didn't eat his head afterward, like a praying mantis!"

He carried on laughing, and Alexia found herself joining in. The tension was broken between them; sharing the joke felt like it had suddenly made them conspirators, close companions.

But something was nagging at Alexia. "Why were you puzzled?"

"About what?"

"When you said you couldn't forget the first time you saw me, and I mentioned the boardroom thing, you looked confused."

Nathan nodded slowly. "That wasn't the first time I saw you."

Alexia didn't know what to say. Not the first time?

"I stopped into the office briefly the day you joined. I saw you talking to Romy. You looked… lost."

The expression in his eyes changed. He looked almost wistful. Alexia remembered her first day, her complete terror. He had seen her that day?

"I thought you looked too fragile to last at the company, to last in this crazy world. But when I saw you with Tony, I thought I must have read you wrong. My judgment about women is sometimes not that good."

There it was again, thought Alexia, that distant hurt. She gazed at him. So much to take in, so much to process, to assimilate. Her need for him was raw now, gnawing at her; the emotion, desire, the frustration of the last three weeks boiled over. She reached up, standing on tiptoes. She put her hands on his chest and kissed him.

For a moment he was startled, then he let out a low animal sound and scooped her up. She felt her feet almost leave the floor; he was, literally and metaphorically, kissing her out of her shoes.

His mouth was on hers, hard now, no gentle kisses to ease her in, but deep and searching.

The air was filled with the scent of him, his natural musk and that oh so seductive aftershave Alexia had come to love. His hands were strong, possessing, but not like Carter, not brutal. This was searing, reciprocated lust.

He was biting her lip and then he was probing her tongue with his. His mouth was like a voracious animal that needed to consume her. She had never been kissed like this, never, and it almost scared her.

Pulled up hard against him, she could feel his erection pressing against her. She'd seen him naked, seen him relaxed, she knew that fully hard he would be much bigger than she was used to. The thought scared and thrilled her in equal measure.

Alexia wasn't prepared for the urgency of his need. Tony had thrilled her, Richard had cajoled and relaxed her, but this—this was different. This was more than primal, this was… She didn't know what it was; there were no words for it, no name. She just knew that she wanted him more than she had ever wanted anything. Not just his kiss, but all of him.

Deep inside her she could feel a thumping pulse, but it wasn't in her veins, in her throat or her cunt. It was all over her, it *was* her.

She wanted to beg him; she wanted to look in his eyes and beg him to fuck her, right there in the changing room. Was he going to? Where was this kiss going?

But she couldn't see his eyes. His head was buried in her neck, biting and sucking at her skin as his hand traced up her rib cage and cupped her breast. She felt a moan escape from her. Her clothes were too tight, too restricting; she wanted to be free of them, she wanted to feel his hands on her skin.

His mouth was back on hers. She bit his lip, just a nip, but it seemed to press a booster rocket somewhere inside him, and she felt his fingers close tighter.

Her nipples were peaking against the lace of her bra; she felt the wires dig into her as she breathed heavily, her breasts swelling to meet his hand.

He was trying to undo her buttons with one hand, but they were unyielding, and they wouldn't come loose.

Suddenly he stood back and turned her around so she faced away from him. She had come out of her heels, and he was so much taller than her. She felt her feet leave the floor as he picked her up and stood her on a low trunk. He was behind her and only a head taller now, looking down over her right shoulder. His arms came around her and she dropped her eyes to see him slowly undoing her buttons. She could see her own fast breathing as the mounds of her breasts rose and shivered in anticipation.

She felt her pussy, flooding with juices, needy, nagging, gnawing, and she knew that at any moment his fingers would touch her straining nipples and she would feel that bolt of fire down to her clit.

The buttons were all undone now, and his fingers traced up her stomach, up her breastbone, so slowly, so agonizingly slowly. She watched them as they inched their way higher. She couldn't tear her eyes away as she watched their progress, willing them to move with more urgency.

Finally his hands were under her breasts, cupping them, feeling the weight of them. She moaned as his fingers moved higher, circling around the side of her breasts to come down over the top of the fabric.

Millimeter by millimeter he peeled down the fabric to expose the pink tips. She had never really looked at herself so fully before. She marveled at how proud her nipples stood, quivering, hard. Then he ran the tips of his fingers over them. It was just a fleeting touch, but it sent her head backward. She closed her eyes tightly as she leaned back against him, pushing her breasts out further. More, more, she wanted more.

Her head was dropped to one side, exposing the tender flesh between neck and shoulder. He bent his head, tracing his tongue then his teeth over it as his fingers played her nipples, stroking and teasing. As she moaned again, she felt his fingers expertly pinch and she gasped this time.

She pushed her arms back and felt his thighs, the muscles tight and hard. She wanted to reach up and touch his cock but it would be impossible, his arms had hers pinned as he massaged and played with her. She could feel his erection pressing against her lower back, and she wanted it so badly, wanted to plunge her hand into his clothing and grasp it, guide it to where she needed to feel it, inside her, in the depths of her.

She felt like she was sinking, falling, drowning. Could this be happening? Was she really standing here, almost stripped to the waist with the man she once could only dream of having, kissing her, touching her? Her mind was whirling. Was he going to take her, would he take her here? They were in a changing room; there were still people in the function room. But she didn't care. Here. Now. Please, now.

His hands were moving down. She opened her eyes to follow their progress as she saw his right hand trace down her middle, his left hand still on her nipple. She stretched up, elongating her body. His fingers were expert, playing her like a musical instrument.

She sucked her stomach in to leave a gap in her waistband, so that his hand could find its way to its destination. He slipped it down under her skirt and she felt the tips of his fingers lift her panties away from her skin.

Her legs were quivering now, the anticipation almost too much to bear. It was too much and not enough. She felt the tips of his fingers make the lightest and briefest of traces along the tops of her curls.

She parted her legs; she wanted nothing between her cunt and his hand, and her clothes were already in the way. She felt his fingers move down, down toward her nub, but not quite.

She moaned, almost in pain. She wanted him to touch her, touch her there. But her clothes were too restraining. The tight skirt was hindering his progress; his hand could get no further.

With a groan of animal frustration he pulled his hand from her skirt. It was sudden and shocking. His other hand left her breast, then she felt his mouth withdraw from her neck, felt the absence of his warm breath.

She suddenly felt alone, half naked, standing on a box… Where was he? She had to wait only a second before his two strong hands were either side of her thighs, hiking up her skirt in one shocking move. She felt the air on her exposed thighs, the soft flesh at the top of her thigh highs.

She felt his breath on her neck again as he leaned against her once more. His hands now traced along the tops of her stockings, up along her inner thighs, where legs meet pussy and flesh meets satin.

One finger snaked its way under the fabric of her panties. She could feel her juices coating it on its way. She felt as if her labia were quivering, as his finger made its way up her slit. It played around the entrance to her sex, curling, toying. It was torture, pure, blissful torture.

She turned her head backward to find his. She needed his kiss. He bent his head around and forward and she found his lips. She was kissing him hard now, ravishing his lips the way he had ravished hers. She was holding his thighs, leaning back hard against him as she tasted his tongue, and his finger wound its way around her pussy.

Then she felt his hand withdraw. No! She moaned the word and he caught her desperation. Then he pushed his whole hand down the front of her panties and she cried as his middle fingers shot down over her clit.

She thought she would come, right there, from one stroke over the yearning mass of nerve endings. Again he stroked and again. She felt the tension building, and he withdrew his hand.

"Don't stop. Nathan, please don't stop!" she was begging him. Tony had wanted her to beg and she'd stayed silent. But now, here, with Nathan, her tongue knew no boundaries. She had to have him. She was alive with need, completely and fiercely alive for the first time in her life.

"Please…"

But something had changed. He stopped. His muscles were tight but completely still. She felt as if he had stopped breathing.

"Nathan!"

She couldn't see his face; he was behind her.

His voice was low, ragged. "No, we can't. Not like this. This is…"

She held her breath. She heard the words "this is…" But this is… *what*? What was he going to say?

He pushed her forward so she was stranding straight and stepped away. "This is wrong!"

Alexia thought her legs would go out from under her. She wheeled around. He was facing away from her. She stepped off the box, unsure if her feet would be steady enough for a landing. But she was on the floor now in her stockinged feet. She was so small next to him. She pulled her skirt down, feeling suddenly naked.

"Nathan, I don't understand…"

"I can't. I'm sorry, Alexia, this is wrong. I've taken advantage of you. I'm sorry."

"No. Nathan, no…"

But his mind was clearly changed. His face was set as he turned to look at her.

"I'm sorry…"

His hands moved, his mouth opened and shut. He didn't know what to do, to say. He ran his hands through his hair. She had never seen him like this. He was always so in control, even when seducing her a moment ago he had been in control, but now?

"Nathan…"

"Please!" The word exploded from him. It startled her. "Please don't. Please…"

He turned away. "I'm sorry. You've picked the wrong man, Alexia."

He moved to the door and grabbed the handle, but didn't turn it. He was going to leave. Alexia watched him but couldn't stop him. He was going to leave, to walk out of her life.

"You deserve better," he said quietly. He turned the handle and then he was gone.

Alexia collapsed on the floor, tears of pain and hurt flowing down her cheeks. She pulled her blouse over her chest, suddenly feeling exposed and used. She felt cheap, much cheaper than Tony had made her feel. She'd opened herself up to Nathan, emotionally and physically, and he'd rejected her. It would have been better if he had told her he had no feelings for her. But to take her, to almost take her completely and then to disappear, it was more than she could bear.

She let all the emotion and misery weep and drain out of her until there was nothing left but emptiness, a howling, hollow emptiness. She sat on the cold, dark polished floor for what seemed like hours but must have been only minutes.

She heard a knock on the door. Panic hit her. She wasn't supposed to be in here. At least with Nathan she had an all areas access pass, but she was alone. But what if it was Nathan? He might have come back, he might have reconsidered. For an instant, she felt hope rise.

"Alexia! Alexia, are you in there?" A woman's voice. She felt the hope melt away.

"Alexia?" The door opened and Sonia stood there. Her expression of concern turned to shock when she saw Alexia on the floor.

"Oh my God, are you all right?"

She helped Alexia to her feet and guided her to a sofa.

"What happened? What did he say?" Sonia saw her unbuttoned blouse. "Or should I say do?"

Alexia told her how she had confessed all to Nathan and looked at her blouse by way of explanation of what happened next.

Sonia didn't speak.

"He just stopped. No warning. He just kept saying, 'I'm sorry, I'm sorry' and 'this is wrong.'" Her eyes were pleading as she looked to the older woman for answers. "How could it be wrong? I don't understand."

She was crying again. Sonia put her arms around her. "I don't know, darling, but he's not cruel, he's no Tony. This isn't him. I really don't know… There must be something…"

Sonia fell silent again, thinking hard. "Come on, we need to get you home. There's a back entrance, you won't have to see anyone. Come on."

Sonia guided them through the corridors and safely out to where her car was waiting. The driver was polite and well trained, and paid no obvious attention to her companion's emotional state.

The car sped its way across London. It was a long way from Wimbledon to Alexia's humble flat and she was grateful to be sitting in the cushioned interior. The back of the car was womblike, and Sonia held her hand like a mother. It was as comforting as anything could be for a girl with a broken heart.

They arrived at the flat and Sonia took her in. Romy was home and horrified at the state of her flatmate.

Sonia took Romy to one side. "She needs some sleep."

Romy smiled and leaned in conspiratorially. "Don't worry, I'll give her a sleeping tablet, knock her out. It looks like that's what she needs."

"See she takes it, she *has* to go to work tomorrow."

"But she can't—" said Romy.

"She has to get back on that horse, believe me. If she doesn't, she'll never get herself together. I have"—Sonia hesitated for a moment—"someone to see this evening, but please trust me when I say Alexia has to go to work tomorrow."

Romy nodded. Sonia was a woman who elicited trust in those she met. "Our other flatmate is away tonight. It's just us, so… I'll look after her, don't worry."

Sonia smiled and left.

Romy put her friend to bed, undressed her like a child, made her a large mug of cocoa, and dissolved the sleeping tablet into it.

Alexia lay in the darkened room feeling as if sleep would never be her companion again, but she was wrong. She slipped into blissful oblivion in moments.

Romy curled up next to her and slept with a comforting arm over her friend.

Chapter 15

THE NEXT MORNING WAS the most excruciating of Alexia's life. She thought it had been hard to walk out of Carter's door, she thought that had taken all the courage she possessed, but it was no match for this particular morning. This morning was a cliff edge.

She wanted to stay in her room, her beautiful little room in green and blue. But Romy insisted.

"Look, I'm back in the office today so you don't have to see Nathan. Anyway, I just looked at the calendar on the company network. He's booked a day off."

"He won't be there?" said Alexia.

"No. I don't know why. He doesn't usually take days off with no notice…"

The idea hung in the air between them. Was it because of Alexia?

Romy busied Alexia so she wouldn't have time to think about it. She hustled her out of the door and soon they were arriving at the offices of Fallon Sports Agency.

Alexia felt weak and insubstantial, as if the wind could blow her away with one strong gust. Her face was pale, giving her a more ethereal look than usual.

The office was buzzing. Alexia could hear mutterings and odd words: "fired," "argument," "Tony." She strained to hear what the others were gossiping about, terrified to hear her own name. She wandered over to the group who were deep in speculation.

"Have you heard?" said one secretary. "Tony's gone. Someone said Nathan fired him. Did something happen yesterday?"

She felt all eyes on her and the floor rippled under her feet. "I—I don't know. Sorry, I didn't really see much of Tony yesterday…"

The group were disappointed at her inability to shed light on what had transpired. They went back to their speculating. A wave of relief swept over Alexia and she left the office to make herself a coffee.

Standing in the kitchen reminded her of Tony, showing her how to use the coffee machine. It reminded her of how she had taken the cup to Nathan and found him half-naked, how she had gone to him and he had…

She almost dropped the cup as someone came in. She picked it up, all fingers and thumbs. She poured herself half a cup, not daring to fill it lest her trembling fingers spill the scalding liquid. She went back to her desk and drank, hoping the caffeine hit would steady her nerves.

The day passed in agonizing slowness; each glance at the clock showed only an incremental move toward the end of the day. Time seemed to have slowed down, drawing out her torment.

At 5:00 p.m. her mobile rang. It was Sonia. Alexia answered quietly. Sonia's voice was firm. "Look, you have to believe everything is going to be okay…"

Alexia started to protest, but Sonia was insistent. "No, listen to me. It is going to be okay, I promise you. Do you understand?"

Alexia thought her friend was just bandaging, covering her wounds in love and concern to shield her from the long agony of trying to get over Nathan.

"You'll see," said Sonia.

Alexia didn't really take in her words. The desk phone rang. "Sonia, sorry, I'm at work. I have to go."

"It's going to be okay. You have to trust me!"

Sonia hung up and Alexia answered the desk phone. She heard the receptionist's voice. "There's a package here that's got to be delivered to Chelsea, and it has to go now. You have to take it."

"What?" said Alexia. "Why can't it go by courier?"

"It can't. It's going to a client and they want someone from the firm to bring it, so it has to be you, sorry."

The receptionist hung up. Alexia looked at the big metal clock on the wall. It read 5:05 p.m.

She sighed heavily. If she had to go to Chelsea it would take her a very long time to get home again through the rush hour traffic, and it was Friday, the worst day of the week.

She texted Romy to warn her she'd be late home and grabbed her coat. She picked up the package and an envelope from the receptionist and went out to hail a cab. There was a spot nearby where cabs often waited in an impromptu rank. That rank had saved her the night she fled from the party, fled from Nathan after Tony and Phillipa's boardroom rendezvous.

She walked up to the first taxi in line and gave the address she'd been handed in the sealed envelope. Clients were very secretive about their addresses, which was not surprising, thought Alexia, given the amount of attention she'd seen them get since she joined the firm.

The cab picked its way through London. Rush hour started at midafternoon on a Friday as tired commuters made their way out of the city for the weekend.

They all have somewhere to go, she thought, someone to go home to. She watched as they rushed on their way and she felt envious of them, envious of their lives. They had a sense of purpose, or so it seemed. Did she have a purpose? Not anymore. She hugged herself, trying to ignore the hollowness inside her.

The cab driver was looking at her in the rearview mirror. "I've picked you up before, love, haven't I? Same place?" She studied him. Was he the same cabbie who had driven her away from the agency that night? The night of the party?

"That's my spot when I haven't got a fare, so if you work there I've probably picked you up," he said cheerily.

He didn't remember; he just vaguely knew her face. Or was it that he knew her distressed face? Twice he'd picked her up, twice it had been when she was leaving Fallon's and twice she'd been beside herself with misery and humiliation.

She smiled politely and put her head down. He understood. She was not a passenger who wanted to chat, and they settled back into silence.

After what seemed like an eternity of traffic lights and turnings, they pulled up at the address. It was a tall, beautiful townhouse. A bright white Georgian façade with shiny black railings. Alexia couldn't imagine what it must cost to live here, in the chicest part of central London. But the agency's clients were not acquainted with poverty. Quite the opposite.

"Would you wait here, please? I've just got to deliver a package."

The cabbie nodded and pulled up the handbrake. The meter, of course, was still running.

Alexia walked up the steps and pressed the bell. She wondered who lived here. She hoped it wasn't one of the soccer players from the hotel. She peered through the large bay window into a sitting room. It was beautiful and stylish, an old-world style. It can't be a soccer player, she thought; far too tasteful, not enough bling.

She didn't have time for more speculation as she heard footsteps approaching the door and a click as the lock was turned from inside. As the large, black door swung open, she found herself openmouthed as she looked at the person standing in the doorway. Nathan.

The world stopped. It actually seemed to stop. The traffic noise evaporated, the chill wind disappeared. The very air seemed to stand still.

He was there, standing right in front of her. Nathan. But he looked different. She had never seen this man who filled the door-frame before. This Nathan was new to her; this Nathan was—was what? She couldn't work out what had changed.

"Is that your cab?" His voice floated toward her from somewhere in the distance. "Is it yours?"

"What?" One syllable was all she could manage.

He stepped past her and she caught a fleeting trace of his aftershave. Her senses came back to life: the traffic noise filled her ears; the wind found its shivery way through her coat; the world turned again.

She turned to see him pay off the cabbie and wave him on his way. He was wearing jeans and a white T-shirt. He was more casual than she had ever seen him. And he seemed softer, easier within himself.

He took the three deep steps in easy strides. He was standing next to her now, looking down at her. Those dark blue eyes.

"Please, come in." He extended an arm to usher her in before him.

She moved, obediently. He showed her into the sitting room. It was beautiful, stylish but comfortable, lived in. There was a smell in the air, a smell of him. He filled the house.

She saw pictures on the mantelpiece. A young army captain, his men, friends, a Labrador, an elderly couple smiling—his parents? No women, there were no pictures of girlfriends.

She turned to face him. He was standing still, looking at her.

"Please, let me take your coat…"

"I have this," said Alexia, holding up the package. It seemed such a silly thing to say. A reflex.

"Ah yes." Nathan dropped his head. He ran his fingers through his hair. He took a deep breath. "Open it."

Alexia was puzzled.

"Please, open it," said Nathan again.

She looked down at the flat padded envelope. She tore open the top and fished inside. There was only one thing in it, a picture of a woman. Alexia studied her. Ash blond hair, blue eyes, an ethereal face.

"You look so much like her." Nathan's voice was flat, emotionless.

She looked up at him. Was this her? The woman who broke his heart?

"Her name was Helen. We'd been together for a few years, but if you added up all the time we were actually together, it probably only amounted to a couple of months. I was fast-tracking through the army—special assignments," he said coyly. "I'd be away for months at a time, and sometimes I couldn't contact her at all. Not easy for a woman."

Nathan paused, thinking about his next words. "Then I got hit. The whole operation was shot to hell. We lost nine guys, it was…" He looked down, unwilling to follow that thought. "Anyway, when I got back, I was a mess, difficult. I thought she'd be there for me, but someone else had moved in on her and she was only too happy to go. You see, it turns out she didn't want the real me, the broken, fallible, ordinary me… No, she wanted the glamorous soldier, the danger man in full dress uniform. Anything less was—I don't know—boring."

There was a long silence, an agonizing silence. Alexia couldn't move; she was afraid to breathe. Nathan was unburdening himself and she was afraid he would stop if she made the slightest noise or movement.

Nathan spoke again. "The crazy thing is, I don't think I really loved her—not truly. But somehow being betrayed when you're at your lowest leaves an indelible mark."

Alexia looked at him. She knew now what she had seen when Nathan opened the door. Vulnerability. She'd seen him without his body armor.

"When I saw you in the office, the day you started, I thought for a moment…" He stopped.

Alexia looked at the picture again. Then it hit her. She had the same coloring, the distinctive ash blond hair falling in waves.

"She was petite too," said Nathan. "Just like you."

Alexia sank down onto the sofa, realization hitting her.

"Oh God, Nathan, you thought I was her. You wanted her, and that's why you stopped. Because I'm not her."

"No!" The vehemence of his denial shook her. With one bound he was on the floor in front of her, kneeling at her feet, looking up into her eyes.

"No, you don't understand. When I saw you my heart stopped for a minute, yes, and I took an interest in you because you were like her. But…"

Alexia searched his face. "But what?"

"You're not her. You're not her, Alexia. I took an interest in you because you looked like her, and I kissed you, that first time when your ex showed up, but that's not why…"

He was struggling, emotions clearly swirling and fighting in him as violently as they were in Alexia.

"That's not why I wanted you later, or why I was so angry in the hotel, when I thought you were with Tony."

"Why were you angry?"

"Because I couldn't stop thinking about you. You, Alexia, not her. You. You're not her; you're nothing like her…"

Alexia couldn't believe what he was saying. She wanted to believe it, but she was still chained to that emotional roller coaster, and she had been on so many highs, she was terrified of another low.

"Nathan, I… Why did you stop?"

Nathan shut his eyes and sighed.

"Why did you stop, Nathan? Why did you say it was wrong? Yesterday, in that changing room. Why did you start if you didn't want—want to make love to me?"

"Oh God, I did… I do!"

"Then I don't understand."

"I was terrified." Nathan gave a small, cynical laugh. "Comical, isn't it? I can face Iraqi insurgents, but you? I was scared of the way you make me feel, and in that changing room… It was wrong. If we're going to…"

He put his hands on hers. She felt the warmth of his skin, just the touch of his hand again. She wanted to cry.

"If I'm going to have you, Alexia, it won't be in some changing room where God knows how many people have torn each other's clothes off."

"Do you want to have me?" asked Alexia, praying for the right answer.

Nathan seemed to hold his breath for a moment. Then he was on her, kissing her, holding her head as his mouth searched hers. She thought that she had felt his passion yesterday, but it had been a shadowy imitation of what she felt from him now.

He pulled back from her and looked into her eyes.

"Alexia…"

She could barely speak, her voice was small, but there was a question nagging at her. "What changed your mind?"

Nathan laughed softly. He looked up at her from under his lashes, bashful almost.

"Sonia," said Nathan.

Alexia couldn't believe it. "Sonia? I don't understand."

"She came here like one of the Furies and demanded to know why I was being such an idiot. She told me it was obvious to anyone with eyes how I felt about you. 'Girls like that don't come along every day, you stupid oaf, and it's time you took a risk' were, I think, her exact words."

Alexia couldn't help herself. She laughed quietly.

"What's funny?" said Nathan.

"She said something pretty similar to me, though without the oaf bit."

They laughed softly, then there was silence between them again. When Nathan spoke, his voice was quiet and somber.

"Alexia, I'm damaged but—I want to try, to try with you."

"I've never wanted anyone or anything more in my entire life," said Alexia.

She heard a low moan escape from him and suddenly she felt herself pushed back onto the sofa as his weight pressed down on her. He was kissing her with such raw intensity that she felt she would catch fire.

He picked her torso up, like a doll, and dragged off her coat. Alexia kicked off her shoes and lay back, watching him as he knelt on the sofa in front of her. His face was in front of her hips and he reached around her and pulled down the zip. She felt his hands grip her sides as he slid off her skirt to reveal black panties and thigh highs.

"Oh God," said Nathan as he leaned forward and ran his tongue over the stocking tops. Alexia wanted to open her legs and pull his head into her pussy, but there was no room on the narrow sofa. She wriggled as she felt his tongue tracing higher and higher.

He pushed a finger under her panties and stroked her wetness. She lifted her knee in an instant reflex. She wanted to feel him inside her; she wanted his fingers in her.

But he pulled his hand away and she moaned in disappointment.

He sat up on the edge of the sofa, his hips jammed against the tops of her thighs. He looked down at her, naked lust blazing from his eyes. No vulnerability now, just raw need.

Alexia couldn't bear it. She knew this time there would be no stopping; she knew for certain he was going to take her. And she needed him, she needed to be fucked by him and fucked hard.

All the weeks of foreplay with Richard and Tony had left her screaming in frustration. No orgasm teased out with tongue or fingers would satisfy her now. She needed him inside her, deep inside her. She craved a complete and total orgasm driven by him, driven from the thrusting of his hips right through to the tip of his cock.

He looked down at her and splayed his hands over her midriff, moving them up. He opened her top button, then the next, again and again until they were all undone.

She shook herself free from her blouse so she could lay in front of him in just her underwear and stockings.

"Beautiful," he said. He stood up, looking down at her prone and waiting body.

He pulled his T-shirt over his head. Alexia felt her pussy flex and her panties get wetter. She looked at his jeans and reached up to touch the hard bulge that strained against the zip. Her hand on his erection was more than he could stand.

He reached down and scooped her up. She was airborne before she had realized what he was doing. She was petite, but the ease with which he lifted her was thrilling. She lay in his arms, feeling the soft hair of his chest against her breast as she curled her arms around his neck and leaned against him.

"We need more space," said Nathan as he bounded up the stairs into the master bedroom. Her face was against his neck and she drank in the smell of him, his musk and aftershave, now her favorite heady cocktail.

He dropped her onto the bed, and as she sank into the mattress he was on her before she had time to bounce back.

The weight of him lying on her was sublime: his heaviness, his maleness. She wanted to feel him crushing the air out of her, to cover her completely.

She reached down and grabbed the button of his jeans. It was difficult to reach so he curled his hip away from the bed to help her, but it wasn't enough for Alexia. She was desperate for him now. She put a hand on his shoulder and, with a force that shocked them both, she pushed him backward and turned to sit up and straddle him.

The look of surprise on his face gave a thrill of power. She ran her hands through the hair on his chest and watched his eyes as she moved down to his trousers.

She flipped the denim so that the metal stud gave way and yanked the zip down.

"Hey, steady there," said Nathan, "you don't want to catch anything in those teeth."

"Sorry," said Alexia as she shimmied down the bed, dragging his jeans and Calvin Kleins with her. Her eyes were transfixed as she watched his erection emerge from the cotton as she pulled it down. She had wondered how he would look erect. Hard, he was more than she was used to. She felt her cunt clench, she wanted to be on him, around him.

"Take your time," said Nathan. "We have all night."

He reached up and pulled her forward so that her pussy rested on his cock. Her panties separated them. It was agony.

Her bra came loose with one flick of his fingers as he sat up and reached around her. He dragged it away from her and threw it on the floor.

"Oh God!" he said, as his mouth fell on a pink and straining nipple.

Alexia gasped. She felt his cock flex against her as he sucked, pulsing against her yawning pussy. Why was she still wearing panties? She felt the satin straining as he leaned against her.

His mouth worked on her breast, his hand taking care of the other, pinching and rolling her nipple in his fingers. He was still in control and she wanted to make him lose it. She wanted to make him as desperate as she was.

His hand was around her, holding her close to him. Alexia started to grind her hips, up and down against his erection, and she felt his fingers dig into her back and his mouth tense against her breast. She ground harder. He moaned and looked up into her face. His expression was getting cloudier.

She put her hands on his broad, hard shoulders and pushed him back onto the bed.

She got up off his lap, kneeling tall in front of him. He looked at her pussy; the satin was damp. She watched as he brought his fingers to the lace. His hands were splayed on her thighs. He brought his thumbs in and hooked them under the fabric. She pushed her hips forward, urging him to touch her, to touch her clit. It was screaming to be pleasured. Alexia felt as if her whole pelvis was a giant nerve ending, pulsating, quivering, needing.

She felt his thumb as it ran along that gorgeous nub and she let out a loud gasp. It was no use, she couldn't play anymore. It had to be now.

She picked up her leg and dragged her panties down and off. She straddled him again, in nothing but the sheer thigh highs.

"Alexia," said Nathan. He was about to stop her, to slow her down, but she could not be stopped.

She took his cock in her hand. It was so hard, she felt as if it were made of metal. It was warm, a dot of precome shimmering on the tip. She raised her hips and ran the tip along her slit.

He raised his arms above his head in one sharp reflex motion and pushed them against the headboard, steadying himself. He took a huge breath. She slid herself down onto him. As the head went in, she bit her lip hard. He exhaled with an explosive groan as down she went, right down to the hilt. She felt her bottom and the backs of her thighs hit his body. She was full, full of him, his cock, and it was agonizing pleasure.

He let out a deep moan and sucked in air through his teeth as if steadying himself against the intense pleasure. She reached back and put her hands on the tops of his thighs, arching her back as she lifted and dropped her hips, her cunt flexing with mind-numbing pleasure as she rode him. She felt his hips push up under her. He wasn't letting her do all the work. He was fucking her from the bed, digging his heels in and pushing against the headboard to drive up into her.

Three, four, five strokes. Six, seven, eight... Suddenly she felt his hands grab her hips and he was turning her.

"I can't... I have to..." He'd lifted her off his cock and flipped her onto her back. He couldn't finish his sentence, but she knew. He had to fuck her. And she had what she wanted. She wanted him to lose control and take her, really take her.

She felt his feet slide in between hers and gasped as he parted her legs in one swift, strong push. His muscles were taut and she felt her pussy give up more moisture as her soft thighs pressed against his rock-hard legs.

He was looking down at her. He looked close already. Richard had taught her to look in a man's face. This was the one man she wanted to look at.

He moved his hand down and placed himself at the entrance to her pussy. Then he took the weight on his hands and drove into her.

The pleasure was explosive. She arched her back and bent her knees so she could take all of him. He was long and she wanted it all. His girth filled her completely. He thrust into her and watched her face as he pushed into her over and over.

It was too much to bear and not enough all at once. The agonizing, driving need of sex. She wanted to come but she wanted it to go on forever. She wanted release but she didn't want it to end.

Over and over he thrust into her. She'd imagined what it would be like to have him on her, driving his cock into her. Her fantasy could never have matched this. Alexia reached down and cupped her hands around his buttocks, feeling the muscles contract and push, reveling in the corresponding feeling in her cunt as he drove into her. He lowered his hips and she felt his pubic bone grind against her clit as he thrust.

"Oh God... Nathan..."

She could hardly breathe the words. At the end of each thrust he paused, just a tiny, momentary pause, enough to press down a little on her clit before withdrawing to drive again.

She knew her orgasm was near, pleasure searing through her

as he fucked. She bucked hard and felt her muscles clench around him, the contractions in her cunt forcing spasms from her hips. He slowed to ride the rhythm of them as she gasped and cried out. The contractions were stronger than anything she had felt before; they spread through her whole abdomen, radiating from the cluster of nerves in her pussy.

She opened her eyes as the waves subsided.

"You have to come too," said Alexia.

"Not yet," said Nathan. He was back in control, damn him, but she didn't care. He wasn't finished with her.

He placed a pillow on the bed next to her hip, then lifted one of her legs and brought it around in front of him. Without taking himself out of her, he flipped her over so she faced down.

Her hips were raised on the pillow, her bottom sticking into him. He thrust into her again; this time the pleasure was insane. His penis was driving against her G-spot now with hard insistence. He reached a hand under her and fingered her clit as he pushed. Alexia had only just climaxed, but she felt an acute, almost painful intensity in her pussy. It took only a few deep thrusts, and she came again. It was short, but so powerful she screamed.

He stopped again. He still hadn't come. Alexia was panting, barely able to move. She felt him take his cock out of her, then turn her over slowly, her hips still raised on the pillow, but now she was facing him again.

He was breathing hard. His hair fell into his eyes and she saw a sheen of sweat over him. He must be close, she thought. How can he not be?

"One more," he said, and pulled her forward and up, so the back of her legs rested against his chest, her bottom against his groin and her ankles either side of his head. She looked up at him, framed by the V shape of her legs.

He pushed himself forward and stopped, looking at her. Her

cunt was pulsating with anticipation. He had just wrung a second orgasm out of her, an orgasm she didn't think possible, but she wanted more. He thrust suddenly and was fucking her again, his hand pressing on her clit, each hard stroke on her nub matching every thrust of his hips.

One more? Not possible, thought Alexia. She'd never had two orgasms, let alone three. But as he thrust, she felt a strange warming in her abdomen and her cunt. Not all-consuming like the last one, but suffuse and toe-curlingly good. He thrust and stroked in perfect rhythm, on and on, and Alexia felt the uncoiling feeling deep inside her.

"Come for me," said Nathan, "one more time."

He was looking down at her, leaning his chest against the back of her legs. The feeling of openness was incredible. Then he looked down at himself as he went into her, reveling in the vision of her pussy, completely open to him as he speared her.

She looked down too and saw his cock driving into her, disappearing into the blond curls and emerging wet and hard, over and over. It sent a spasm of illicit pleasure through her. The sight of him inside her was enough to send her over the edge. She came again; this time it was a swooshing, flooding sensation, like the last shuddering crash of a foaming wave.

As she clenched around him, he lost it. He gave one huge thrust, almost pushing her up the bed, and let out a guttural cry that seemed to last for three or four more thrusts. She felt him spasm inside her, then the flood of his warm wetness as he spilled himself completely. She didn't care; he was hers and she was his, completely.

He leaned against her legs, panting. She felt her pussy quivering around him. He was struggling to bring his breathing back under control and she saw strands of his hair, damp with sweat, clinging to his face.

He pulled out and fell back beside her. Her legs flopped onto the bed as if her bones were liquid. Her entire body felt like a melted candle.

The room seemed to melt away too, and Alexia disappeared into a floating dream accompanied only by the sound of their breathing.

—⁓—

She came to. Nathan was propped up on one elbow, looking at her.

"I think—I think I passed out," said Alexia.

Nathan laughed softly. "Not quite, but you certainly zoned out for a minute there. Not long—you made a quick recovery!"

"I'm not surprised. I…"

She looked at him. She didn't know what to say. There was so much, but she couldn't think of a single word.

He leaned over and kissed her.

"Thank you," he said quietly.

"For what, letting you have your way with me?"

"No." Nathan laughed. "For bringing me back to life. For showing me it is possible to love again…"

He kissed her, a hungry and searching kiss, looking for salvation in her lips. To love again? He'd used the word, the word she was terrified to say. She curled her arms around him and held him tightly as she kissed him, kissed him as if she could breathe life back into him.

When he withdrew, he looked serious. "I'm not an easy man, Alexia. I have demons and it's going to take me some time to be open and to share things with you. It might be a bumpy ride."

He looked so vulnerable. Her big, strong, beautiful man needed her, wanted her, loved her. Alexia loved him more at that moment than she thought possible.

"Do you think we can do this? I mean really do this?"

He needed an answer. Alexia smiled a coy and naughty smile.

"I think, Mr. Fallon, we have a sporting chance!"

She giggled and flashed him a wicked come-hither look.

"Mmm. Just for that, Miss Wright, I think I'm going to have to test your powers of recovery a little harder…"

He covered her body once more. He was hard already.

Awakening

by Elene Sallinger

He will open her eyes to the ultimate pleasure…

The minute Claire walked into his shop, she aroused every protective instinct Evan ever had. She looked so fragile, so lost. He ached to be the one to show her a world she'd never dreamed of, to awaken within her the passion she was so ripe to share. It only takes one touch for him to see how open and responsive she is to his dominant side. But the true test will be whether he can let go at last and finally open his heart…

Festival of Romance Award Winner

What readers are saying:

"If *Fifty Shades of Grey* intrigued you, *Awakening* will take you to a whole new level of desire, submission, and unforgettable romance."
—Judge, Festival of Romance contest

"One of the absolute best BDSM novels I have read. (And I've read quite a few.) This one is absolutely amazing!" —Autumn Jean

"Finally! A well-told story that shows the characters' vulnerabilities and how they learned to trust and love again." —A. Hirsch

"Exquisitely beautiful, touchingly heart-wrenching, and hedonistic enough to keep your body on fire." —*Coffee Time Romance*, starred review

For more Xcite Books, visit:

www.sourcebooks.com

Restless Spirit

Sommer Marsden

Three men want her. Only one can truly claim her.

When Tuesday Cane inherits a cozy lake house, she's not expecting to find love as part of her legacy. But how can she choose between Aiden, the loyal and über-sexy handyman she's known for years; the charming and wealthy Reed Green, a former TV star; and the mysterious Shepherd Moore, an ex cage fighter.

The only way to know for sure is to try them all… Surrounded by so many interesting men and erotic temptations, Tuesday has no intention of committing. But deep down she longs for that special, soul-deep connection. Only, which man can entice this restless spirit into finally settling down?

What readers are saying:

"An intense emotional and sexual journey
that is quite compelling." —Kathy

"One of the best adult/erotica books I have ever read.
The characters are real and believable, and the sex
scenes are absolutely scorching hot." —Rebecca

"Themes of domination and submission are fantastically well
varied throughout the story… Realistic and relatable characters
with steamy encounters at every turn." —Michelle

For more Xcite Books, visit:

www.sourcebooks.com

Control

by Charlotte Stein

Will she choose control or just let go?

When Madison Morris wanted to hire a shop assistant for her naughty little bookstore, she never dreamed she'd have two handsome men vying for the position—and a whole lot more. Does she choose dark and dangerous Andy with his sexy tattoos? Or quiet, serious Gabriel, whose lean physique and gentle touch tempt her more than she thought possible?

She loves the way Andy takes charge when it comes to sex. But the turmoil in Gabe's eyes hints at a deep well of complicated emotions locked inside. When the fun and games are over, only one man can have control of her heart.

What readers are saying:

"Forget *Fifty Shades of Grey*…take a look at this and see how long you can stay in control!"

"This is honest to God, hands down, the best erotic fiction I've ever read."

"Highly addictive!"

For more Xcite Books, visit:

www.sourcebooks.com

The Initiation of Ms. Holly

by k.d. grace

The stranger on the train

He came to her in the dark. She couldn't see him, but she could feel every inch of his body against hers in the most erotic encounter Rita Holly ever had. And now he's promising more…if she'll just follow him to an exclusive club where opulence and sex rule. She can have anything she's ever dreamed of—and more—but first she'll have to pass the club's initiation…

What readers are saying:

"After reading *Fifty Shades of Grey*, I didn't think I would find another book as well written, but then I read *The Initiation of Ms. Holly*, and I was immediately taken in. This book is sexy, erotic, and explosive. I didn't want to put it down." —Dani

"Very, very erotic and sizzling!!! Wow, I could not put it down." —Theresa

"Everything you want in a romantic, erotic, sexual novel." —Jean

"For a fast-paced read with enough twists and turns to keep the story fresh and entertaining, you couldn't ask for a better book." —Christine

For more Xcite Books, visit:

www.sourcebooks.com

Telling Tales

by Charlotte Stein

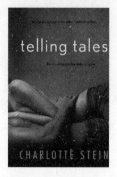

The only limit is their imagination.

Allie has held a torch for Wade since college. They were part of a writing group together, and everything about those days with him and their friends Kitty and Cameron fills her with longing. When their former professor leaves them his mansion in his will, it's a chance for them to reunite. But there's more than friendship bubbling beneath the surface.

As relationships are rekindled and secrets revealed, they indulge their most primal desires. With the stakes getting higher, Allie isn't quite sure who she wants…fun-loving Wade or quiet, restrained Cameron.

For more Xcite Books, visit:

www.sourcebooks.com